Anyra

Lanasting Trilogy, Volume 1

Juniper M. Limerick

Published by Juniper M. Limerick, 2023.

ANYRA

First edition. March 7, 2023.

Copyright © 2023 Juniper M. Limerick.

ISBN: 979-8215246375

Written by Juniper M. Limerick.

Table of Contents

Dedicated to Lucas and Brandy

Thank you for always believing in me

Prologue: Sylvia Lanasting

First came the heat. That came long before anything else. That brought forth the fear that had been simmering just below the surface for weeks now. Sylvia had to keep reminding herself that this was an honor. She was the chosen Gift that would satiate the Totem, soothe her anger. This was the heroic death of a warrior, a savior, a brave defender protecting her people. Why didn't she believe it?

Xavier was sobbing as he staggered toward the edge, the heat beginning to tease the line between pleasant warmth and searing pain. *This is a gift. I am a Gift.* The thin linen gown allowed the hot wind of the volcano to meet Sylvia's skin with little resistance. The fear began to grow, twisting around her gut like strong, black tentacles. She could see the orange-red glow from within the pit waiting to receive her.

Beyond her control, Sylvia's body began to react. Her heart began to race, her breaths coming quick and shallow. She had no bonds, no rope or chain barring her escape. She went into the mouth of the monster willingly as very few Gifts before her had. Now she second-guessed that willingness. She clutched the back of her brother's shirt, terror filling her as the edge drew ever nearer.

As her last act, Sylvia glanced over her brother's shoulder, catching sight of her family several feet back from the edge. Evelyn, Xavier's wife, was crouched on the volcanic rock, sobs wracking her body as she clutched her two precious daughters to herself. Gwendolyn, the smaller of the two, was curled into her tearful mother, weeping as well though she couldn't understand what was happening.

The elder, Adelaide, was staring back at her aunt in shock and confusion. She had always been so clever. At a mere four years old, she didn't understand what was happening, but she certainly grasped the weight of it. Tears slipped silently down the girl's cheeks, confusion and sorrow making her eyes seem so much older than they were. She showed no fear. Rather, Sylvia could sense her anger.

"This is wrong," Sylvia gasped. She looked into her brother's grief-stricken face, his mouth twisted with pain. He knew it too, yet he had no choice. "Xavier, this is wrong!"

Sylvia locked eyes with Adelaide once again. The girl she would never get to see grow up. For a moment, it was as though her eyes betrayed her. She saw a tall, young lady in Adelaide's place, her broad shoulders squared and tense as a bobcat ready to strike. Then the small child returned, beginning to grow agitated as her father stepped ever closer to the edge. Sylvia prayed her two nieces would not meet the same fate. No more empty promises. She gently shook her head, and Adelaide shook hers in return, her tiny brow furrowed and little jaw set in anger. No more.

She watched as though time had slowed as Addie's expression shifted to one of horror. Her eyes went wide, her mouth opening to release a short, broken cry as Sylvia fell. Then she was gone. The black stone flashed before her eyes, seemingly glowing red with the light cast from the magma. A brief instant of horrid, soul-breaking, unimaginable pain overwhelmed her. Then there was darkness.

"She's here!"

"They've done it again!"

"I don't think they'll ever stop."

"Damn the Temple! Damn the Totem!" The voices were all female, yet there was still only darkness surrounding her. Sylvia searched for any source of light, but there was none to be found.

2

"What is your name, sister?" a calm, authoritative voice asked. The tone of her speech was firm, yet gentle. Her voice was high, light and lilting like that of a child, yet it carried the weight of great wisdom and knowledge. Seemingly at the sound of her voice, all the others fell silent.

"Sylvia Lanasting," the newest Gift answered, unsure of how she spoke. She could not feel her body, no motion of her jaw or tongue, yet she could still think and speak. As she strained to see in the darkness with impossible eyes, a soft, blue-white glow seemed to creep into this strange sense of sightless vision. It was wispy as smoke from incense, yet as she watched, it began to take a form.

"Welcome, Sylvia. You need not be afraid. You will be here for quite some time."

Chapter One: The Temple

"Do you know when this year's Choosing is?" Valerie asked from her workbench across the room from mine.

I paused with the hammer raised above my head, ready to pound the reflective steel into the shape I needed. At the current stage of craftsmanship, the metal was rough and jagged, waiting to be smoothed into a nearly mirrorlike cylinder. I racked my brains, the hammer hanging precariously overhead.

"I don't know," I realized. The hammer fell to my side as I turned to her, but she seemed unbothered.

"Must not be for a while then," Valerie shrugged, and she returned to her work. I did the same. I nodded to myself as I raised the hammer once more and let it fall, a prick of fear tingling in the back of my mind now.

The familiar clang of metal against metal rang in my ears as I hammered at a new staff for the High Priestess, Rhoda. The reflective surface threw light at all angles, and when it flashed in my eyes, I flinched. Rhoda had requested a new staff to replace the old, seeing as the garnet staff she carried now had become dull, ragged, and chipped over time. Though how it had come to be this way eluded me. What kind of abuse was she putting it through?

Shrugging away the question, I refocused on my work, bringing the hammer down to pound the steel into the tapering shape I needed. Rhoda's staff had to be perfect, the symbol of the Totem's weapon. Just as the Totem was said to wield a great, glimmering sword with a ruby pommel, so would the High Priestess wield a staff forged in its image. I chuckled mirthlessly to myself, finding this appropriate. The chromed surface was smooth and long, and at the top in a clawed hand would rest the incredible gem.

In a box on the shelf sat the ruby, nestled safely in the luscious purple fabric that lined the inside of the case. The priestess that delivered the gem had dodged my questions about the ruby's source. Ever since Rhoda had requested the staff, rumors had flown around our forge of how she had come by it. Old Delilah was certain that it was a gift from the Totem herself, given to Rhoda for her good work as the mouthpiece of the goddess. Caleb had a theory that it washed ashore from some ancient shipwreck. His nieces and nephews had immediately run to play pirates at the sound of that.

It was my firm belief that Rhoda had broken a centuries-old law. For decades, Anyra had stood in solitude, forbidden from contacting the outside world. If anyone left, they were barred from returning to their homeland. I doubt any of them saw another shore regardless. Anyra was completely self-sufficient, with no need for trade with other cities or countries. In truth, part of me wondered if there truly were any other people out there.

I glanced over at an unfinished bread knife I had been crafting for myself. I would need it for my wedding in a month's time when my husband and I would break bread together as one for the first time. Yet it had fallen to the wayside for now. Rhoda had requested the staff only a week before, paying a great sum for it to be moved to the top of my list of projects. There was a grand total of three forges in the whole of Anyra, and ours was by far the most popular. As the only forge run by women, we specialized in detail.

I laid the hammer down on the workbench, gazing at the progress I had made. The staff was about halfway complete, the shape mostly pounded out. Now the long process of detailing could begin, but my stomach made it clear that it would have to wait until after I was fed.

"I don't think The Choosing is till after the wedding," I continued, now able to focus on conversation.

"I hope so!" Valerie agreed. She dunked the metal she was working into the bucket to cool. The piece she drew out was a twisted sculpture, the metal wrapping around itself in intricate patterns. "What about Gwendolyn? How is she handling it?"

"She's always been decently scared about it. You know Gwen, she's nervous in general." I glanced out the window on the bright day. It was growing close to afternoon. "I think Xander will propose soon."

"What?!" Valerie cried, drawing my gaze. "They're so young!"

"Why is that a problem? My parents were only a little older than them when they had me," I reminded her. I poured water over the rough metal, and it sizzled away, giving off a cloud of steam. Valerie winced away from the heat, but I smiled as the vapor kissed my skin.

"I don't know. They shouldn't be marrying just to save her from the Choosing," she insisted.

"I don't see a problem with it. They've known each other long enough, and they're incredibly happy together. I think they should," I argued.

"Might as well get married when you and Sebastian do. Have two weddings in one," Valerie jabbed sarcastically. Her grin showed that she was only joking, and I gave a small smile in return. In truth, I wanted Gwen to get married sooner rather than later. The Temple could steal her life away before she had the chance to live it.

I wanted the same. I grew frustrated as I strained my mind to remember if the Choosing would fall before or after my wedding day, but I couldn't find the date. As I removed my heavy leather forge-wear, I fell into my thoughts once more. I would wed Sebastian in only a month. In a month's time, I would be safe. On my wedding night, I would no longer be eligible to be chosen as the Gift, as I would no longer be a virgin.

7

"Addie, it's past noon," Valerie reminded me, drawing me out of my thoughts once again.

"It is," I nodded. "What are your lunch plans?"

"Caleb and I are meeting Mama for lunch. At the same restaurant that's catering your wedding!"

"Oh, I forgot that was today!" I realized. "Tell her I say hello. I'm going to pick up some lunch for Sebastian there."

"Then you may bump into her yourself," Valerie corrected. "But I'll pass on the message."

"Have fun!" I called as she went into the house to wash up. Rather than follow suit, I simply dunked my hands into a bucket of clean water and wiped them on my tunic. I left through the forge rather than the house, excited to see my betrothed and surprise him with lunch. As the Chosen of the Temple and my betrothed, he had a lot of stress on his plate. He deserved a good meal on it as well.

Using just one of the hundreds of coins from Rhoda, I bought a large pastry for myself and a basket for Sebastian, a preview of the first meal he and I would share as husband and wife. I stopped for a moment to say hello to Valerie and her mother, Rachel. Caleb was running late, though none of us were surprised. With a quick hug and a wink from Rachel, I was on my way toward my beloved.

I came to the Temple courtyard where the Memorium stood. Here, all the names of the Gifts and their Chosens were carved into stone, a permanent reminder of the yearly sacrifice. On the stone farthest to the right, Sebastian's name was already carved in the next blank space. Another stone would need to be added soon. To the left of his name, the space for the Gift remained blank, waiting for the name of the girl that would die as Anyra looked on.

As I approached the monument, my eyes immediately found the name that truly meant something to me. Sylvia Lanasting, the aunt that I hardly had the chance to know, and beside her name was that of Xavier Lanasting, my father. As if it were a cruel trick of fate,

Papa had to throw his own sister into the mouth of a volcano. The words of High Priestess Rhoda rang in my head: "Anything for the Totem." A tear spilled down my cheek, and I quickly wiped it away. I remembered that day well.

At only four years old, I had not been old enough to be chosen as the Gift, but Aunt Sylvia was nineteen and unwed. The Temple enforced strict chastity laws in order to keep young girls from committing adultery in order to escape being selected. They called it adultery, for each young woman was said to be wedded to the Totem until they were wedded to another. No one knew how they discovered if a woman had committed adultery against the Totem, but they knew, and women found guilty were punished harshly. So harshly that most would rather face death than the Temple's fury. Even if that option had been open to her, Sylvia revered the Totem. She went into her fiery arms willingly.

On that day so many years ago, I watched the priests placed Sylvia in my father's arms, and he sobbed as he approached the mouth of the volcano. His steps staggered as if she weighed a thousand pounds despite the fact that she was incredibly thin. She hadn't been able to bring herself to eat in the weeks leading up to her execution. My mother was crying as well, but I didn't fully understand the scene unfolding before my eyes. I had never known the heavy ache of grief. All I knew was that something terrible was happening, and I must fight to stop it from happening again.

"I'm so sorry," my father sobbed, his words strangled with the grief and guilt that wracked his body. I could see his form trembling even from where I stood several feet back from the edge. I could remember how the warmth of the lava kissed my skin.

"Don't be," Sylvia assured him, but the tears on her face said otherwise. "It's an honor to be the Gift." I saw her mouth moving, but I could no longer remember what she said. With great difficulty, Papa let his sister fall into the mouth of the mountain.

She disappeared but didn't scream. Sometimes the Gifts screamed and sometimes they didn't, and likewise, some were willing, and some were not. Sylvia was one of the Gifts who went willingly, so no bonds were needed to bar her escape, no force taken to keep her from fighting back. She allowed herself to be sacrificed. We had watched helplessly as she slipped from my father's arms.

There was no sound to mark Sylvia's entry into the lava and subsequent death. No splash as if she had jumped into the ocean, no agonized screams as the heat took her life. To fill the void of silence, Papa let out a shriek, the weight of carrying the murder of his sister proving to be too much. He took a glance back at me, my mother, my sister, and I reached out for him, offering comfort. Papa simply shook his head and jumped into the volcano after his burning sister. Jumped truly wasn't the right word. He more crumpled and plummeted over the edge.

I blinked hard and brushed my fingers over the names, forever etched in stone, and after a moment I moved past the Memorium and mounted the stairs into the Temple. The structure was a large, boxlike thing, rising stark white out of the platform on which it stood. The Temple had stood longer than any other building in Anyra, but it had been kept so well that there was hardly any wear on the stone. The marble was pristine, the swirls of grey like smoke caught in time. Everything was sharp and square, even the steps remaining stark angles despite the thousands of feet that had climbed them.

I entered the large open structure, admiring the beauty of the craft despite my inherent dislike of the Temple's ways. The space was open and arid, with large windows allowing sunlight to fill the space. Fresh flowers decorated every available surface as gifts to the Totem, adding color to the neutral palette of stone and marble. There were several stained-glass windows depicting important scenes of Anyra's history. The Totem's arrival on the peninsula one thousand years ago, the terror she wrought on the ancient people, the first Gift that quenched her wrath, and many more besides that. I grimaced at the red glass as if it were stained with the blood of all those Gifts.

"Addie," a voice called, and I turned to see Sebastian coming down the steps from the Sanctuary, the scarlet curtain fluttering in his wake. His jet-black hair was slicked back against his head, his normal curls tamed for his duties as the Chosen. Though he was not permanently a priest of the Temple, for his time as the Chosen he must act like one for the most part.

"Hi, sweetheart," I greeted him. He placed a hand on my waist, drawing me close to peck my lips. "How has your day been?" Sebastian shook his head, his eyebrows furrowing as his expression became grim.

"Tomorrow is the day the Totem will choose her next Gift, so tensions are riding a bit high," he informed me. My eyes grew wide in surprise.

"I didn't think the next Choosing Day was for another month!" I took his hand. Gently, Sebastian rubbed his thumb over my knuckles, the action meaning to soothe my sudden nerves. It failed to help. A thought struck me, and I clutched his hand tighter. "Seb, what if the Totem chooses me? What if she chooses Gwen!?"

"I'm sure she won't, darling, our wedding is barely a month away." Sebastian wrapped his arm around my shoulders and pressed a kiss to my temple.

"That would be just like the Totem though, to pick a girl about to reach safety. A girl from *my* family." I argued. I saw Sebastian roll his eyes from my peripheral. Anger flared inside me once again. "People say the Lanasting name is cursed, Seb! Seven Gifts have come from my family! Not to mention the four Chosens as well."

"Your name is not cursed, Addie," Sebastian countered. "The Totem does what is necessary. She cares about the good of Anyra, the welfare of each of its citizens. She chooses the strongest, most heroic girls as her Gifts. If anything, it's a compliment."

"The Totem does what she feels like, she demands blood every year! It's not right, Sebastian!"

"Addie, we've talked about this," he huffed, drawing back. Cross, he folded his arms over his chest and began rubbing the bridge of his nose as though he had a headache.

"Look at the windows, Sebastian!" I flung my arm up toward the high windows, gesturing to the memorial of the first Gift. Her face was obscured behind the shoulder of the man that carried her and by her long, dark hair blown by the volcanic winds. The story of her sacrifice said that it was her own father that sacrificed her, convicted by the Totem in order to show her will. Directed by the Totem herself, he had tied his daughter up in her sleep and carried her to the mountain to burn. She had been a mere fourteen years of age, setting the precedent for the youngest age a girl could be chosen. "You can't tell me that's not cruel! Tell me what happened to Papa and Sylvia isn't cruel!"

"Adelaide, stop it!" Sebastian hissed. "We are in the Temple. Rhoda could hear you!" He grabbed me by my arms as I opened my mouth again. "You are blaspheming against the Totem in her own Temple! She could strike you down where you stand!"

"Let her!" I cried, wrestling out of his grip. "A girl will be sentenced to a gruesome death tomorrow, and it very well could be me or my sister!" An idea struck me, and I snatched Sebastian's arms. "Seb, marry me tonight."

"What!?" he shouted, tearing away from my grip. His face conveyed the horror he felt at the idea. Why he was so certainly pitted against it, I had no clue. "Adelaide, we can't."

"Why not? I'll be safe! *We'll* be safe, Sebastian. We can still have the celebration in a month as we planned, but we have the wedding ceremony tonight. Please, Seb!" He hesitated and slowly began shaking his head. I searched his eyes, desperate to reach safety. I wanted my future. I would not be an empty promise as Sylvia had been. "Sebastian, think of our future!" I snatched his hand and pressed it to my stomach. I imagined what it would feel like to have a tiny life there one day, the ultimate creation. "Think of our children!"

"I can't do it, not without my father here," Sebastian argued. He drew away from me, and I stumbled back as though he had slapped me.

"Sebastian, your father left you seventeen years ago, I'll be surprised if he ever returns to Anyra at all."

"You don't know that! I've been praying, the Totem will bring him!" he cried. He pulled away and stormed up the stairs, returning to the Sanctuary. I let out a heavy sigh, trying to see from his perspective. I would wait a thousand years for even the smallest chance to see my parents again. Although, my mother hadn't chosen to leave me while Sebastian's father had walked away willingly. All the same, some deep part of me understood that longing of a wounded, abandoned child.

"Sebastian, wait!" He stopped at the top of the stairs but didn't turn to face me. I took the basket up from the ground where I'd dropped it before quickly ascending the steps, and I placed the handle in the crook of his arm. I had brought him roasted chicken with seasoned potatoes and a slice of raspberry pie, his favorite. "I'm sorry, Seb. I love you." He stepped into the Sanctuary, letting the curtain fall behind him. Tears prickled in my eyes as I stormed down the steps and made the return trip to the blacksmith shop.

I SWEPT INTO THE SHOP, the heat from the forge washing over me with a welcome familiarity. The door slammed behind me, and Valerie looked up at the sound. She paused in her work to watch me as I snatched my heavy leather apron from its peg and angrily began dressing for work. Catching her eye, I found a concerned, expectant look on her face.

"What happened?" she asked. She knew me far too well for my own good. My temper had a tendency to match the fires I forged with, flaring and dying at a moment's notice. She had learned to ride the waves better than any other. Sebastian often had difficulty dealing with my bouts of emotion, usually feeding it right back, and my sister drew away in concern, but Valerie always knew how to either quench the flames or forge something useful from them.

"Sebastian and I had a bit of a tussle," I informed her. "As it turns out, tomorrow is Choosing Day, and I'm still a virgin. I asked him to marry me tonight to ensure my safety, but he refused."

"It's tomorrow!?" Valerie stood, bumping the workbench so it wobbled on its legs. I lunged to steady it as she tore off her metalworking gloves. "Does he not understand that he could lose you?"

"Evidently he cares more about his father being in attendance for our vows than making sure that those vows actually happen," I commented. I replaced the few tools that had tumbled off the bench as rushing footsteps approached the door. Caleb came through like a bull, his eyes wide with concern.

"I heard shouting. What's wrong?" he demanded. His orange hair was wild, and the dark circles under his eyes showed how little he had slept as of late. He'd been staying up working on projects again.

"It's alright, Caleb, I just got into an argument with Sebastian," I explained, taking a breath. I needed to calm the rage before it got out of hand. It had been a problem in the past, and Caleb was much more sensitive to my emotional swings than Valerie.

"Did you just wake up?" Valerie asked, a wry grin on her face. Caleb nervously twisted the iron wedding circlet on the chain around his neck. The surface had been worn smooth and shiny from how often he did this.

"Perhaps," he dodged. His presence dispelled my rage and Valerie's rising concern. I chuckled as Valerie smiled and pecked his cheek. He grinned like they were newlyweds when she did, but he quickly shook his head as he remembered why he came downstairs. "Now, what were you arguing with Sebastian about?"

"Tomorrow is Choosing Day, and I asked him to marry me tonight to make sure I won't be chosen to be the Gift. And he wouldn't, and he got angry with me for disrespecting the Totem, and..." I took a pause as the hot, angry tears welled in my eyes again. "And I'm none too pleased with him right now."

"That's understandable, I understand why you're upset," Caleb assured me, nodding as he processed my situation. "Sebastian is very particular, you know that well. You're not wrong to be upset with him. But I do think it's unlikely that the Totem will choose you. There's plenty of girls to choose from, and hopefully the Totem will be merciful."

"Doubt it," I grumbled. "And with the curse, I'm more worried that it will be Gwen than me."

"I think your curse is more a coincidence. Lanastings simply tend to be strong-willed, and you're no exception." I shot Caleb a glance, and he shrugged his shoulders helplessly, his point a valid one.

"You never know," Valerie consoled, slinging an arm around my shoulders. I allowed a small smile to cross my lips. "I mean, I hate the Totem just as much as you, and I still doubt you'll be the Gift."

"I suppose we'll find out tomorrow," I shrugged.

Chapter Two: The Punishment

T he clangs were loud in my ears, the work a comfort, yet the project a burden. The sooner the staff was complete and out of the forge, the happier I would be. It wasn't until the visitor was pounding on the door with strong fists that I noticed the sound. I dropped my tools on the workbench and rose, removing one glove in order to answer the door.

"Addie!" I had hoped to find Sebastian, begging forgiveness, but another much younger man stood at my door. "Addie, I'm sorry. I made a mistake, I'm sorry." The man was Gwendolyn's lover, Alexander or simply Xander as he preferred. His face was blood red, and his chest heaved with heavy breaths. A wild fearful look had overcome his eyes.

"What happened?" I demanded, shutting the door behind him. "Where's Gwen?"

"They have her," he answered vaguely, still catching his breath.

"Who has her!?"

"The Temple." He finally recovered enough breath, and he stood upright. At only seventeen, he was not much taller than me, yet he seemed so much smaller from the fear crippling his body.

"You had sex," I deduced, my shoulders sagging. "You two committed adultery against the Totem." Xander could only nod. He braced himself, expecting me to scream in rage, expecting me to blame him. I couldn't bring myself to do it. "I honestly can't blame you. I asked Sebastian nearly the same thing, but he refused to marry me today." Xander could only stare at me for a moment, jaw slightly agape.

"How could he do that?!" he demanded, shaking his head in disbelief. I nodded, my gut twisting as I wondered what they were doing with my sister. She was too fragile for the Punishment, for all we knew it could kill her.

"When are they Punishing her?"

"Soon, I don't know exactly when, but soon."

"We have to get to her, now," I reasoned. I quickly began stripping off my forge gear, hanging it haphazardly on the rack. We had no time to waste. Xander shuffled on his feet, wanting to help but unsure of how. Before he had time to think of something, I was ready. I nodded, running out the door ahead of him.

Unlike this morning, this was not the time for a leisurely stroll to the center of the city. Knowing the pain that would come from running in my heavy work boots, I broke into a sprint, Xander easily running alongside me. People whizzed past, some calling out in confusion as the he and I flew past shops and restaurants.

I was heaving for breath by the time we reached the Temple, but I only slowed enough that I would not trip as I thundered up the steps, taking them two at a time. I was first to burst through the doors, but Xander was the first to speak.

"Gwen!" he cried, the shout echoing on the marble walls. Still catching my breath, I searched for Sebastian. As the Chosen, he would know where she was. As much as I didn't want to see my betrothed, I would do anything for my sister. I would not lose her too.

"Sebastian! Where is she!?" I snapped. A young priestess drew back the red curtain that divided the waiting chamber from the Sanctuary, and she quickly retreated to retrieve someone of higher authority. I began storming my way up the second set of stairs, unafraid of any consequences I may face.

I tore my way through the curtain, Xander following closely behind. Priests and priestesses began shouting, demanding we leave. A heated glare sent them scurrying back to their cushions where they had knelt before the statue of the Totem, the demonic creature they'd been brainwashed into loving. The statue loomed over the room, dark and menacing. She looked almost as if she were a pair of conjoined twins standing eternally back to back. I took the nearest priest by the shoulder, and he drew his fearful gaze to my face.

"Where is my sister?" I growled, low and angry.

"Below, in the dungeon," he answered quickly. He winced as if in pain, rubbing his shoulder when I released him.

"Take us," I commanded.

The young priest guided us down yet another set of stairs to a level I had never seen before. Sebastian had never mentioned the cold, stone prison beneath the Temple, yet I knew a place such as this must exist. Crime was rare in Anyra, but when some idiotic soul committed a sin against the Temple, they were punished. I should have known they would have to be held somewhere as they awaited their consequence.

"Gwen!" Xander called. His voice echoed here as well, but in a different way. It reverberated louder, and the echo made it seem as though a hundred voices were calling her name one after the other.

"Xander!" Gwen's voice cried, also echoing toward us. She reached through the bars of her cell, her arms pale and thin like twigs from a birch tree. We sprinted down the hall, both of us desperate to see her. I slammed into the bars, gripping them with strong hands.

Gwen had taken on the appearance of an injured bird, small and fragile. She stood just on the other side of the bars trembling like a leaf about to fall with the sobs that wracked her small frame. As I looked her over, I already saw injuries. Large chunks of her hair had been ripped out, and long, strawberry strands were scattered about the floor of her cell. Red scrapes marred her skin from where they had gripped her arms and thrown her into the cell, and her nails were broken from fighting back.

"What did they do to you?" I demanded, reaching through the bars to take her face in my hands.

"They grabbed me as I was leaving Old Delilah's," Gwen gasped. "I don't know how they found out, we tried to be careful. They threw me into the carriage and brought me here." I took her cold hand in mine, squeezing it tight. Her shame and guilt wracked her body as she looked up at me. Her sobs began anew. "I'm sorry! I'm so sorry, Addie."

"No! No, Gwen, it's alright, you did nothing wrong," I assured her, hushing her as she struggled to remain standing even with the bars, Xander, and myself supporting her. "You did nothing wrong, they did."

"Did they throw you in there by your hair?!" Xander asked, placing his hand gently on her head. She nodded gravely, sniffling through her tears. He pressed himself as close to her as he could with the bars separating them. "I'm so sorry, darling. I should be in there with you, I'm just as guilty."

"Except they only punish women," I commented angrily. "The horrid bastards and their blasted Totem."

"I'll be alright, Addie," Gwen promised. "I did this, I have to face the consequences." She gave me a determined gaze, her slender jaw set. "Mama did it, I can too."

"Mama was also about fifty pounds bigger than you," I reminded her. "When are they going to do this? What does the punishment consist of?"

"Did Mama ever tell you about it?"

"No, we were too young, and she died before she got the chance."

"Adelaide!" I turned to find Sebastian storming down the hall. Before he could continue, I took my own step. I marched to meet him, and though I was smaller than him, I felt much bigger.

"Did you know about this!?" I cried, fuming with anger. "How could you let this happen!?" He shook his head, unable to answer as tears welled in his eyes.

"Addie, he's the one that got me," Gwen called gently. I froze, so filled with rage that I could hardly move. My chest heaved with fast, heavy breaths as I attempted to keep myself from acting violently toward him.

"You're the one that arrested her?" I growled through gritted teeth. I stared at the stone floor, knowing I couldn't look at him. If I did, I would most certainly lash out.

"That's part of my duty as the Chosen, Adelaide," he answered. "It's not like I had much of a choice!"

"She is my sister, Sebastian!" I shrieked, finally tearing my eyes up from the floor. "My father was the Chosen, he never did that! He didn't agree with it!"

"I don't *want* anyone to get hurt."

"Yet you're facilitating it! You're throwing innocent, young girls into jail cells by their hair!" He finally broke and began to fire back at me.

"She's not innocent! Not anymore! She broke the Chastity Order, she had sex out of wedlock, and defiled herself in the eyes of the Totem!" He was shouting as well now, and that only stoked the fire in my chest more. How dare he.

"She's sixteen and afraid of dying for the Totem! She wants her life, is that too much to ask!?"

"Being the Gift is an honor, she would be protecting her people!" he shot back. "She chose to be selfish and protect only herself!"

"Don't you call her selfish, you hypocritical twat! You're the one that refused to protect me!" I shrieked, finally releasing what I had wanted to say to him earlier.

"Enough!" The click of the garnet staff echoed against the stone walls as Rhoda walked toward us. The High Priestess making herself known. "Adelaide Lanasting, your sister committed a crime, and she will pay the price."

"I'll take it for her," I assured the High Priestess, squaring my shoulders to face her.

"You cannot," Rhoda informed me coldly. "You have committed no crime. Gwendolyn did, so she must face the Punishment." As if on cue, a priest unlocked Gwen's cell and dragged her out. She screamed, her cries wordless, and Xander and I leapt into action.

"You can't do this! Leave her alone!" I screamed, latching onto one of the priest's arms, attempting to wrestle him off of her.

"Adelaide, that's enough!" The voice belonged to Sebastian, but at this point I didn't care if he approved of my actions or not. They were going to hurt my sister, and there was no way I would stand by and watch. A pair of arms encircled my waist, forcefully pulling me away from Gwen and her captors.

"Let me go!" I began howling. From out of the corner of my eye, I saw three priests holding Xander down against the stones as he struggled, attempting to fight his way to his love. "Seb, this is madness!"

I tried to fight my way out of Sebastian's grip, but there was nothing I could do. Gwen disappeared up the stairs, followed closely by Rhoda. Just before she disappeared, she pounded the stone steps twice with the garnet staff. I recognized it as a signal. Instantly, Xander and I were released, and we both sprinted up the stairs.

By the time we reached the Sanctuary, Gwen was already screaming in agony. Xander and I burst through the curtain to find all the priests and priestesses in a circle at the foot of the statue of the Totem. I assumed Gwen was in the center. And they were already nearly finished with her. As I reached out to pull one of the priestesses away and reach my sister, her screams died.

"Gwen!" She lay on the marble floor, curled into a ball. She was visibly shaking in pain, tiny groans escaping her chest. Yet somehow there wasn't a single mark on her. No physical evidence of any torture. I rose, shaking in fury, as Xander gathered her into his arms.

"What did you do to her?" I demanded. Every single priest and priestess averted their eyes, refusing to look at me. Rhoda stood at the foot of the Totem, her eyes closed as she breathed heavily. Apparently, whatever the Punishment consisted of had taken a great effort.

I turned to Xander to find that he had lifted Gwen into his arms, cradling her with tender care. Her face was tucked into his neck, hiding the tears that came with the quiet sobs hitching in her chest. I turned back toward the Temple dwellers, outraged. Even Sebastian's betrayal hadn't made my blood boil like this. I had protected Gwen from so much in this life, yet the Temple left me powerless to defend her against it.

"Damn the Totem!" I yelled, throwing the words like weapons. "Damn any creature that demands an innocent, young girl be punished as recompense for protection. Damn a goddess that knows nothing but bloodlust! Damn the Temple!"

"Adelaide!" Sebastian cried, trying to silence me.

"Blasphemer!" Rhoda howled, her knuckles white on her chipped garnet staff.

"And damn you, Rhoda! May the volcano devour you along with whatever poor girl you throw into it!"

I whirled around, urging Xander to run as I moved. We took the steps quickly, running home to care for Gwen before they could do the same to me. Blaspheming, let alone in the Temple, was certainly a punishable crime.

"Where do we go?" Xander asked as he carefully picked his way down the stairs, Gwen in his arms. He cradled her close, her unconscious body so small in his arms.

"Back to the forge. We have plenty of medical supplies," I reasoned. Unsurprisingly, the journey home seemed so much longer than the frantic sprint to the Temple. I darted ahead, planning on readying a place for Gwen to rest.

No one questioned us on this pass. They bowed their heads as we ran by, able to assume what fate had befallen poor Gwen. Punishments were few and far between, but there seemed to be at least one every year as the Choosing approached. Gwen was simply this year's casualty, the one young lady everyone knew would not be chosen. She was untouchable, and though I hated the pain she'd been put through, at least I knew she would live.

We ran to the front door of the house, and I shouted for Caleb as I entered. Xander was on my heels as I snatched pillows off of the plush chairs, and he settled her on the gorgeous velvet couch. Valerie's parents were well-off from the success of her father's furniture business. His craft was just as painstaking and skilled as our blacksmithing. This also meant that Valerie had some of the finest furniture in Anyra. Even Gwen's own bed was not this comfortable.

The soft golden fabric seemed to cradle her body. It was the perfect length for her, allowing her head to rest comfortably and her feet to relax. I snatched a woven blanket from the chair and unfurled it, draping it over Gwen. I didn't know whether she was warm or cold, but the blanket meant well, nonetheless.

"What now!?" Caleb cried as he came thundering into the room for a second time today. This time he came from the forge. He had clay and dirty water smattered all over himself, his fingers caked in the beige substance. His skin went sickeningly pale at the sight of Gwen. "What happened?"

"She was Punished," I answered, rising to speak to him. "I don't know what to do. There are no physical injuries!" Caleb's shoulders sagged as he moved to wash his hands. My breath failed to slow, and Xander wiped at the sweat on his brow before clasping Gwen's hands in his. Valerie followed behind her husband, and she moved to me as Caleb knelt to examine Gwen.

"She's going to be alright," she assured me, wrapping an arm around my shoulders. Safe in my friend's arms, I let my body relax. "It doesn't cause any physical injury. Just pain and fatigue. It'll seem as though she's ill for about a week."

"A week!?" I cried, shocked.

"How? When we came in, she was screaming, but there seemed to be nothing happening," Xander asked.

"It's been said that the Punishment shaves one year off a girl's life as a form of payment for denying the Totem her right to choose her as the Gift. Rather than her whole life, the Totem feeds on one year of it," Caleb explained, never taking his eyes off of Gwen. He placed a gentle hand on her head. Her body had finally relaxed fully, a peaceful almost-smile on her face as she slept. One year of my sister's life, now gone.

"That's sick," I commented. "There shouldn't be so high a price for something like that. She just wanted to live."

"That's the Temple's exchange," Caleb shrugged, his face sour. "It is sick. But at least now she's safe." He turned to Xander. "We'll need to keep an eye on her. Give her plenty of rest, water, good food. But she will be alright."

"Thank goodness for that," Xander nodded. His eyes hadn't left her face, despite the fact that there was no threat anymore. "And you're right, Addie, damn the Totem. I want out."

"Out?" I asked.

"Out," he nodded gravely. "Out of Anyra. I want to take Gwen and give her a life away from the Temple and the Totem. If we have daughters, I don't want to fear for their lives." His hand drifted down to rest on her stomach, and my eyes narrowed, but I shrugged the questions away for now.

"So do I, but where would we go? We have no idea if there even is another civilization out there."

"There has to be. There has to be something better than this forsaken hole," Xander growled.

"There is," Caleb confirmed. "People have been leaving. They have to be going somewhere."

"Then we go there too," I decided. "A new life free from the Temple's reign. I'd give anything to go."

"What of Sebastian?" Xander asked, finally tearing his eyes away from Gwen to look up at me. "He's your betrothed, but he's the Chosen! He wouldn't betray the Temple."

"I'd give him a chance. I'd tell him I'm leaving and that he may join me, but if his allegiance truly does lie with the Temple, there's no saving him. He has to choose between me and the Totem, and I think I know which he'd choose."

Chapter Three: The Choosing

At precisely midday, almost the entire population of Anyra gathered in the square to find out what unfortunate girl would be chosen to meet her demise. Rhoda stood front and center, her garnet staff clenched in her left hand, and the priests and priestesses stood behind her on the raised stage. The stone pedestal that would choose the Gift rested before the high priestess. Sebastian had been sent to the mountain to retrieve the Sacred Fire for the ceremony. He'd left early in the morning before I'd had the chance to talk to him. As soon as we saw the orange glow of the torch, Rhoda addressed the crowd.

"People of Anyra, the Totem smiles upon you on this day," she cried. I only half-heard what she was saying. I clutched Caleb's hand in my left and Valerie's in my right, sweat beading on my brow despite the crisp chill of the autumn wind. "Today, our Totem chooses the virgin who will give her life to appease her and protect us from her wrath for another year. The Totem thirsts for blood, and she will take it from all of us if one girl does not bravely give her life for the greater good."

"Like she has a choice," I growled, and both of my friends squeezed my hands tighter, silencing me. I could see Xander and Gwen in front of us. Her small body was still sore and fatigued from the Punishment. Xander had his arm firmly around her as if he had to protect her, despite the fact that she could not be chosen. As much as I hated the Punishment she received, I was glad for it. Xander had protected her in a way none other could. Though it caused her pain, he had saved her from a worse fate.

"The Totem will reveal who she chooses with fire drawn from the volcano where the virgin's blood will be spilled. And we, people of the Totem, may live in peace for another year. Rejoice!"

Many of the people cheered, but many more remained still and silent. Some in fear, others in reverence. This was an honorable, difficult sacrifice. The many young virgin girls of the Anyran population and their families waited in anticipation. Some girls seemed to have a savior complex and longed to be the sacrifice to the Totem, remaining unwed and *pure* to the end of their days. Others were fearful, desperately trying to find a man to marry or breaking the law as Gwen had, taking pain over death. I was so close to safety, yet my life still hung in the balance.

Sebastian arrived, carrying a torch he had lit with the lava from the volcano where the virgin would be sacrificed. A different young man did so each year as part of his service to the Temple, each one serving in his 21st year. This year Sebastian was the Chosen. He retrieved the fire that would doom the Gift, and he would be the one to throw her to her death. He very well may be the one that would throw me into that damn volcano.

"Come, Chosen of the Totem, and reveal to us who will be our Gift this year," Rhoda instructed. The same speech she had given for as long as anyone could remember. Old Delilah was one of the few people left who could remember the previous High Priest. Sebastian approached the pedestal as two young priests placed the stone bowl upon it, filled with kindling. The crowd was silent, collectively holding its breath in anticipation. Sebastian placed the torch in the bowl, setting the wood ablaze.

Sebastian stepped back and Rhoda took his place, her garnet staff clicking on the stone. She held a piece of parchment above her head for all to see before dropping it into the flames. I rolled my eyes at her dramatics, sickened by her praise of the gruesome practice. The flames died within moments, not a sound but the wind whistling between the buildings. Rhoda fished the piece of paper from the smoking ashes, and as always it was miraculously still intact, only lightly singed on the edges. She read the name as the crowd watched with bated breath.

"Please don't be me," I breathed, hardly audible. Caleb, Valerie, and I clutched each other with vicelike grips. I was surprised we didn't break one another's bones with hands hardened from labor as ours were. Xander looked back at me, scared and saddened by the prospect of my death. He was a good man, and he would hate to see Gwen in such sorrow. Rhoda glanced over her shoulder to where Sebastian stood with the priests.

"Please," I begged.

"Adelaide Lanasting!" Rhoda cried, raising the paper high above her head. The world seemed to freeze around me. The cold cobblestones met my skin, my knees scraping on the rough edges without me truly registering it, and I pulled Caleb down with me. Valerie's scream rang from her chest, certainly deafening with her powerful singer's voice, but the sound was muffled as if my ears were stuffed full of cotton. The cruel Totem had chosen me.

The loudest sound in my head was that of my own heart, pounding at a deafening volume and rising in speed. I didn't realize I was crying until the cracks in the cobblestones blurred and I saw twin puddles beginning to form. I deftly felt Caleb's strong hands on my shoulders, taut as if they were metal wire from working the clay he used for pottery.

Slowly, the world around me grew louder. Valerie was shrieking with grief and rage, the sounds waking my heart from the numbness the shock had brought. Gwen had also crumpled to the ground, pulling Xander down with her. She lay in a heap, motionless as if dead. Xander pulled her into his chest, but his horrified gaze never left me.

My surroundings came back to life as hands seized me, dragging me toward the stage as Valerie and Caleb attempted to keep the prying fingers of the crowd away from me. They couldn't fight them all off. I went limp. I was in shock, unable to believe that my fears had come true. The shambles that were my world had come crumbling down around me in mere moments. The crowd threw me onto the stage at Rhoda's feet, and I shakily began to rise.

"People of Anyra, I give you your Gift!" she announced. After a moment's hesitation, the people began to applaud. No whoops and hollers sounded, as this was not a joyful noise. It was a sounding of thanks for what I would do for them. I was their martyr if an unwilling one. I caught sight of Caleb's wild, orange hair and found him clutching Valerie in his arms. I'd rarely seen either of them cry, but now they were both sobbing.

Rhoda stepped up behind me and placed an arm around my shoulders. Only her palm actually touched me, withdrawn as always. I stood trembling as if I had a fever, and a noise drew my attention. Some hollow, desperate howl echoed behind me, an otherworldly bellow of agony. I turned to find Sebastian on his knees, his head in his hands, hunched over as if he were wracked with unbearable pain. He let out another deep, guttural shriek, and the sound bounced off the limestone into the air.

"I'm sorry!" he screamed, finally putting words to the sound. I stumbled a few steps toward him and fell to my knees as well, hardly able to support my own weight. He looked up at me, his face twisted in a grimace full of guilt and regret. He placed a trembling hand on my cheek, looking at me as if I were already dead. "I'm a fool." My breathing grew harder as Rhoda announced the end of the ceremony.

"You're damn right you are," I growled. He blinked, surprised by the malice in my tone. I shook with anger now that the shock had begun to wear away. The crowd began to disperse as Sebastian and I sat on the stone dais. I had one month to live out the rest of my days as best I could. I could do anything I wished so long as I remained pure in the Totem's eyes. I had mere weeks left to live thanks to *him.*

"Addie?" he asked as I stomped to my feet, the rage that had been smoldering inside of me since the day before growing uncontrollably. For the first time, I let it consume me, and I unleashed it with no holds barred. No longer was I tamed like the fires of the forge. I had become like the volcano that would kill me, boiling over in a horrifying display. I'm certain my face was as red as the lava that would eat through my skin and devour my bones in only a month's time.

"*MURDERER!*" I screeched. The word ripped my throat raw, and I tasted blood. Sebastian flinched away from me, and the remaining crowd stopped to stare at our altercation. "You did this!" I snatched the engagement necklace at my throat with such force that the chain snapped.

"Addie, please, I couldn't have known!" Sebastian argued. I threw the symbol of our union at him, and he caught it with open palms. He gasped and dropped it as if the metal were freshly smelted.

"You *did* know! I warned you that this could happen!" My stomach began to ache as my breath hitched with sobs. "I'm going to die, Sebastian! And the blood will be on your hands, you selfish twat!"

"Addie, please!" I turned and stormed away, running into Caleb and Valerie's outstretched arms. Finally, I broke, mourning my own death before it happened. I sobbed as I had when I was a child at the triplet funeral held for my parents and Sylvia. Gwen threw herself into our huddle, sobs wracking her petite form. She had always been so small, but now she seemed even smaller, liable to shatter like glass at the slightest touch. She clutched at my shirt, unable to form words.

We remained in that position for a long time, crumpling to the cobblestones as the effort of standing became too much to bear. Gwen lay across my lap just as she had as a child, her body shaking. Caleb and Valerie remained connected to me and to each other, some form of physical contact the only comfort in this bleak moment. Xander hesitated for a moment, his chest heaving violently. No doubt his young mind was overwhelmed by all these changes and pains. Sebastian was still on the stage, lying in a heap.

"Come on, we have to go home," Caleb coerced me. Xander pulled Gwen onto his back and with a nod, began his journey home. After her Punishment, they had chosen to begin living together so he could better care for her as she recovered.

Caleb then pulled me and Valerie away, and we began the miserable trek home with wet faces even before the grey skies opened to pour down on us. We passed few people on the streets as rain drizzled out of the clouds above. Many were making preparations to open shops and cafes for the remainder of the day. When the Anyrans we passed caught sight of me, they stopped what they were doing and stood in solemn reverence as I passed them by. The Gift of the Totem selected to follow in my family's footsteps and die before my time. The name of Lanasting was cursed indeed.

The three of us were silent when we reached Caleb and Valerie's home. We entered through the front door of the house rather than the smithy in the back as we normally would. Without needing to communicate, we moved to change our clothes. I had been living with them for a few months as I prepared to move into the home I would have shared with Sebastian. We exchanged our damp clothes for warm, dry attire, and without thinking we began to prepare the evening meal.

Few words were spoken as I chopped potatoes. Working in tandem beside me, Caleb prepared and roasted the chicken, and Valerie set the table. She laid out three place settings of their fine wedding dishware, passed down from mother to daughter for five generations. Once the table was set, she quickly gathered ripe strawberries from the garden, the last of the season, and placed them on the table with a large bowl of sweetened cream. She knew they were my favorite. Caleb and I placed the steaming food on the table, the smells making the dining room warm and welcoming.

The three of us sat down in our usual seats with Caleb at the head of the table, his wife to his right and myself to his left. We were not like some pious families who thanked the Totem for each meal. We saw her for the violent, cruel thing she was, on this night more than most. None of us moved to begin filling our plates. I gazed at the chicken, my stomach in knots, as an image of my own flesh feeding the Totem flashed through my mind. I would not let this own me for what time I had left.

"Come on then, you two," I commented, reaching forward to pull the drumstick off of the chicken. "I won't let all this delicious food go to waste. I'm living these last few weeks however I wish." I ripped into the poultry, the succulent flavor filling my mouth. Instantly, the discomfort in my stomach was eased, and the hunger came flooding in. As if they had suddenly become famished themselves, Caleb and Valerie began filling their plates, their faces softening as they relaxed. We briefly forgot the harrowing events of the day as we tucked into a hearty meal and good friendship.

After the dinner table was cleared and the dishes washed and put away, Valerie pulled a box from a cabinet. She shook it twice, drawing Caleb's and my attention. It was a board game; the same one Caleb, Gwen, and I had played as children. We played for hours, laughing and talking as if today was not the one that sealed my fate. Long after the sun had set, we were still playing. We had long since lost track of how many games we'd played or who had won the most. Exhaustion crept into me, and I went to bed, entirely drained but now filled with joy.

33

Chapter Four: Familiar

Valerie wouldn't allow me to enter the forge the morning after the Choosing. She insisted I take a day to rest, visit family, and decide what I would do with my time. It was left unspoken, but we knew that I would not allow my life to be taken. Being thrown into the mouth of the monster simply wasn't an option. I would not follow my aunt's footsteps into the Totem's lap or allow a curse to dictate my death. Somehow, I would live. How I would do that was uncertain.

I made my way through the town, revered by many I passed. As I walked through the market, past shops and restaurants, they bowed their heads in respect. I was their martyr, the one who would make the ultimate sacrifice for them. How could they allow it? How tight was the Temple's clutch on the fearful, subjugated people of Anyra?

As I walked, the city fell away behind me. I hadn't left with the intention of coming here, yet I found myself on Uncle Quinton's doorstep. His cottage stood a fair distance from the city proper, surrounded on three sides by tall grass waving in the breeze. The fourth was flanked by sand, leading to the ocean. The wood had been worn from years it had endured being battered by the salty ocean winds and sea storms. A thin tendril of smoke rose from the chimney as always. I hesitated, but I knew I had to talk to him at least once more, even if it broke my heart.

I raised a hand and rapped on the door twice, softly so as not to startle him. My uncle had changed so much since I was a child. A crash and a scuffle came from within before the door swung open.

Wide eyes greeted me, the same as those of my mother. The siblings had always looked so alike. Gwen had been mistaken as Quinton's daughter so many times. No one questioned for a second whether I was my father's.

The years had not been kind to my uncle. He had never married, claiming he was wed to the sea. He had wasted away to skin and bones, his hair thinning and unruly. So absorbed in his works of fiction, he had always had a bad habit of forgetting meals. His eyes were wide as if permanently startled.

"Addie," Quinton breathed, "oh, my little thing." He pulled me into his arms, and I allowed it. He hadn't been present for the Choosing, but there was no doubt that word had spread to him. No doubt that Old Delilah had told him. No doubt she did so proudly.

"Why?" I begged him as tears began to gather in my eyes once again. "Why do they do this?"

"I don't know, Addie," he crooned, holding me tightly. He gently ran his hand over my hair, tugging at the long, ruddy strands. "It's not right." We went into the house, and he placed the kettle over the weak fire on the hearth. Tea fixed just about anything in my uncle's eyes, and if it didn't fix it, tea certainly helped. He sat down in the armchair across from me, folding his hands.

"How've you been?" I asked, attempting to make conversation. "Anything new?" I glanced around the small house, finding little change since my last visit. There were books everywhere, shelves lining the walls filled to bursting. They were stacked on tables or the floor, tea mugs scattered around with them. Some of the books he read, some he'd written. So many worlds inside his head. Maybe that was what drove him mad.

"It's been good," he nodded. "Your mother has been a lot more active lately; she always is as the Choosing approaches. This year more than most. I guess she knew it was going to be you. Maybe she was trying to warn me."

"Q, you know what I say about that," I replied, shaking my head. "There are no ghosts! Mama's gone, she died trying to save us. She did her best."

"She wasn't done with this world. She never wanted to leave you and your sister behind." Quinton suddenly had fire in his eyes, as he always did if his notion was challenged. He'd claimed for years that he was haunted by the ghost of my mother, that she was trapped in the sea and spoke only to him. "She was trying to save you, Adelaide! And you should appreciate it!"

"I do, Quinton," I assured him gently. "She did all she could. Now she's in the sea, resting." My uncle calmed at my words and relaxed back into his chair. His gaze moved to the window where the surf lapped at the shore.

"She is in the sea, you're right about that," he ceded. He gently began rocking in his chair, mimicking the waves. A fisherman at heart, Quinton had always been more comfortable on the water. "Resting, not so much. She'd do anything to save you."

I nodded, matching his gaze to the waves outside. The water that had taken my mother from me. She had drowned trying to escape to find a place for me and my sister. She would not feed us to the volcano as well. My mother was not a sailor, nor did she know what the water would be like. The very day my aunt and father fell into the volcano, she had fled.

As soon as the sun set, she bundled us up with all we could carry. At four years old, I couldn't carry much, so we only took the absolute necessities. She strapped my sister onto her back and lead me by the hand to the very house where I sat now. She handed Gwen to her brother, kissed us each on the head, and told him she'd be back for us when she found land. Once she had found somewhere safe where the Totem couldn't reach us.

She never returned. Quinton's boat, or at least what was left of it washed ashore a week later. It was as if the Totem herself had whipped up a storm to keep my mother from leaving. Nothing would escape her grasp. Evelyn Lanasting was never found. She was buried in spirit alongside her husband and his sister. We had no bodies to bury but three people gone.

"You need to go," Quinton announced, his voice calm but serious. I looked to him to find his eyes wide, his body stiff. The chair was no longer rocking. He seemed to stare through the waves rather than at them. "Get out, Adelaide. Run!"

As his words grew louder and more urgent, I rose from my place beside him. "Uncle Q?" I asked. I received no answer. He remained motionless, frozen with glassy eyes. The only thing that moved was his mouth as he shouted louder and louder. "Run! Get out! Anyra will kill you!"

"Quinton, what's wrong?" I asked, rising from my chair. The kettle had begun to boil, the rushing water beginning to spill over. A drop of sweat fell from the tip of my uncle's nose, staining a perfect circle on his shirt.

"You have to go! They're going to kill you! The Totem is dead!" The voice didn't seem to belong to Quinton. It was as though something, some force was speaking through him.

"Q, what do you mean the Totem is dead? She's not real?"

"The Totem is dead!" He raged, still rigid as a board. "She is a lie! She is the power the Temple holds!" His head slowly turned to me, eyes unmoving, staring straight through my soul. I shrunk back in fear as he began to rise. My feet left the floor as the kettle finally whistled, and I knocked a mug from its place atop a precarious stack of books. Quinton didn't even flinch when it shattered at his feet.

"Quinton, stop!" I cried, forced to shout to be heard.

"It is in you! Get out! Before they steal it! Rhoda will steal everything from you! Go!"

"I don't understand," I begged, backing toward the door. Quinton drew close, placing a hand colder than the heartless sea on my arm.

"Get. Out." I couldn't move as he stared at me, never blinking, completely void of emotion. "GET OUT GET OUT GET OUT GET OUT GET OUT GET OUT!" Finally, I followed his instructions and fled. I stumbled over the clutter as I moved, but he didn't follow. I slammed the door behind me, but I could still hear his voice bidding me to run. His words haunted me as I trudged back to the city. Get out. But go where?

Shaken, I followed my feet once more. I simply moved, no destination in mind. What I needed was difficult to find, but once I realized it, I knew where I must go. I needed a mother. Seeing as mine was unavailable, my subconscious had taken me to her closest relation, Uncle Quinton. Now, my substitute mother could surely help.

The bell rang cheerily as I entered Old Delilah's flower shop. I had been raised in these walls, along with Caleb and Gwen. Old Delilah had no blood relation to me or my family, but she took us as her own. Caleb's parents had died of disease when he was a toddler, so she had already adopted her grandson. He gained two playmates when she brought us home.

"Addie!" she cried at the sight of me. She dropped a glass vase, and it shattered on the counter as she rushed to greet me. Another thing broken.

"Delilah, are you alright!?" I demanded, but she gave no heed. She pulled me down into a hug, kissing my temple fiercely.

"Oh, my little Addie," she gushed, her voice choked with tears. I returned the hug, desperately craving the security. Old Delilah was no replacement for my true mother, but she was a good substitute and all I had. My heartrate finally slowed, relaxing into Old Delilah's gentle touch. "I'm so proud of you." The tension instantly crept back into my muscles again, no respite finding home in my heart.

"What for?" I asked, my brow furrowing. She pulled away, looking me over and placing her hands on my face.

"You are the Gift of the Totem, dearie, it's an honor!" she explained, smiling with tears in her eyes. "It's a beautiful thing. You're so selfless." It took me a moment to speak as I fought to control my temper.

"What?" I demanded tersely.

"And following in your aunt's footsteps. She was so eager to save her people."

"Delilah," I said, my voice stern as she turned to walk back to the counter. "You see this as a blessing?"

"Of course! You have been selected! You are the fairest, most brave girl in the city! It is a compliment!" The smile had not faded, but tears still fell onto the flowers as she gathered them into a bouquet. "Your purity did not go unnoticed. I'm very proud. I'll miss you terribly, darling, but I know you'll never truly leave me." She placed the bouquet in a new vase and laid a hand on her heart. "You'll always be right here." I couldn't speak for a moment, and Old Delilah simply stared at me. Finally, she took notice of my distress and her smile faltered. "What's wrong, Addie?"

"I am going to die!" I shouted, my voice deep with the power of the bellows in my forge. "I'm going to drown in lava! I'm going to be sacrificed to the damn Totem! To Rhoda!"

"Adelaide, be quiet!" Old Delilah shot back, horrified.

"I'll die in the same fires as my father and my aunt! All for nothing!"

"Adelaide Lanasting, you need to have some respect! They died to save you!"

"They died for NOTHING!" I shrieked, my voice shrill and choked by tears. "You're blind."

"You are blind! The Totem is a good caregiver! She requires a small price for the wellbeing of all Anyra! She is merciful!" Delilah screamed in response.

"She isn't benevolent! I refuse to believe it!" I fired. Old Delilah stopped cold, drawing away. I didn't stop, my mind racing as my caregiver, the woman who raised me, simply accepted my death. "The only thing you worship is Rhoda and her power over you! The Totem is dead, that's what Quinton said."

"Get out, Adelaide." Delilah leveled her finger at the door, new tears shimmering on her cheeks.

"Gladly," I said curtly. The bells jingled cheerily as I slammed the door behind me. I ran, stumbling home to my forge and the family that wanted me to live.

Chapter Five: Heretic

Two days after the Choosing, I awoke cold in my bed. I had no desire to drag myself out even as the first rays of sunlight reached my eyes through the open window. Anyra was just waking up from the long, dark night. As I lay still in the groggy morning haze, I listened, the sounds of the city beginning to float through the open window.

I could hear the shopkeepers opening their stores two streets over, the familiar tinkling of bells as they unlocked their doors for business. The scent of frying eggs and freshly baked bread wafted in as the restaurants served breakfast to the early risers. The clank of wood against wood as they opened the awnings, offering shade from the ocean sunshine.

From within the house, I heard the whistle of the kettle as Caleb prepared his morning tea, and the heaving clang of Valerie's hammer in the forge echoed over the sleepy city. Breathing deeply, I let myself rest in that moment, the sounds and smells of my home. The good parts of Anyra. I still had a life to live in the meantime.

Quickly, I rose from the bed, and dressed for the day, braiding my hair down my back. My forge clothes were clean, but they appeared as though they were not from the stains and scorches Valerie and I could never seem to scrub out. I found it charming in an odd way, clean and dirty in the same instance, rather like Anyra itself.

I found Caleb at the table as I bounded down the stairs, sipping his rather large mug of tea and reviewing his plans for the day. Several pots and pitchers lay in the sketches before him, along with one particularly elegant set of tableware. Only one stained glass window was sketched out, a beautiful scene of the sunset on the ocean. 'Barnable House' was scribbled on the bottom, denoting where the piece would end.

"Morning, Lubby," I greeted him, invoking the childhood nickname. He chuckled at the sound of it, remembering what a hard time Gwen had pronouncing his name as a toddler.

"Morning, Laidey," drawing a giggle from me as well. "I'm glad to see you up and about. I wasn't sure how you'd be."

"Me either. I figured I should live, no matter how much time I have left to do so," I shrugged, pouring myself a much smaller mug from the teapot. Caleb met my eyes as I sat down with some bread and cheese.

"I'm proud of you for that," he smiled. My eyes misted as the closest thing I had to brother placed his hand over mine.

"Thank you."

"What are your plans for today? Working in the forge I take it?"

"Yeah, thought I would. Get a few more things done in my month. Maybe some projects for myself, have a little more fun with it," I shrugged. I took a sheet of blank paper and a piece of charcoal from Caleb's pile and began sketching, something I rarely did.

"What about the staff?" he asked. The charcoal screeched on the paper, and I froze, remembering the wretched work I had begun. I thought for a moment.

"That's not getting finished. That wretch doesn't deserve my handiwork," I commented, returning to my drawing. From the corner of my eye, I saw a smug grin flit across Caleb's face.

"Good. Now, I need to get to work." He stood and squeezed my shoulder for a brief instant. "You know where I'll be."

He left for his potter's wheel, and I continued eating my breakfast, drawing with one hand and eating with the other. Beneath my pencil, the form of a statue took shape. Rhoda would not get her ruby staff. If she wanted my life, I would take something in return.

My boots clomped heavily on the stone floor as I walked into the forge, melding with the clang of Valerie's hammer on the metal she was working. She looked up at me as I moved to the pegs on the wall, quickly putting on my protective forge gear. An anger burned in my heart as I moved, and I would use it.

"Addie, I didn't expect you in here today," Valerie commented, pausing in her work. I shot her a wicked grin.

"I have something I need to do." That was all it took for her to understand. She nodded with a sly smile and returned to her work. I knew deep down she disagreed with what I was about to do, but she didn't object. I needed this, and Rhoda deserved it.

I took the rugged, half-formed scepter up with my tongs and shoved it into the forge, heating the metal. It quickly reached the red-hot stage I needed. Moving with speed, I withdrew the oblong piece and began hammering at the larger end. I flattened it into the anvil, forming what would have been the clawed hand into the base for what I would create.

Moving on, I softened the metal and cut it into six long strips sprouting from the base. I did all of this instinctively, not truly knowing what I was going to create. I had a rough idea of what I would make in my head, and an even rougher iteration on the paper beside me, but the metal knew what it wanted to become under my hands and tool.

The long metal pieces almost seemed to twist and braid themselves into form as I worked, spiraling around one another in complex shapes. They formed a nest at the top as they cooled, and I used a torch to melt the ends together once again. The heavy shears cut at the metal with a satisfying snap as I cut prongs out of the smooth curves to hold the gemstone in place.

Satisfied with the shapes I had created, I plunged the entire mass into my bucket with a hiss of steam, cooling it instantly. Water splattered to the floor as I shook off the excess, and I set it back on the workbench. I ripped the heavy leather gloves off and threw them to the side as I reached for the box on the shelf.

It was only then that I realized the forge was silent if not for the roaring flame. Valerie had halted her work, watching me in my craftsmanship. I glanced over my shoulder to see tears on her face. I didn't comment.

The ruby glinted in the firelight, throwing red and orange light around the forge as I removed the gem from the fabric cradling it. I settled it into the nest of metal, finding that it fit perfectly, held secure but not choked by the steel. Taking up a small mallet, I tapped the prongs into place around the jewel, ensuring it would never come loose. My creation complete.

I stepped back, admiring the handiwork. I smiled, finding solace in the fact that what was meant to be a symbol of the Totem's power now sat before me as a beautiful sculpture. I wiped the sweat from my brow, and I realized my stomach was grumbling with hunger. I turned to Valerie, and she reached out to hug me.

"You need to go eat some lunch," she told me.

"How long was I working on that?" I asked, only just realizing that I had become completely blind to the time in my work. It had been a while since I'd gotten so lost in a project.

"It's been five hours, Addie." I froze, my eyes wide staring at the finished piece.

"Oh," I gasped. "Alright."

"Let's go get washed up," Valerie coerced me, untying my leather apron and pulling it over my head. My breath hitched in my chest as she did this, though I couldn't quite pinpoint why. In that moment, I seemed to revert to that scared little girl I was once.

"Alright."

NEITHER VALERIE NOR I heard the knocking at the door, so we were surprised when a priest barged into the shop. I dropped the goblet I was shaping but kept the hammer in hand as he approached. He was an older priest, his graying hair receding back. Unless he was incredibly fit underneath his robes, there was no way he could take me by force.

"Does no one realize there's a bell?" I demanded, frustrated.

"Revered Gift, your presence is requested at the Temple," he stated, noticeably avoiding looking me in the eyes.

"Use my damn name if you're going to barge into my forge," I spat, "and you can tell Rhoda to shove it. I have work to do." I turned back to my bench, but the priest remained adamant.

"My Gift," he said through gritted teeth, "I insist."

"What did I just say?" I commented, not looking up as I reheated the goblet in the furnace. "Get out of my forge."

"I understand that you may want to say a few final words to your uncle before his execution." My eyes grew wide as the words fell from the priest's lips. I took the cup from the fire and brandished it at the priest as a knight may wield a sword.

"Pardon?" I demanded, advancing on him with the red-hot metal clenched in the tongs I held. The sly grin disappeared from the man's face in an instant.

"Quinton Marason has been found guilty of heresy!" he cried, scrabbling backward toward the door. "He will be executed this afternoon!"

"OUT!" I roared, and finally he complied. The goblet and tongs clattered to the floor as I once again began ripping off my forge gear.

"Why in the Totem's name was he tried for heresy!?" Valerie demanded, and I glanced over to see her doing the same as I, ripping her heavy leather gloves and apron away. She would not let me go to the Temple alone again.

47

"He was acting strangely yesterday. It was like he was possessed! He started screaming that the Totem was dead and that I needed to get out."

"Maybe he still is possessed, if that is what happened," Valerie guessed. "If he is going to die, Gwen should get to see him too."

"Send Caleb to get her and Xander," I suggested. Valerie darted into the house, and reentered the forge seconds later.

"He's going to go get her." I nodded, my chest tightening with fear and anger.

"Then let's go to Quinton."

For the second time, I raced toward the Temple, this time with Valerie on my heels rather than Xander. My stomach churned and boiled as we mounted the steps yet again. I didn't call out this time. I knew now where to go. I darted past the steps leading up to the Sanctuary and began thundering down the staircase to the dungeon, neatly tucked away and nearly unnoticeable.

I could hear the commotion as Valerie and I raced down the row of cells, following our ears toward the screeching. A chill ran through my body as Quinton's voice echoed down the stone hallway, the same as it had been when I had visited him. He shrieked the same words as before.

"The Totem is dead! The Totem is dead! The Totem is dead!"

He repeated the phrase over and over, hardly stopping to take a breath. I understood why they had accused him of heresy. They should have exorcised him instead. Something had come over him, and I was beginning to believe in his notions that my mother was haunting him.

Two priests armed with spears stood to either side of Quinton's cell, looking visibly uneasy as he screamed and carried on. Valerie and I approached warily. I looked between the two guards, both young and frightened. It was almost as if they knew that what he was saying was true yet didn't want to admit it.

"Leave us. I wish to speak with my uncle in private," I demanded quietly. For once, they took no convincing. Immediately, they scurried off at the behest of their precious Gift. I sneered at the power I abused, but my face fell again as I turned toward Quinton. My heart plummeted into my already upset stomach.

He was chained to the wall by his arms, spread wide to either side, but he didn't seem to have struggled against them. His blank, sightless gaze stared forward, fixed on some point lost in emptiness. The words poured from his lips in a continuous stream, only stopping to suck in a great heaving breath when he could speak no more.

"The Totem is dead! The Totem is dead! The Totem is dead!"

"He's either possessed or gone completely mad," Valerie commented. Her wide eyes hadn't left Quinton's thin, pale figure since they had fallen on him.

"Both are fairly likely," I nodded in agreement. "Uncle Q, it's Adelaide and Valerie. We're here to help."

Quinton gave no response other than to take in another gulp of air and continue his tirade of words, the one sentence still repeating. Before we could entreat him further, more feet came thundering down the steps to our left. Caleb, Xander, and Gwen came down, Gwen moving slowly and shakily as she was still recovering from the Punishment.

"Why is he screaming like that?" Caleb asked, coming to wrap an arm around his wife.

"Remember how he said he was haunted by my mother's ghost?" I asked. Caleb and Gwen nodded, Xander gaping wide-eyed, first at Quinton, then me, then back again. "I'm starting to think he may have been right."

"Uncle Q?" Gwen's strained voice asked, still hoarse from screaming and crying both during her Punishment and when I was selected as the Gift. Again, he gave no response, his repetition never ceasing. I took a wild stab.

"Evelyn," I said, more commanding than questioning. Quinton fell silent, his eyes finally focusing on mine. My heart joined my stomach at my feet as the entire hall became deathly silent, the very stones seeming to hold their breath. For the first time, I realized why he had been screaming. The shrill pitch of his voice better matched a woman's voice than his deeper male tone.

"Adelaide," came the reply, "the Totem is dead."

"Yes, I know," I nodded, a chill of fear running through my body as if my veins were filled with ice. There came a pregnant pause, silence making each of us somehow even more uneasy than the knowledge that Quinton had spoken true. He had been haunted by our dead mother, and now she had taken his body as hers. A tear slipped down my cheek as I stared at the amalgamation before me. The reunion with my mother should have been a joyous event.

"You are the Gift," my mother said through Quinton's mouth. I knew the eyes looked like my mother's, now more than ever. Was this what drove him mad?

"I will fight," I argued, fighting now to keep my voice steady.

The strange being chained to the wall gave no response. The silence grated on my nerves until a sound shattered the quiet. Gwen gave out a shrill, broken scream, piercing the air with the high clarity of the sound, and causing the rest of us to jump out of our skin. I heard the priests beginning their descent down the steps and the sharp *click, click, click* of Rhoda's staff against the stone steps.

"Get out!" I cried, staring deep into the strange eyes, both my mother's and Quinton's, yet somehow also neither. The phantom within him seemed to heed my words. The body of my uncle went limp against the chains, finally falling into a state of rest. He began to stir as if waking from a deep sleep, his head lifting to reveal clear eyes.

"What?" he murmured, finally returning to his senses from days of possession. I suddenly regretted forcing my mother to leave him. Perhaps she would have been laid to rest if we'd had more time. I turned as Rhoda approached our troupe.

"My Gift," she addressed me, bowing her head in what must have been feigned reverence. "I apologize, but the time has come."

"He is innocent," I argued, placing myself firmly between Rhoda and the cell door.

"Please, I do not want to go through this a second time in the same week," Rhoda huffed, her shoulders sagging. "He committed an act of heresy against the Totem, and the penalty is death. You are lucky you are not receiving the same sentence."

"Except I am, you intend to kill me regardless!" I argued, my chest swelling in indignation. "He was possessed by something. Quinton is not to blame."

"He was not possessed. I know his allegations of your mother's ghost. There is no such possibility," Rhoda dismissed.

"Adelaide," Quinton called, his voice hoarse but now returned to his normal range and tone. I turned to him, and he seemed more awake and coherent than he had in years. "It's alright," he smiled. "It's time for me. This is not the war you need to fight."

"No, Uncle," I begged, but he cut me off.

"Girls, I love you," he promised, his eyes clear and unafraid. Gwen's were filled with tears, but mine held nothing but rage. "All will be well." Two priests stepped forth, one holding the key firmly in his hand for fear I would snatch it away from him.

"Your uncle has accepted his punishment. I suggest you do the same," Rhoda shot, the faintest suggestion of a smile tugging at her lips. Reluctantly, my chest heaving as I had to watch the last surviving adult in my family surrender himself to a fate he did not deserve, I stepped back to allow the priests to remove Quinton from his cell.

Gwen reached out and took my hand, grasping it firmly, although I could hardly feel her squeezing with my work-worn hands. Xander held her wrapped in his strong arms, her shoulders shaking as she cried once again. Her short life had been filled with far too much turmoil. Shakily, she lifted her head to look at me.

"I can't watch this, Addie," she whispered, knowing her strength was failing. Yet another person she loved, dead before her very eyes. I nodded, clasping her bony hand gently in my strong fingers.

"You don't have to," I promised her. I shifted my gaze to Xander. "Take her home." He nodded, and she collapsed into him, fully and thoroughly exhausted. I turned to Valerie and Caleb, and they nodded as well. They would stay, despite having no connection to Quinton themselves. As Rhoda disappeared up the steps, I squared my shoulders and followed.

The somber procession led up to the Sanctuary, and the priests and priestesses of the Temple stood waiting for the so called "criminal" that would be executed. They were lined along the walls, plates of smoking incense in their hands. The priests holding Quinton's arms were not rough or cruel to him, as he did not fight back. He went quietly, without protest, though also not throwing himself at the Totem's feet.

He knelt with his back turned toward the massive obsidian statue, somehow peaceful for the first time in many long years. Deep down, I knew he was looking forward to resting at long last. Rhoda and Sebastian stepped up behind him, and she looked me dead in the eye. I was not the first to look away. My former betrothed stared solemnly at the knife resting on the velvet cushion in his hands.

A taut ball formed in my stomach as Rhoda began to speak, her words almost sounding like a string of sounds, no language discernable from the noise. She reached over and gracefully lifted the knife out of Sebastian's hands, the blade shining brilliantly in the afternoon light. It was curved, the tip almost impossibly sharp, and I knew it would cut through fabric, skin, and sinew like it was nothing but air.

I couldn't watch any longer. As Rhoda placed the tip of the knife on his back, Quinton closed his eyes, and I did the same. There was no sound as the knife pierced his heart, and he didn't cry out as the life faded from his body. The only noise came when he slumped to the floor, and I finally looked. Rhoda still held the knife poised in the air, dripping with crimson, and Quinton lay face down on the marble floor.

"The Chosen will dispose of your uncle's body, so you need not worry about funeral preparations," Rhoda assured me, the faintest impression of a smile on her face. I had no will left to throw words at her as weapons. I looked to Sebastian who still avoided my gaze.

"Be sure to mark his grave so I can visit it," I requested, staring at the top of Sebastian's head as he stared at the floor. "Go ahead and mark mine beside it, though I doubt *you* would place any flowers there."

Chapter Six: Exodus

In the dead of night, I was shaken from a deep, dreamless sleep by Valerie, speaking urgently. She bid me to rise and get dressed despite the fact that sunrise was hours away. I did as she urged, quickly dressing as she instructed. Rather than my smithy clothes, I donned a heavier outfit meant for travel in the chill air. My rugged hiking boots found their way onto my feet, and I followed Valerie into the hall.

"Is something wrong?" I asked groggily, pulling my jacket on.

"We're getting you out of here," she explained, her voice grim and her jaw set. I stopped cold, hardly able to process her words.

"What?!" I shrieked in a whisper. She turned and hushed me violently as Caleb rounded the corner, still dressed and holding two bags.

"We're not letting them kill you. You have to leave," he explained.

"I don't understand," I argued as Caleb piled the packs into my arms. "Where will I go?"

"There's a group people living in a settlement in the woods," Valerie explained. "People like us who see the Totem for what she is, people who turned and fled from Anyra's ways. They'll accept you as their own."

"What about Gwen? What about you!?" I asked, the questions I grabbed from the whirlpool of queries and protests in my head.

"She and Xander can leave in a few days when she is strong enough," Valerie promised as she wrapped a scarf around my neck. "We'll watch over them while you're gone."

"We'll follow in a week or so. Till then, we'll cover your escape. Lead a search party in the wrong direction," Caleb explained.

"But Sebastian. He's still with the Temple," I argued. Even after his many betrayals, he was still one of my main concerns.

"He's made his choice, Addie," Valerie said. She laid a hand on my cheek, and I melted into her touch, comforting in its solidity with the whirlwind of confusion in my mind. "I know it's sudden, and I'm sorry for that. You'll have time to process when we settle."

I was simply at a loss, overwhelmed by the sudden developments in my quickly approaching fate. I could only croak out two words.

"Thank you," I breathed. Valerie and Caleb quickly took me in their arms, holding me fiercely for a brief moment before pulling away.

"Now go," Valerie instructed, helping situate the knapsack and satchel on my shoulders. "Follow the path of the moon. You'll find them, or they'll find you. We'll be there soon."

They gently pushed me out of the door, and I found myself alone on the dark, empty streets that I knew so well. After a moment of dumbfounded indecision, I began to walk. The entire city was fast asleep, safe in the knowledge that soon enough, another sacrifice would keep the Totem at bay. Little did they know that I would not succumb to that so easily.

I reached the edge of the city in a quarter of an hour, facing the farmlands that surrounded the city proper. The fields of wheat, barley, and corn stretched out for only a few miles before abruptly ending in a perfect line. There was only a few hundred feet of empty field between the crops and the trees. I quickly searched the stars, and I determined that I only had about an hour until the first rays of light would filter through the trees. I set out across the fields, finding myself allowing hope to bubble up in my chest. Perhaps I would survive longer than the few weeks I had been sentenced.

THE WOODS WERE COOL and calm, the green just beginning to fade into the beautiful golds, reds, and oranges of autumn. I had always been told never to venture close to the trees, yet I had not understood why they were hailed as evil. Only the most skilled hunters dared brave the forest, and their numbers had dwindled over the years. I had always assumed there were dangerous animals in the woods that had killed the hunters. Now I knew that some may have defected.

I entered the woods just as the sun came up, the dense trees providing not only shade, but shelter from any prying eyes in Anyra. The city looming at my back and the unfamiliar territory I trod toward caused a pit to form in my stomach. My friends had assured me that I would find this sect of rogues easily, but I had no idea what I was trying to find.

As I continued moving, weaving through the trees and stepping over rocks and fallen branches, I began to feel more at ease. The natural environment was soothing, a place that was seemingly in no way hostile. Nothing here was trying to kill me. The more distance I put between me and the volcano, the more I appreciated the woods I'd been taught to fear. I witnessed squirrels darting about in the trees, rabbits running through the brush, and even a buck standing serenely in a clearing.

I stopped and gazed at the deer for a moment as he nibbled on the grass. The antlers on his head were sprawling, branching out as if they were twin trees on his head. As I watched him, he slowly lifted his head as if waking from slumber. He locked eyes with me. In that moment, I knew he was something more than just a stag. There was some form of incredible intelligence in those eyes. I lowered my head, and the buck darted off into the woods. Feeling somehow different, I moved on.

Nearly an hour after the sun rose, my stomach started grumbling. I felt as though I was at a safe distance, so I took a break from my hike. I began unpacking the bags to see what Caleb and Valerie had sent with me on my journey. In the knapsack, there were extra clothes, a thick blanket, and a flint kit for a fire. Caleb knew I was capable of making a fire from what I found, but he provided it for me regardless. In the satchel I found two large water canteens, nearly a pound of dried meat, and several apples.

In the very bottom of the bag, I found a small jar full of strawberries with a note resting on top. It was in Valerie's hand. *Addie, I know this may be frightening, but you have nothing to fear. Follow the moon's path, and you'll find the Village. Gwen, Xander, Caleb, and I will join you soon enough. We love you, Addie. Be safe.* She was all too right about this sudden change frightening me. As much as I welcomed the escape, I was afraid of the unknown. I had left behind my family and the only home I had ever known. There was no familiarity for me anymore.

After a small, quick meal of dried meat and an apple, I repacked my bag and began moving once more. With no clue as to how deep into the forest these runaways were, I resolved simply to get as far from Anyra as I could. The air warmed as the sun climbed toward its peak, and I shed my outermost jacket as I walked. A pit was forming in my stomach as I marched forward with little sense of direction. Yet I pressed on.

The hours droned on as I forced myself to march onward, away from Anyra. Away from Sebastian. The pang in my heart at the thought of him nearly caused me to stumble, and I took a moment to breathe. These long hours of hiking allowed me time to think, though this was not my preferred activity. Normally, I would go to my forge, allowing my hands to twist metal and gems into the shapes of my emotions, placing them into a tangible object. By the time my piece was finished, I normally had a solution for whatever problem I had been contemplating.

Here I had no physical marker of what was in my mind. Only the faint footprints I left behind marked my cognitive work, pointing my direction in every sense. I had to get away from him. He had done this to me, driven me out of his life. I began to realize how true that was. He and I had grown apart over his months as the Chosen.

Every moment he had was spent in the Temple, praying, counseling those who sought the Totem's help, acting as Rhoda's lackey. The few moments we had spent together, he seemed distracted. Something had always hung like cobwebs in the back of his mind, tangling his thoughts and pulling him away from me.

He had always been more verbal than physical, showing his love through his words, through notes and reminders of his affection. For so long, I would wake up to notes throughout the house, hidden in different places every time. It was his own Choosing that triggered this change. He had all but disappeared from my life, taken by the Temple. He may as well have been the sacrifice himself. How could I have been so stupid? Our marriage could never have changed the way things were. Sebastian was no longer the man I'd fallen in love with.

The hours stretched out long and tiresome as the day went on. I watched as the sun slowly climbed to its apex, hanging over my head as if by a string. Yet once more it began to fall lazily back down to the horizon. In a few hours, the blazing orb would meet the sea, setting the water alight in a brilliant display.

I would not be able to see it. I had always loved watching those sunsets, where the colors thrown off the ocean were too beautiful to match. No gemstone or flower could capture the beauty created by the last drops of golden light meeting the blue-green sea. Yet I may never see it again. Perhaps I could watch the sun rise on a different sea, hundreds of miles away.

It had been on a day like that when Sebastian had proposed. I didn't think that day would ever fade from my memory despite our falling out. I had suspected it for a week beforehand, yet I cried all the same when he put the necklace around my throat. He'd had Valerie forge them in secret, trusting none other to get the job done correctly. She hadn't charged him, but he'd hidden some coins around the shop and the house for us to find. He had always been excellent at hiding things.

How much had he hidden from me? Was he having second thoughts about our marriage? Was that the true reason he had refused to marry me? Yet something deep in me believed that it was the Temple. Rhoda and her penance to the Totem had stolen him away from me, away from all those he had loved and that loved him in return.

The Chosen was truly the first Gift, drained of the life in him and returned as an empty husk. Would my father have been the same had he not fallen into the volcano? So many Chosen went the way of my father, jumping in after their Gifts either moments or months after the sacrifice. They simply couldn't live with what they had done.

By the time I was drawn from my thoughts and my wandering, the sun was beginning to dip below the trees, throwing shadows around my feet. For the first time, I began to realize why the forest had always been forbidden. What lurked in the dark spaces between the trees, where the moonlight was blocked by the canopy overhead? What was waiting to leap out from the wood and snatch its prey in talons like swords? What creature would make me its prey?

I found a small clearing between the trees and began quickly making a camp for myself. I gathered branches from the surrounding wood, haphazardly stacking the boughs into a tented structure, just large enough to offer shelter. Using the smaller sticks I'd found, I built myself a campfire with the flint kit Caleb had packed me. The light the fire gave offered some comfort as the last rays of sunlight melted away into the night.

I settled down next to the fire, eating another meager meal from the pack. Tonight, I indulged in a few of the strawberries, reminding myself of the home I had left behind. So many times, Delilah had chased little Caleb, Gwendolyn, and me out of the strawberry patch with mouths stained red from the sweet fruit. As we got older and she recruited us for the harvest, we had popped smaller strawberries into our mouths as we gathered them, hoping Delilah wouldn't notice. Our red lips always gave us away.

I threw a few more branches on the fire, hoping it would be enough to ward off anything that may come across me in the night. Even if the Anyrans were searching for me, they would never dare venture out into the woods at night. The pit of fear in my stomach kept my tired body from sleeping, so I sat and took in the forest around me. The sounds seemed to be amplified during the night, each cricket chirp or hoot of an owl a hundred times louder than it should be.

I whittled at a branch, trying my hand at a new medium. I had only ever shaped metal and occasionally dabbled with clay on Caleb's potter's wheel, so wood was a new challenge for me. I had chosen a relatively easy shape, but it was still giving me some trouble. And I listened. All my thoughts had been spent for the day as I walked, so now my mind was ready to receive new ideas from what lay around me.

The soundscape of the woods unfolded around me, singing as if to show me that it meant no harm. The howl of wolves in the distance gave me a start, but I realized that their song was not a threat. They simply lifted their voices as one, calling to one another. As I watched, a few bats swooped through my little campsite, chasing after insects for their dinner.

Owls hooted to one another, each call coming from a different direction in my environment. They were talking, their late-night conversations certainly full of deep thought and wisdom. Even the crickets rose up in a chorus, no sound ever left without response. I realized that in this forest, I was completely alone. Not another human soul was to be found. For the first time in my life, there was no togetherness. No safety of home and hearth. No one but me.

Leaves began crunching softly nearby, and I turned my head toward the sound. Perhaps I was wrong. I took up my carving knife, preparing to face an Anyran should one stumble across me. Though the tread seemed too light to be a priest or the Chosen. Perhaps it was a child or some creature of the night wandering its way home. The truth surprised me.

Into the clearing, a buck stepped daintily out of the trees. The deer seemed to know exactly what he was doing, the king of the forest come to see the newest resident. This was the same buck I had seen earlier during my journey, the enormous antlers unmistakable. I remained motionless, resting my hands on my knees so as not to spook the majestic creature.

He blinked at me with large, brown eyes full of soul. Somehow the buck seemed to know me. Could he possibly remember me from our previous meeting? He stepped carefully closer to me, the crackling fire causing him no fear. With a gentle toss of his antlers, he approached me. I couldn't move. I had never heard of a deer behaving like this toward a human. I did all that I could think of.

"Hello," I greeted the creature. He gazed into my eyes, blinking slowly as if to communicate that he understood. With a surprising air of comfort, he stepped up to me and began settling himself down. I was stunned, but I didn't react. I didn't want him to leave. Something about this felt familiar. I stared into the fire as a heavy weight came to rest on my leg, and I looked down to find the buck's head on my lap, his antlers tilted away from me.

We gazed at each other for a moment before I moved. How strange this day had been. I carefully placed a hand on his head, petting him as if he were a dog begging for affection. A heavy sigh heaved out of his chest as he closed his eyes. Perhaps he and I were both alone in this wood, finding comfort in one another. As the buck drifted to sleep, the fire began to die, but the fear of the dark was no longer festering in my gut.

Chapter Seven: The Chosen

"No, no please." Sebastian thrashed in his sleep, the sheet tangling itself around his legs. The heat burned his skin to a crisp and scorched his dry eyes. He looked up into the eyes of his lover, turned black and hollow. "Adelaide!" He huffed as the hot air stifled him, seeming to reach into his very chest and burn him from the inside out. Sweat dripped from his brow, sizzling away midair.

Somehow, he was inside the volcano, dangling from a rope, and Adelaide leaned over the edge, gazing down at him. For the first time, he was terrified of her. Her eyes were pure black, offering no view into her thoughts as they usually would. It was as if she was possessed, yet he knew she was in the body somewhere. Her face was relaxed but betrayed her interest, innocent in her wispy confusion. It was as if she didn't know who he was. She stared at him with curiosity, calm and unafraid, but also unsure.

Her attire seemed strange until he realized that it had been burned away. The fabric was almost gone, parts of it simply ash on her skin. He had no idea what the garment once was. It may have been her usual attire, or it could be the traditional linen gown that each Gift wore on sacrifice day. Her body was marred with festering burns, bone and sinew exposed by the fires of the mountain. Her hair was blackened and shriveled; the long, soft, ruddy brown waves he was used to turned into a ragged nest of fibers. This is what he had done to her.

The only relief was that she didn't seem to be in pain. Though her body was covered with bubbling, charred skin, she showed no signs of discomfort. Perhaps she had surpassed the point of pain so much that her body no longer registered the extent of her injuries. Perhaps she'd already died and no longer had the capacity to feel pain. Sebastian couldn't help but keep coming back to her eyes, as black as coal, the whites and caramel irises lost in the darkness.

"Adelaide! Help me, please!" She didn't seem to hear him. "Addie, I'm sorry!" He continued to cry out, but she simply stared, wide-eyed as if she did not know the language he spoke. A few times, Sebastian reached up and began to climb, but with each attempt, a gust of wind blew him back downward. Finally, Adelaide began to move.

"What are you doing?" She reached down and took the rope in her hand. "Yes! Please help me, Adelaide!" Smoke began wafting from her hand in graceful ribbons, and suddenly the rope snapped. As Sebastian fell, he gazed up in horror as a wicked grin smeared across Adelaide's face, revealing sharply pointed teeth.

Sebastian shot out of his terrorized slumber, tumbling to the floor with a heavy thud. A twisted cry escaped his lips as pain ravaged his body. His skin was damp with sweat, and bruises marred his skin. The beating he'd received in the Sanctuary was merely the latest of a long series.

It took a moment for Sebastian to drum up the will to rise from the floor. Stumbling, he drew back the curtain and squinted out of the window to find the sun just barely peeking over the horizon. There was no use attempting to get any more sleep now. With hindered speed, Sebastian dressed for the day, unwilling to face the continued torture. Not even sleep could offer him some respite.

Sebastian entered the Temple to find that Rhoda had become frantic. This was the side of her that Sebastian saw on a daily basis, but now she was on display for the rest of Anyra to see as well. She was crazed, shouting at the young priests and priestesses who scurried to do her bidding. Sebastian heard the sounds of a muttering crowd in the Temple common area below, many of them shouting, some wailing or crying. One voice seemed to rise above the rest, a woman shouting and sobbing loudly.

"Where is she!?" the woman begged. "Tell me where she is!" Fear began to grow in Sebastian's gut as he moved toward the curtain. "What happened to Adelaide!?" Sebastian froze, suddenly recognizing the voice as Old Delilah's. If she was this frantic, something horrific must have happened to Adelaide. Sebastian burst through the curtain, thundering down the steps where Delilah lay across them. She seemed to already be prostrate with grief.

"Delilah, what's going on?" he demanded, gently pulling her to a sitting position. The crowd of Anyrans began murmuring. Sebastian caught fragments of what they were saying, several repetitions of his name or "The Chosen" hoping that he could offer some explanation. "What happened to Adelaide? Why are all these people here?"

"How do you not know?" Delilah asked, dumbfounded by his ignorance. "She's gone. No one can find her. Caleb and Valerie woke the city screaming her name."

"What?" Sebastian breathed. He felt as though he was a cripple and someone had kicked his crutch out from under him. He fell to his knees on the steps, gasping for air. How could she be gone? Had she run? Where would she go, there was nothing for miles, if anything at all. He shook his head.

"I think she ran, Sebastian," Delilah confessed. "You know her as well as I do, she's always hated the sacrifice. She must have fled!" Still hardly able to process the weight of the situation, he nodded vaguely before turning to retreat back into the Sanctuary. The crowd began shouting at him, demanding answers. As their Chosen, they trusted him as the direct servant of the Totem. With a heavy sigh, Sebastian squared his shoulders and turned to face the Anyrans.

"People of Anyra!" he called, evoking Rhoda's typical greeting. The crowd instantly fell silent, receptive as he took authority over them. "There are treacherous rumors flying around the city. It is as yet unclear what is true and what is false. Allow your Temple and your High Priestess some time to understand the situation and form a plan of action. Please remain calm." He paused as the people below collectively nodded. "Once the High Priestess has made a decision, you will be notified and called to action."

With that, he turned and climbed into the Sanctuary as the people began to murmur once more. Delilah's sobs echoed through the curtain, evidencing her grief though whether it was for Adelaide's death or her insubordination was unclear. Perhaps it was both. Delilah had always been devoted to the Temple. How her adopted daughter had become so adamantly against it could only be explained by the loss of her biological family.

Sebastian quickly gathered information from the priests and priestesses, moving frantically in an attempt to piece together the full story. Eventually, the group came to a conclusion. Adelaide had most likely fled from Anyra, never to return. The Gift had slipped off into the night, leaving the Temple without a sacrifice. Many thought she had thrown herself into the sea, but Sebastian knew she was far too strong-willed for that. She would not escape one death only to embrace another.

Once the others had dispersed, Sebastian sat in the Sanctuary, completely alone. The rest of the priests and priestesses began searching the land surrounding Anyra, scouring it for any trace of Adelaide. Sebastian simply couldn't bring himself to join them. Deep down, he wanted her to live, and more than that, he wished he was with her.

He sat cross-legged on a cushion facing the great, dark statue of the Totem. The obsidian monument was enormous, standing twenty feet high, and it was carved into a dual image, depicting two women standing back-to-back yet melded into one being. Sebastian had stared at this statue for countless hours over the course of his life, and he could not see where the kindness ended and the cruelty began, the line blurred so much that there was no distinct separation. The two sides of the Totem, one adored and one to be feared.

The woman on the left was a kind, benevolent goddess offering a bountiful harvest. She had long, flowing hair curling gently away from her face. The skin on her face was smooth, and she wore a pleasant expression. In her hands were bales of barley or wheat and luscious fruit. She was kind and giving, a loving deity ruling over the people of Anyra.

The woman on the right was the precise opposite of the figure on the left. She was a vengeful, warriorlike figure wielding a fiery blade. Her hair was in matted braids, her scant battle clothes stained with grime and blood. The sword in her hand was massive, said to be forged in the fires of the volcano where the sacrifices took place. She held it above her head as if preparing to strike down a foe before her. Her right hand was leprous, filled with disease and rot that she would cast upon the people at her feet.

These were the two sides of the Totem. So long as the angry side was fed with a sacrifice, the kind side would bless the land. This was the way of things for hundreds of years. Every year, a virgin was thrown into the fires of the volcano, appeasing the Totem's wrath. The blood of the innocent and pure taken from her, and for what? Was it worth the loss anymore? Was it worth Adelaide?

Though it seemed as though Sebastian was praying, sitting in the Sanctuary surrounded by burning incense and offerings of gold, food, and much more, he was doing the exact opposite. Screaming with rage in his mind, he cursed the Totem and her cruel ways. Knowing Adelaide could be chosen as the Gift until he married her, Sebastian embraced being the Chosen in an attempt to appease the goddess. If he performed his duty well, the Totem would spare his beloved Adelaide until he could save her. The Totem had gone back on her promise.

The blasphemous thoughts filled his mind as hot, angry tears spilled down his face. *We had a deal. How **dare** you! She was going to be safe in no more than a month!* Sebastian began drawing quick, heavy breaths, the crushing weight of the grief on his chest beginning to choke him. *I should have saved her when I had the chance.*

"Where is she!?" Rhoda howled, bursting through the curtains and breaking Sebastian from his thoughts. "What are *you* doing here?! You should be out searching! She's your Gift!" Sebastian was made bold and reckless by the anger and grief in his heart. He shot a livid glare at the High Priestess, the fires of the volcano itself in his eyes. For the first time in months, he stood against Rhoda.

"She is not mine to give!" Sebastian fired back, rising from the floor. He shook with the rage and sorrow filling him, tears still wetting his face. "If she was my wife, then she would be. But then she would not be the Gift." Rhoda simply stared at him with wide eyes, surprised that he would fight back. The moment passed, and she gripped the garnet staff tightly in her hand.

"You would speak to me like that?" she asked, her voice filled with quiet outrage. She was horrifically calm as Sebastian took a step back. "You are *mine!*" The crimson staff met his cheek with great force, knocking him to the ground. Blood spattered on the white marble floor, his nose and lip dripping the substance.

"I could follow her," Sebastian suggested, spit and blood flying from his lips in a fine spray. "What if I went her way and ran? I could escape this life, too." Even as the words left his mouth, he knew they were not true. He felt the icy grip wrap around his body, effectively immobilizing him.

"You think you have that kind of freedom?" Rhoda asked, almost laughing at the absurd thought. She flicked her wrist toward herself, and Sebastian's feet dragged across the floor as her magic pulled him closer. Her rank breath would have made him gag were he able to move. She grinned as she puppeteered him, turning to hold him up to the statue of the Totem. "Do you have any idea what you are fighting against?"

"I don't care." Sebastian spoke through gritted teeth, hardly able to force the words past his paralyzed lips. His stomach dropped as she released her hold, and he stumbled as he caught himself.

"I am the power of the Totem!" The small knob of gemstone met his shoulder this time, driving him down to the floor again. He knew the order by heart at this point. The muscles in his back instinctively became as hard as the metal that Adelaide worked in her forge. If he was the metal, Rhoda was the hammer twisting him into the shape she wanted.

Three blows landed in quick succession, first directly between his shoulder blades, knocking the air out of his lungs. He coughed and sputtered, spraying more blood on the floor. The second blow fell low on his spine, causing an audible crack to ring out. A jolt ran through Sebastian's body, ending at his head and filling it with a horrible, ringing pain. The third landed perfectly on the back of his neck, causing his forehead to slam into the floor.

The final blow was the worst. Rhoda lowered the perfectly spherical knobbed end of the staff to the floor and drew back to drive it into Sebastian's tender flank. He was overcome with a violent, hacking cough as Rhoda stepped back, satisfied with her fit of rage. She took a stained kerchief from within her robes and wiped the blood from the already blood-red staff.

"You never learn, Sebastian," she sighed. Through gasps for breath, Sebastian shot a glare at her, his face red and bloodstained. She simply shook her head. "Now clean this mess up." Trembling, Sebastian clambered to his feet, hardly able to stand. He spat a glob of blood onto the floor.

"What if I said no?" he demanded. Rhoda was taken aback. "What if I decided that I love Addie more than I fear the Totem? Or you?" Brazened, Sebastian took a step forward. "I refuse to do it! You can't make me kill her!"

Rhoda suddenly marched forward. She worked her staff in her hands, twisting the small knob off to reveal a dagger concealed within. Fearful, Sebastian scrambled back, but she advanced too quickly. Rhoda snatched Sebastian's shirt, balling it in her fist and using it to keep him in place.

Slipping her dagger beneath his shirt, she sliced into his unharmed left flank once, twice, thrice. Three slashes in his skin, stinging and oozing blood. The cuts barely broke his skin, but they stung like fire. Sebastian thrashed, attempting to wrench himself out of her grip. Threads in the fabric of his tunic snapped with tiny pops, but she held firm with strength she should not have. Blood trickled down from the triplet gashes in his side, almost tickling the unharmed skin below.

"I want you to remember this, you insolent child," she hissed, her rancid breath filling his nose and stinging his eyes. "I own you! You step out of line once more, and I will do much worse. I'll make you scream and beg for mercy! I'll throw your bride into the volcano myself if I have to. Then I'll slit your throat!"

Rhoda dropped him to his knees with a heavy thud then disappeared through the curtains again, leaving Sebastian alone once more. Unable to stand, he keeled over, curling into himself on the floor, and began to sob. He clutched at the necklaces he wore, bringing Adelaide's to his lips, wishing he were kissing her rather than her memory. A dark, empty hole seemed to open in his chest, a monster fed by his grief and pain. One way or another, she may as well be dead.

After a long while, Sebastian lifted himself from the floor and removed his shirt. He had grown thin, the softness of his youth stolen by Rhoda and her wicked Temple. His ribs stood out from his skin, giving the appearance of a skeleton. His skin had become pale, as he had rarely left the Temple since becoming the Chosen. Then there were the scars. There were too many to count, too many of Rhoda's beatings to keep a record anymore.

This was the true reason he had refused Adelaide's offer of marriage. Not because he was awaiting his absent father, but because he refused to let her see him in this state. His father was most likely dead, never to be seen again. Although Sebastian would never truly know. It was unclear why he left, but Sebastian remembered the day well.

His parents had argued that night, shouting at each other as Sebastian lay awake, listening. He just remembered his mother screaming "No!" over and over again. Then in the middle of the night, Theodore was gone. No note, gone without a trace. Disappeared into the night. Just as Adelaide had done. Neither gave a warning, nor even a farewell.

Sebastian smoothed the shirt in his hands and used the garment to clean the blood from the floor and from his face. The movement caused his aching limbs to complain, but by now he was rather used to the soreness that came. Deftly he went to his quarters to change and tend to his wounds. The jar of salve he used to prevent infection and promote healing was nearly empty. He rubbed the substance over the places Rhoda had marred, his hands knowing exactly how much pressure to use to minimize the pain.

Sebastian took a plain, brown tunic from the closet and pulled it over his head. His dark hair had become mussed. Sebastian gazed at his reflection for a moment before deciding that he did not care. He exchanged the bloodied trousers for a new pair before reporting to evening prayers. He spoke beautiful words of reverence, the malice in his heart hidden away for none to see. Yet it festered like gangrene.

AS HE SHUFFLED DOWN the steps, his body voicing its complaints as he moved, Sebastian found a large group of people in the Temple. The morning sunlight shone through the stained glass windows, illuminating the faces of the Anyrans with a warm glow. They chattered among themselves, and it seemed the Temple itself hummed with worry and confusion. This was unprecedented. Sebastian half smiled. Of course it would be Addie to break the tradition. She'd broken the mold from the day she was born.

As Sebastian joined the crowd, Rhoda appeared from the Sanctuary, wielding the garnet staff as always. He cringed away from her, shuffling back into the group as they fell silent. She would never attack him with witnesses present, but regardless he wanted to be as far from her as possible.

"People of Anyra," Rhoda began, her usual greeting. "Brave volunteers. You know why you are gathered here today. Our precious Gift has fled her choosing, and it is up to us to find her." Sebastian drew inward, letting his thoughts drown out Rhoda's drawling. Was there any way to drive the search party away from Adelaide? He had no clue in which direction she'd gone, therefore no plans on how to lead the group astray.

He was once more pulled out of his thoughts as the crowd began to move, and Sebastian was swept up in the stream of people. Once again, he was powerless. The men and women determined to find the doomed girl marched with ferocity, eerily quiet as groups of people broke off to search in different directions.

One party splintered off toward the coast, theorizing that Adelaide may have followed the shoreline to safety. A second went off toward the docks to dredge the shallow ocean floor of the bay for Adelaide's remains. These people firmly believed Addie had drowned herself, dying by her own hand in order to spite the Temple. Sebastian knew this simply was not the case.

The third and largest group which Sebastian had joined entered the woods. This was the densest area, and the most likely route she would have taken. Anyra had been cut off from the rest of the world for so long that no one remembered what was on the other side of the vast forest. Perhaps the trees went on forever, and there was no other side at all. Regardless, if she could survive in the wilderness, which Sebastian was certain she could, Adelaide would be able to hide from Anyra for a lifetime.

The group spread out to cover a wide area, each one staying within twenty feet of the next searcher. Unlike any usual search party, no one called out. They had to take Adelaide by surprise. The trek was long and boring, yet peacefully beautiful. The wilderness had been left untouched by the people of Anyra for decades, only a few hunters ever returning from their journeys.

Sebastian marveled at the tranquil forest scene, eyes wide. He drank in the sight of something so wild, untamed by the will of humanity. Nature had created something beautiful and untainted. As rabbits loped through the brush and squirrels darted in the trees, the tension in Sebastian's body began to unwind. He somehow could feel Adelaide's presence in the forest, as if the trees whispered of her passage through the woods to safety.

A small, bashful smile crept onto Sebastian's face. Addie would love the forest, and he was certain she was somewhere in the wilds far away enjoying the scenery. Maybe she had already made it past the trees if there was an end to them and found some other land. Some country that did not worship the Totem and her wicked ways. Perhaps she had already befriended them.

Sebastian came to a clearing, almost perfectly circular and dotted with bushes and flowers. He paused for a moment and realized that there were no other Anyrans to be seen. Somehow, he'd wandered away from the others. There was a rustling in the brush, and

Sebastian looked up, expecting to see another person, but what emerged was far more breathtaking.

A beautiful deer stepped out from the trees, his long, slender legs seeming to allow him to float rather than trod on the ground. The antlers adorning his head were sprawling, red and gold leaves caught on some of the prongs as if he had two saplings sprouting from his skull. Sebastian froze, hardly breathing to avoid scaring the creature away.

The buck turned his head slowly, no doubt weighing a great deal with the enormous rack on his brow. He swung his gaze left then right as if scanning for any other life forms before training his eyes on Sebastian. The large eyes stared directly into his, and Sebastian began to sink into a crouch, moving as if through molasses. With the sustained gaze, the deer seemed to reach through Sebastian's eyes and into his very soul. A tear fell squarely onto a leaf at Sebastian's feet.

Without warning, the beast became agitated. He huffed and began prancing on his hooves, tossing his head back and forth in a show of aggression. Sebastian put his palms out, unable to form words in his surprise. What had he done? The buck reared back, thrashing the air with his front legs before crashing back down onto the forest floor and charging across the clearing.

Sebastian's instincts kicked in. He knew by now how to take a hit, and his body moved into its defensive position seemingly of its own accord. As the buck thundered toward him, Sebastian dropped to his knees, curling into the smallest space he could, covering his head with his arms. He simply hoped the deer's sharp antlers wouldn't pierce anything vital.

He waited for the blow, but it never came. The thudding hoofbeats slowed and came to a halt, and Sebastian felt the heavy breaths moving the soft fringe covering his brow. Slowly, he looked up into the knowing face of the buck, its eyes once again soft and seeming to know more than any deer could. This was no buck. As

Sebastian's posture relaxed, the deer nuzzled his wet nose into his cheek.

The affection surprised the Chosen, and he paused, unsure of how to respond or if he even should move. The deer took a step back, looking at him as if trying to communicate something, but Sebastian could not understand. The deer slowly bowed his head, surrounded Sebastian's head and shoulders in the prongs of his antlers, before blinking at him one last time, and darting off.

"Sebastian!" A member of the search party came into the clearing, finding Sebastian still crouched on the ground. The sun would soon meet the horizon, making the forest a dark and dangerous place. "We thought we lost you, too!" The young priest crouched at Sebastian's side, placing a caring arm around his shoulders. "Are you alright, Seb?"

Sebastian shuddered at the sound of the nickname. That was Addie's word, only she had ever called him that. The thought of her only brought more pain bearing down on his chest, threatening to suffocate the life from his heart. He shook his head, rousing himself from the stupor.

"Please don't call me that," he requested, beginning to rise. "I'm alright. It's been difficult, but I'll be alright."

"Yes, I'm sorry," the young priest nodded, drawing away in shame. "But you scared us! We thought we may have lost our Chosen, too."

"Couldn't have that, could we?" Sebastian asked, his voice distant and his eyes focused somewhere deep in the trees. He longed to sprint into the forest, following the deer tracks the buck had left behind. Anywhere would be better than here where he had to search for his betrothed in order to kill her. The thought of running had crossed his mind so many times. Yet those who did were almost always found dead if they were ever found. The Totem would have her revenge on those who tried to flee her grasp.

"Yes, now come on," the priest urged him. "We must be getting back. It'll be dark soon." Without another word, Sebastian stood, walking silently back toward the wretched crater he called home. The pair walked together, and more Anyrans came into view. As the sun crept toward the horizon, the searchers returned home. Those who stayed in the forest overnight were certain to meet danger. Perhaps Adelaide would not be killed by the volcano.

Chapter Eight: Dark Magic

In her study, Rhoda sat at her desk smiling. She turned the parchment from the Choosing over in her hands, the singed edges leaving smudges of ash on her fingers. She always had to leave the edges, though she would prefer the paper be whole. Though she couldn't see the words, Rhoda knew what the paper read. Adelaide Lanasting. The Chosen's own bride chosen to be the Gift.

Rhoda chuckled to herself. What a trick that had been. Sebastian was devastated, just as Adelaide's father had been fifteen years prior when his sister was chosen to be the Gift. What a wonderful day that had been. Xavier had fallen to the floor sobbing just as Sebastian had, but Sylvia's behavior was so different from Adelaide's. Where Adelaide had been angry, Sylvia comforted the man who was to kill her.

Rhoda passed the paper over the lamp, and the words appeared in the heat. In her own neat handwriting, the name took shape once more. Adelaide Lanasting, the Gift that ran away. But she would be found, and her Chosen would throw her into the mountain according to plan. Rhoda would stop at nothing to find her. If the ceremony had to be postponed, so be it. So long as the people believed in the Totem, the people believed in Rhoda.

Rising from the desk, Rhoda took up her garnet staff. How she did want the new staff. She had hoped Adelaide would finish the work before the choosing, but Valerie could pick up where Adelaide had left off. Although how ironic that would have been. A new staff forged by the next Gift. She would have given two things to the Totem.

By this time, night had fallen, and Anyra was asleep. The people's fear had been calmed for the moment at least, Rhoda and the Chosen assuring the people that the Gift would be found and thrown into the mountain as they had promised. As it had been for longer than anyone could remember. The people would even be able to help in their own salvation, hundreds having signed volunteer lists to go search for the runaway. Rhoda had no doubt that Adelaide would be returned to Anyra by Sacrifice Day.

She stepped out into the courtyard, the night hanging heavy around her. There was only the slightest curve of silver moon to light the courtyard where she stood. This was the best time. The magicking hour dawned. In the dead of night, with no witnesses to be found. Breathing in that crisp air seemingly charged with magic, Rhoda began the short trek to the volcano.

The crickets in the grass seemed to hush themselves as Rhoda passed, knowing that some powerful force was moving amongst them. The garnet staff left a third, round footprint on the soft ground. She did not need the staff to walk, it was solely there as a weapon. This item was one of great power, capable of summoning powerful dark magic. Yet the steel and ruby staff would be capable of even more. Rhoda would be able to perform incredible feats with that weapon in hand.

Rather than hike to the summit where Adelaide would be sacrificed, Rhoda's path diverged to the opposite side of the mountain where few people thought to tread. This was her sanctuary, a place where generations of High Priests and Priestesses had come before her. A place of dark magic and deception. A place that would bring her runaway Gift back home.

Rhoda made her way around the mountain, coming to the stone outcropping. The surface had been worn smooth by the many feet that had trod it before hers. Her heart began to pound with the excitement this place brought. Here her power was uninhibited. The garnet staff pounded the ground twice, and the lamps surrounding the space flickered to life. Rhoda smiled, basking in the warm light.

The magic ran through her veins, filling her with energy. The ache left her old bones, and her muscles lost their stiffness. She felt young once more. This was the birthplace of the Totem, where the old Anyrans had formulated their plan. It was here they had discovered how to face the blight that had infected their sinful land.

Rhoda closed her eyes, the corner of her mouth pulling into a smile as she listened to the mountain. Trapped within, deep in the heart of the volcano, she could hear them. The Gifts were all still there, screaming in their endless torment. The newest Gifts were loudest, the older ones falling quiet after a time, realizing there would be no end for them. Sometimes Rhoda could pick out words from the ruckus of howls.

This was one of those nights. As the anniversary drew nearer, the Gifts grew louder, screaming their pain and sorrow, the injustice they had suffered. They suffered together at the least. Rhoda could hear last year's Gift, Cecily, screaming above the rest. She had been willing, requesting to walk into the volcano herself. She was denied her plea.

The words were garbled, but Rhoda could make some of them out. Cecily was howling with agony, begging to be set free. She pleaded for help that would not come. The name Jeremiah was called several times, as if she were looking for him. Jeremiah, Cecily's Chosen, had killed himself shortly after, following her into the magma just a week later. He had been a particularly compliant Chosen, and Rhoda had liked him. It was a shame he had chosen to end his life rather than becoming a priest.

Oddly enough, no male voices could be heard. Rhoda was unsure if it was simply because there were so few of them that they were drowned out by the screams of the Gifts or if they were not trapped as the Gifts were. Rhoda shrugged, unsure but not truly caring enough to find out. She was certain her predecessors would have recorded any information about people other than Gifts that died in the volcano. She had more pressing matters to attend to than revisiting old history.

Rhoda had work to do before the night was done. Words began to flow from her lips, softly at first, but rising in volume as she continued. The language was strange. Had anyone been around to hear her, they wouldn't have been able to make out what she was saying. Not even she could define all of them. She didn't need to.

The words grew into a kind of chant, the rhythm and song of it forming as Rhoda began to move. She marched around the circle, pounding the staff on the ground in time with her spell. She knew not what she was summoning, only its purpose. No one in Anyra would be able to find the lost Gift. Something stronger was necessary.

Heaving breaths approached, and Rhoda grew excited, curious to see what her spell had brought her. As the chant came to a triumphant close, Rhoda slammed her staff to the stone, and a great bear heaved itself onto the platform. Rhoda's shoulders fell as she looked at what she had summoned.

"Brilliant," she grumbled. The spell had brought forth a black bear, but it was old and decrepit. Rhoda was surprised it hadn't died on its journey to her. It must be past the normal lifespan of a bear, its fur almost completely gray. Its skin hung off of it like an overlarge tunic, and it took slow, weary steps. Rhoda shook her head as the beast collapsed in the center of the stone circle and heaved out one final breath.

Rhoda paused, waiting for a moment to see if it was truly dead. It's small, beady eyes had become glassy in death. For good measure, Rhoda reached out with the end of the staff and gave the carcass a solid shove. As the corpse rolled back toward her, the stench came over Rhoda in a great wave. The beast had been rotting on its feet.

"It will have to do." Once again, Rhoda began chanting, this song more aggressive than the last. It made the heart shrink deeper into the chest for fear of the darkness. One by one, the lanterns flickered out with the stamps of the garnet staff. As the last flame winked out of existence, a great rush of air was drawn into the bear's lungs.

Rhoda's staff slammed into the ground over and over as she marched around the bear, chips of garnet breaking off with each strike. The beast's impossible breaths came heavier and faster, life filling him up once again. But it came at a cost. The skin tore in places as he struggled to stand, exposing the sinew and grey muscle underneath. It opened its eyes to reveal dull black orbs like scuffed marbles in his skull.

It took a step, and the muscles ripped themselves apart. They had already become stiff in death, hardly able to move. Yet the bear would not be stopped. He shook himself, tossing wet clumps of grey hair over the stone. Black blood seeped from the cracks and crevices. As if used to the stench, Rhoda smiled as she came to stand before the bear, her spell having worked its magic.

"That'll do, now won't it?" She extended her hand to the creature, and he bowed his head in submission. Rhoda smiled, her lips stretching over her teeth in a wicked grin. The Gift would come home. She produced a scrap of cloth from Adelaide's shirt. In her shock during the Choosing, Rhoda had snipped it off of her, suspecting that the girl would not go down without a fight.

The bear lifted its head and took a deep inhale, catching the scent of the fabric. As if in a trance, his head swung left and right before he settled on the scent trail. He turned toward the forest which was on the other side of the neighboring mountain but paused as if asking Rhoda for permission to go.

"Bring her back to me," she told the creature. With unnatural bones creaking, the bear began lumbering toward the forest, making his way around the mountain. There was a chance the bear would bring Adelaide back close to dead, but Rhoda didn't care at this point. So long as she lived long enough to drown in the lava, Rhoda would be satisfied.

Chapter Nine: Haven

I awoke cold and sore on the forest floor, the buck long gone and the fire nothing but a pile of ash. The buck had guarded me from the creatures of the night. I rose, stretching the stiffness from my limbs. The light had woken me as it filtered through the trees, rousing me before the Anyrans could make their way into the forest. Moving as quickly as my fatigued body could manage, I dispelled my campsite. I kicked the ashes aside, scattering them amid the sparse grass. I tossed the branches back into the trees, making sure they were not in piles. I would leave as little trace as I could.

I started back on my trek, once more letting the hours drone on. How long would I walk until something appeared before me? Perhaps I would find these fabled rebels, or even some other civilization. Or perhaps there was nothing. I could reach the end of the forest and find nothing but ruins, the rest of the world truly fallen. Yet despite all, I pressed on another step.

I'd been walking for another hour, my stomach and legs both beginning to complain, when I heard a rustling in the leaves to my left. I thought nothing of it at first, assuming some small animal was making his way through the brush. Soon however, I realized that not only was the sound growing louder, but larger. This was no small creature. The leaves began to rustle, shaking as if being thrashed like barley from within.

Fear blossomed in my chest as I picked up my pace, glancing over my shoulder to try and see what was stalking me. It couldn't be terribly large, for no part of it showed through the sparse bushes.

Perhaps it was one of the rogues. The leaves began to shake, and I found myself frozen in fearful curiosity. I could do nothing but watch. At long last, the creature burst forth from the shrubbery, revealing itself.

The animal that had been stalking me was a great, black bear, but not like any I'd seen. The thing was skin and bones, his hips and shoulders jutting out at odd angles. His hide was torn, revealing the greying muscle beneath. The eyes glittered from deep in his skull, his teeth bared in desperate hunger as he charged at me with a heavy limp. Instinctively, I flung the jacket in my arms at its head, hoping to blind it and allow myself a lead, and I took off in a dead sprint. My feet thudded against the cold ground as my heart pounded out of my chest.

The beast batted the garment away and kept on, gaining ground despite his injuries and age. His heavy footfalls sounded like those of a giant from a children's bedtime story. I spotted a tree with low branches, and hoping the bear couldn't climb as high as I could, I leapt onto the lowest branch. My muscles strained as I began heaving myself upward, but a force pulled me back to the ground. My hands stung as they scraped against the bark, and I landed with a heavy thud. The creature had caught my satchel with his paw and brought me down to the ground.

I rolled onto my back, and the ragged monster roared in my face, spittle and a putrid odor filling my mouth and lungs. I screamed in reply, letting the howl rip from my chest. My hands instinctively came up to protect my face, and the beast flinched back as if he was surprised that I had a voice of my own. Using my feet, I scrambled from under his body, but a large paw came down on my abdomen, pinning me in place.

I screamed again as his overgrown talons pierced my skin, the weight of him pushing all the air from my lungs. The volcano wouldn't be what killed me after all. As I squeezed my eyes shut, preparing to be torn into, the beast was ripped away from me with incredible force. I could only breathe, staring at the canopy of leaves above me in disbelief. By some miracle, I was still alive. My life had become a pendulum, swinging between short and long at a moment's notice.

The scuffle as the bear fought my rescuer drew my attention, and I warily stood to help defeat the beast. My help was not needed. A group of around ten people surrounded the creature, battering it between them with spears. They were a mixture of men and women, most of them several years older than I.

They seemed to communicate without words, each one knowing when to jab and when to retreat, keeping the beast distracted so he could not set his sights on any singular one of them. When the bear turned on one member, two more would jab at its flank or legs, pulling its attention elsewhere. With their number, the beast couldn't focus long enough to land an attack.

At long last, the creature grew frustrated as my rescuers toyed with it. The bear reared up onto its hind legs, and exposed its soft, rotting underside. One young man leapt forth and buried his spear deep in the creature's belly, over half the spear's length disappearing into its hide. I could see the tip emerging from the bear's back, piercing its skin as if it had already been tanned and stretched to dry. The bear sputtered, stumbling on his feet before crumpling to the ground. Dark blood seeped into the soil beneath him, and the hunters fell back as if they would become infected by it. Perhaps they would.

With my chest still heaving for breath, I stared at the bear's corpse dumbfounded as the people turned their attention to me. Their faces were surprised, but they looked no different than the people I had been surrounded by as I was raised in Anyra. Rather than finding the rebels myself, the rebels had found me.

Only one of them was entirely unfamiliar to me. A tall woman with dark skin and broad shoulders stepped forward, extending her hand to me. Her hair was cut close to her scalp, and her brow was set with the stern face of a warden. Even with her commanding demeanor, her eyes were kind.

"Stranger, are you hurt?" she asked, her voice deep for a woman, but strong and clear. I could tell she was the leader of this small band if not the rebels as a whole.

"Only mildly," I replied. I pressed my hand against my stomach to find it damp with blood, but not as badly as the pain had made it seem. "Thank you for saving my life, thank all of you." I scanned the faces, searching for a familiar one, but there were none. Two of the men looked incredibly similar, possibly twins, but the only familiarity was a tug at the back of my brain.

"It is no difficulty, we are glad to help," the woman assured me. "When did you flee Anyra?" The young man that had landed the fatal blow stepped up behind the woman, studying me with a furrowed brow as if he recognized me. I couldn't say the same of him, though there was an odd twinge in the back of my mind as I looked into his face. His brown hair glinted with a golden-blond sheen in the sunlight, falling into his face in soft curls.

"I set out early yesterday morning. My name is Adelaide Lanasting, I was chosen to be the Gift, so I fled." Several members of the party gasped, surprised. I was the first to escape my Choosing.

"You are a brave soul indeed, my dear," the leader commended me. "We too disagree with Anyra's ways and the giving of Gifts every year. Join us, Adelaide. We are many, and we will protect you." My shoulders relaxed as the young man stepped forward with a boyishly crooked smile.

"Thank you, thank you so much!" The woman took both of my hands, hers surprisingly gentle for how large and strong they seemed.

"You have nothing to thank us for," she said. "I am Edrei, I care for our society. You will be safe in our midst."

"I have no doubt of that," I agreed. The men and women in the group quickly welcomed me, introducing themselves in quick succession. I knew I'd have difficulty remembering their names. They guided me deeper into the woods, off the vague deer trail I'd been following. The man that had stabbed the bear came to walk beside me.

"Adelaide," he addressed me. "I'm Zakariah."

"Nice to meet you," I smiled, clasping his hand briefly in mine. "I saw you kill the bear. I can't thank you enough for saving me."

"Don't mention it," he replied, "but I think I admire your bravery more. No one has fled their Choosing before."

"It honestly wasn't my own doing. I was chosen a few days ago, then in the night, my friends woke me to packed bags and sent me to find you." He playfully raised his eyebrows, another mischievous grin crossing his lips.

"Oh, they sent you to find *me*, did they now?" he teased, chuckling under his breath. I lightly bumped his arm with my elbow as he grinned and ran a hand through his curls. He smiled, but I grew solemn. His flirting reminded me of Sebastian, though he hadn't been jovial with me for months. Ever since he began his apprenticeship at the Temple, he'd become aloof and serious.

Shaking my head, I reminded myself of what Sebastian had done. I smiled at Zakariah, the pain of the betrayal and grief still fresh in my heart. But I would not let that keep me from this new life. In the woods, I would find new hope, new purpose, and I could not let the pain of the past hold me back. Based upon my first impressions, Zakariah was joyful and adventurous, fearful of little, and brave to the point of rescuing a stranger. If nothing else, I was certain he'd be a friend.

"So, were you born into this society, or did you come from Anyra as well?" I asked.

"My family left Anyra and its ways when I was around ten, and that was twelve years ago now," he explained. "My sister was sacrificed earlier that year. We couldn't bear living among the people that killed her."

"I'm so sorry. The pain the Temple has caused is truly unforgivable. I lost my aunt to the volcano, and my father as well," I related. His story was tragic just as mine. He looked to me with wide eyes.

"That was *your* family?!" he demanded. I nodded with silent respect. "I remember that day! No one could believe it!"

"Neither could I. Still can't really. Papa simply couldn't bear it. He knew that what he'd done, what the Temple had made him do was wrong. He should have run to the woods and your society instead of leaping in after her."

"He should have, and taken you and your family as well," Zakariah agreed. "Then you would never have been chosen."

"True. Uncle Quinton would still be alive, and Gwen would never have been Punished for adultery. She wouldn't have had to commit it in the first place." I paused, remembering the days of joy I spent in Anyra as well. "Then again, I wouldn't know Caleb and Valerie, the friends that sent me into the woods," I smiled. "I wouldn't have been raised by Old Delilah. I wouldn't have met Sebastian."

"Sebastian?" Zakariah asked, raising his brow. His eyes darted to my neck, checking for an engagement necklace. I was certain the marks on my skin from when I'd ripped it off were still there.

"Yes, Sebastian," I replied. "That is a whole story in and of itself. But he was the Chosen." Zakariah reeled back in surprise, his eyes growing wide. I realized how shockingly blue they were.

"He would have had to throw you into the volcano!" he stated, horrified by my plight. I nodded, pressing my lips firmly together.

"It seems my family is dogged by tragedy as it were." I shrugged, relinquishing the pain of it for the moment. "But I'm here now, so I won't fall victim to that."

"Absolutely," Zakariah confirmed, smiling at me. "I wonder what they'll do. They've never had a Gift run away before you."

"I'm sure other Gifts have, they've just never succeeded before I suppose," I argued. "Do you think they'll choose a new Gift?"

"They will not," a man walking behind us replied. I turned to see an older man, his hair just beginning to go gray, with a thick beard trimmed close, and a strong build despite his age. "They will come looking for you and do anything short of killing you here in the woods to get you back." My eyes grew wide with fear, and I turned to Zakariah for aid. He knew these people and their ways. I was quickly beginning to trust him. Yet he was just as dumbfounded as I.

"Calvin?" he inquired of the man. Calvin's face softened, and he offered me his hand in greeting.

"But you don't need to worry about that, lass," he assured me, clasping my hand tightly in both of his. The tension left my body as Calvin's eyes grew warm and comforting. "We'll protect you. Edrei would never allow them to harm you." We continued our journey toward their base, and my mind drifted back to Anyra. What was happening there in my absence?

We reached the camp in less than an hour, though I had difficulty calling it merely a camp. It was more like a village condensed so that it hardly took up space on the ground. Rather, it grew upward. I gazed up in amazement at the structures stacked one on top of the other, built into the trees. It would take no more than ten minutes to walk from one end of the Village to the other, but the massive trees allowed it to house nearly a third of Anyra's population.

I squinted into the sky and spotted small buildings almost sixty feet up.

The structures on the ground seemed to be mostly family homes for those with small children or elderly. I could hear the wail of an infant, but the cries were quickly soothed. As I craned my neck to look above, I realized there were storehouses for food and smaller living quarters built into the branches. Ropes and ladders were strung between them like spiderwebs, and several lift systems were in use to carry greater amounts of cargo. The limbs of the trees were woven into the buildings like thread holding together fabric.

People milled about both overhead and on the ground, busy with the chores of the day. Men and women alike performed each task, whether that be repairing buildings, caring for children, or working the gardens that filled almost the entire ground space. Some of the fruiting vines crept up the tree trunks, creating vertical gardens for food. Tomatoes, berries, and beans sprung from the trees, and I smiled as I saw several trees sporting strawberries.

The people smiled and welcomed us as we entered, many greeting me as a newcomer and exchanging names and kind words. People of all ages welcomed me to my new home from kindly older men and women, to babbling toddlers. I already began to feel at home in their midst. I couldn't believe the number of people here. How had I never noticed so many people leaving Anyra and never returning?

"Welcome home, Adelaide," Zakariah said, grinning from ear to ear.

With nearly alarming speed, Edrei and two other members of the group that had rescued me, Joshuah and Katharine, settled me into a guest bungalow. They had an enormous tree near the northern edge of the Village dedicated solely to these small, one-person structures. They were always prepared for refugees from Anyra, and none more important than girls running from the Totem.

I trailed behind Edrei as she mounted a rope ladder, climbing swiftly. She selected a bungalow roughly twenty feet off the ground for me, and held the door as Joshuah, Katharine, and I entered. The space was small but arid as the large windows allowed light to fill the space. There was no glass in the openings, so the air flowed through freely, though any strong winds were blocked by the trees. In one corner a hammock was strung up with a pillow and a few blankets.

"This will only be a temporary home for you, dearie," Katharine assured me. "Soon enough, we'll get you a home of your own."

"Thank you," I smiled, satisfied even with this small space. "I simply can't wrap my head around all this. I expected something much smaller."

"Most newcomers are surprised when they arrive," Edrei assured me. She took the pack from my shoulders and set it gently on the floor. "We are many. You will be safe here."

"I have no doubt of that," I agreed.

"Settle in and get some rest. There will be a banquet tonight," Katharine smiled, patting me on the shoulder.

"I swear we're going to have one every week with everyone fleeing!" Joshuah added. "Especially now, so close to the Choosing. We'll become a city-state ourselves."

"A banquet?" I questioned. Edrei shooed the two others out with the wave of her hand, and she motioned for me to sit. I did as she asked, swiftly dropping to the floor with my legs crossed, listening attentively. She descended to the floor much slower than I, elegantly settling herself before she spoke.

"For every newcomer, we hold a banquet, celebrating that their lives are no longer enslaved to the Temple. We don't agree with Rhoda and her ways. Many here don't believe in the Totem at all."

"My uncle claimed she was dead after I was chosen as the Gift," I agreed, my chest tightening with the fresh grief and fear of Quinton's death. "The Totem, I mean. She took everything from me. Or more the Temple did." Edrei nodded in understanding.

"I personally don't believe in the Totem. I think there is a higher power, but not her. Not something so violent and cruel." Again, I found myself nodding. These were the things I had thought for years, but whenever I expressed them, those who feared the Totem and her Temple would silence me.

"Tonight, there will be a banquet. Another family came to us three days ago. A couple and their twin daughters. The girls are about to come of age, and their parents wouldn't let them be chosen."

"I'm so glad," I agreed. "I want more people to come here, but I fear the Temple will take notice. My sister and our friends are going to be coming here soon. They seemed to know this place existed."

"There are some in Anyra that do. They tell those who agree with us of our existence, help them to reach us. She was probably one of those," Edrei explained. I nodded. How long had Valerie and Caleb kept this from me? We could have been gone long since.

I shook my head, reminding myself of my connections. I had been engaged to be wed to the Chosen himself. I wouldn't simply abandon him, nor could I have convinced him to leave with me. He was loyal to a fault. Once that tie was gone, they knew it was safe to tell me.

"Now, get some rest, get settled in," Edrei instructed, rising from the floor. "Katharine will be back with some more medical supplies for your injuries." She nodded toward my stomach, and I looked down to find my tunic stained a murky brown. "The banquet starts at sundown."

"Thank you," I breathed once again, still reeling from all that had happened.

"Welcome home, Adelaide," Edrei smiled before climbing back down the ladder.

I settled into the hammock, my feet aching from the miles I had walked. The exhaustion finally crept up on me. So much had happened in the span of only a few days, and still there was more yet to do. I gazed out the window at the leaves waving in the soft breeze and the dying light.

I startled awake as a gentle knock sounded at the door. I hadn't realized I was beginning to doze off until the sound roused me. I nearly fell as I rose from the hammock, and a pang shot through my body. The puncture wounds in my stomach complained, the scabs that had formed cracking with the motion.

"Come in," I called, my hands coming away wet with blood. Katharine opened the door, and her eyes went wide with the sight of me.

"Adelaide, are you alright?" she quizzed, rushing inside. She dropped a large, linen bag on the floor, taking my arms in gentle hands.

"I'm alright," I promised, "I got up too fast and broke the scabs."

"Here, sit down," the healer instructed, and I again plopped down onto the floor. She knelt to dig in the bag and began pulling out the supplies she would need. I watched with fascination as she pulled rolls of bandage, cloth, and jars of salve out. "Lift your shirt or take it off if you're comfortable."

I slipped the tunic over my head, as I wore a short camisole over my chest. For the first time, I got a good look at my injuries. The monster's claws had punctured my shirt and dug into my stomach, piercing the soft layer of fat under my skin. Luckily, my rescuers had torn the beast off of me before the talons could dig deeper and reach the muscle.

Katharine handed me a jar of some balm and instructed me to apply it liberally. The scent stung my nostrils, and I sucked in a breath through my teeth as the substance smarted in the wounds. I worked quickly. Luckily, there were only three tears in my skin that needed dressed. Katharine pressed a strip of linen treated with herbs and oils over my stomach, then she began winding the strip of bandage around my midriff.

I was aware of her muttering to herself, but I didn't think twice of it. The pain and fatigue clouded my judgement, but the stinging quickly eased as she tied off the bandage, fitting it in the small of my back. She patted my shoulder twice, signaling the end of her work. I reached for my tunic and slid it back over my head.

"There we are," she said, smiling as I turned to her. "Just leave that on until this time tomorrow, then you should be fine to take it off. Do you have any other injuries?"

"No, I'm feeling better already," I shrugged. "Thank you so much."

"Of course! If you have anything else you need, the healer bungalow is on the ground close to the center of town." She swiftly packed the bag and headed for the door. "Don't forget, the banquet starts at sundown!" I glanced out the window to see the golden tinge of the setting sun staining the evening like aged paper.

"I wouldn't miss it," I smiled.

THAT NIGHT, THERE WAS a feast held to celebrate not only my arrival, but the arrival of the family that had come to the Village just days before. There was a father and mother along with their twin daughters. I sat with them at the end of a long table spanning the entire width of the encampment. Edrei sat at the head of the table, smiling with contentment and sipping from a glass of blackberry wine as she watched the fellowship down the table before her.

The twin girls, Orchid and Willow, sat to my right. Smiling broadly, their parents sat across from their daughters. Finally, this family could rest at ease, free of fear. I took note of how young the parents were to have a pair of thirteen-year-olds. My best guess was that they were similar to my parents. They had sex out of wedlock to be safe from the Totem, and as result had become parents very young. Like my parents, they had chosen to view it as a blessing.

At only thirteen years old, the twins had not quite yet become eligible for the Choosing, but their parents simply would not allow either of their daughters to meet that gruesome end. The poor girls had lived their entire lives in fear of being chosen. As I spoke to them, I saw how much this had tormented them. They told me that when they were very small, they feared they would both be chosen as the Gift together, seeing themselves as two halves of the same whole. Once they grew a little older, they realized that even more horribly, only one of them may be chosen, leaving the other without her best, most constant companion.

"Is your place comfortable?" Zakariah asked as the girls turned into one another, discussing amidst their giggles. I believed they found Zakariah incredibly handsome. I couldn't disagree with them.

"Yes, it's lovely," I replied. "I cannot believe how beautiful this place is! I was expecting a few ramshackle structures and maybe two dozen people, not... *this!*" I gestured to the camp around us, the buildings and the people who built them. "I can't believe this!"

"Sometimes, neither can I," he agreed, smiling broadly. As we spoke, an older woman meekly approached, hoping for a break in our conversation so she could interrupt. I took notice of her first and pointed her out to Zakariah with a tip of my head. He smiled.

"Ramona!" Zakariah greeted her, extending his hand. She approached, the skin around her eyes crinkling with a smile. "I suppose you'd like to meet our new guest. Adelaide, this is Ramona, one of our Village Elders. She's a Seer." I turned to her in surprise. The historical accounts kept in the Temple claimed that Seers were once common, but now were incredibly rare. These women were born with the ability to peer into the future, and could read people's histories and fortunes by touching their skin. I could see how they may view this as a blessing or as a curse.

"Glad to meet you," I greeted her, extending my hand. She shrunk back.

"It is lovely to have you with us, Adelaide, and I do not mean to be rude, but if I touch you, I will be able to see things about your past, present, and future," she warned me, bobbing her head in anxious joy. I let my face soften as she backed away.

"I have nothing to hide," I assured her. "If you are comfortable and willing to read me, I have no problem with you doing so." The excitement on her face was palpable. Seers were feared and revered for their gifts, and many superstitious people avoided them with great prejudice.

"I hope to see you staying with us for many years," Ramona assured me. She took both of my hands in hers, and immediately her brow furrowed. The crinkles around her eyes returned as she squeezed her eyes shut, studying the visions that must be dancing behind her eyelids. Or perhaps she was listening intently for things only she could hear. I searched her face for any indication of what she might be seeing. A glance at Zakariah showed that he was as intrigued as I. She began mumbling under her breath, allowing us some insight.

"A child, drifting alone in a sea of tears. Found and lost and found again, though the one who claimed to love her most held love outweighed by fear. Flames, licking at the walls. A great legacy of beautiful, flaming souls to follow. A child of fire and brimstone. The blackened heart that wields the greatest love and anger. Change, such great change. A Gift that carries a gift of her own."

At long last, Ramona withdrew, opening wide eyes filled with a thousand different emotions. Zakariah and I exchanged a glance, but neither of us had any idea how to interpret the words that had tumbled from Ramona's mouth. Some references were obvious, allusions to my orphanage and Sebastian's betrayal clearly stated. Others were entirely obscured. A gift that carries a gift of her own.

Shuddering, Ramona thanked me profusely and scurried off before I had the chance to inquire of any deeper meanings in her words. I looked at my hands as if hers would have left a mark. Some evidence of all she had seen. I shook my head, entirely at a loss of what to think about what I had heard. Zakariah's hand came into my field of vision, gently replacing Ramona's. Sensing my confusion, he pulled me into a hug.

"I've got you," he assured me quietly. His hands were heavy on my back, the weight a comfort to me. I collapsed into him, allowing myself the support of his body for a brief moment at the least. I needed him. The pain I had been staving off for days now came rushing into my heart, spreading throughout my body like tea in boiling water. The home I had known all my life, the man to whom I had chosen to give my heart, body, and soul had betrayed me. I hadn't realized how much it hurt, let alone had time to process all that had happened.

"You're going to be alright, Addie," Zakariah promised me, drawing me out of my own melancholy state. I lifted my head from his chest, where I could hear his heart beating quickly. "Whatever she said about the past, that's gone. You're home now." We shared one last tight squeeze before I pulled away with a heavy sigh, allowing all of the tension to leave my body with the great release of air. I nodded, smiling up at him. His expression was warm and comforting, the light from the lanterns dancing in his eyes.

"I'm home," I confirmed.

Soon, the amount of food on the long table dwindled, and people began to rise, moving into conversations. The tables were cleared away, and the bonfire in the center of the Village was lit with many torches, sending the flames up toward the treetops. I could feel my body pulling toward the familiar sense of heat and fire.

"Come on!" Zakariah cried, grabbing my hand and pulling me closer to the fire. A band struck up, and people began to dance. I laughed as Zakariah pulled me into a large circle, and I quickly caught onto the steps as he guided me through the movements until my feet knew what they were doing. We danced late into the night, enjoying the music, the company, and the wine perhaps a little too much.

Chapter Ten: The Seer

"Edrei! Edrei!" Ramona reached for her leader's shoulder, but she stopped short of touching her skin. Even after so long, Ramona still forgot about skin-to-skin contact. "I need to speak with you."

"Yes, my Seer?" Edrei responded, turning toward the Elder. Edrei held a deep respect for Seers, and Ramona had proven her ability to be useful. Many times, she had predicted that runaways would be arriving, and helped search parties avoid capture by Anyran patrols. Yet above that, she was kind, and Edrei valued such a quality.

"Adelaide, the Gift that ran away. I read her," Ramona began, hardly able to get the words out. She was choked with emotion, her eyes wide with fear and excitement.

"Not here," Edrei hushed the older woman. Glancing about, she gestured for Ramona to follow. In the wee hours of the morning, few Villagers were awake, especially after such a raucous celebration. Even still, Edrei chose caution. It was not her fellow runaways she feared, but others. No one could predict what trees may have ears, even a great Seer like Ramona.

Edrei led Ramona to her own personal bungalow. Edrei's was one of the few on the ground, so that she was able to respond quickly in case of emergency. She ducked into the small living space, holding the drape open for Ramona as she trailed behind her.

"Tea?" Edrei asked, gesturing for Ramona to take a seat at the table. Nervously, Ramona nodded and quickly seated herself. Edrei placed the kettle on a burner and stoked the fire in the stove. "You take honey, don't you, Ramona?"

"Yes, but Edrei, this is a pressing matter," Ramona fretted.

"No business is more important than tea before sunrise," Edrei argued as the water began to boil. Smiling, she took it off the flame then carefully poured it into a teapot. She selected an herbal blend from the pantry and added a few spoonfuls to steep. "That is, aside from rescue and childbirth." The pleasant aromas filled the room as Edrei placed a jar of honey and a wooden honey dipper before her.

"I suppose," Ramona ceded, "and yet I still think this is important."

"I have no doubt that it is," Edrei agreed. She sat across the table, smiling warmly as she waited for the tea to finish steeping "Now, what did you see when you read our latest newcomer?"

"It was mad, Edrei!" Ramona burst, finally able to release the tension she'd been holding. "This poor girl's past. She lost her mother, father, and aunt in a matter of days. Her betrothed was the Chosen, and he chose the Temple over her. Her sister was punished mere days ago for adultery against the Totem then they killed her uncle. She's been dragged through fire!"

Edrei nodded, suspecting the latest Gift's past was a storied one. She lifted the teapot and carefully poured two cups of beautiful, deep red tea. Scents of cinnamon and ginger filled the bungalow. "What of her present? Her personality and traits?"

"Oh, she's strong. She's doing well all things considered. She's astonishingly full of hope. Sad and angry, but hopeful. She could fill your shoes one day if you help her."

"I could sense a fiery spirit in her," Edrei smiled. From the moment she'd met Adelaide, she knew there was a spark of leadership and rebellion in her.

"Fire is right. That was all I could see in the future," Ramona revealed. Edrei stopped cold with her cup halfway to her lips.

"What?" She looked up to find Ramona nodding, her eyes wide.

"I'm not certain what it meant. If it was fire within her or what she will bring about. But there was so much fire. Some form of legacy of fire. She is going to change everything. But as of now it is unclear to me whether that is for better or worse."

Edrei sat back in her chair, nodding in deep thought. "Perhaps that part is up to us. If she gets the help and support that she needs, she may be able to bring down the Temple as a whole. Perhaps she's destined to overthrow the theocracy."

"There's more." Edrei's eyes darted back up to Ramona's face. "There's something in her. The sentence that came to me was 'a Gift that carries a gift of her own' and I don't know what it means. She has something inside her, perhaps this fire or the ability to spark change. Something strong."

"Well, we must help her learn to use it for good then," Edrei nodded.

"How!?" Ramona asked. "There is such great potential, but also such fear. She could burn everything. This Village, the work we've done. What if she turns against us?"

"She will not," Edrei soothed her. She set down her tea, staring at the tabletop in deep thought. "She is set against the Temple, that is undoubted. I believe she has the potential to hurt innocents in her fury. But there is definitely a future with her."

"For the first time in my life, I am uncertain Edrei," Ramona confessed. She tugged at her skirt, pulling the cloth through her hands. "I have never seen such a blurred future as that of Adelaide Lanasting." Edrei remained silent, still in her head as Ramona looked to her for guidance.

"This will take time," she murmured. "We cannot take the Temple in a day, or even before the day that Adelaide was to be sacrificed. We must protect her first."

"Edrei!" The leader didn't seem to hear her. She rose, leaving her tea untouched, and began to pace. Ramona knew this well. As the plans and ideas churned in Edrei's mind, she moved, dancing to create something new and real and good. Comforted by the familiar practice, Ramona sat back and watched, allowing Edrei to process. Ramona lifted her cup, holding it close to her chest as the steam wafted into her face.

"A gift that carries a gift of her own. What could it mean? Was she given something, or will she give it?" Her feet swept across the dirt floor, leaving faint traces of her musings. "I must lead her, guide her. She never had that teacher, but I can fulfill that for her. But how to protect her as she grows?" As Ramona began to drift off, Edrei whirled around and slammed her hands down on the table.

"We have to go."

"Where? I thought this was the most private place to discuss such matters?" Ramona questioned, beginning to rise.

"No, not us, not right now. All of us." Edrei's eyes were alight with the idea as Ramona scrutinized her, eyes narrow and brows furrowed. "We have to leave Anyra, fully. Get as far as we can."

"But where will we go?"

"Ramona, look at me." The sudden demand took the Elder by surprise, and she stopped. She turned toward Edrei, looking deep into her dark, intelligent eyes.

"I am, Edrei."

"I'm not like anyone here. No Anyran has my skin, my hair, my eyes."

"I know, Edrei," Ramona agreed. "But that doesn't make you different or an outcast."

"I know, it's not that," Edrei placated her. "I mean that I'm proof. I'm proof that there's somewhere else. I came to Anyra as a little girl, as an orphan that hardly remembered her homeland. But I remember enough to tell you that it's real."

Ramona nodded, understanding Edrei's intent. The plan was communicated with no words, the same idea blooming in both minds. A future, a safe haven, a new land free of the Temple that worshipped a false goddess. A new beginning.

"So that's where we go," Ramona nodded. Edrei returned the nod to confirm.

"We won't all leave immediately. Adelaide said that at least four others are coming. Once they're here, I'll take a small group including Adelaide, and we'll go find it."

The first rays of sunlight streamed through the curtain, casting a blue-grey glow through the room. A new day. A new future. Edrei gave Ramona a soft smile before sending her on her way to rest. Edrei took up her mug and sipped the warm tea. She leaned against the doorframe, watching the sunlight filter through the branches. The future was not here, but she would find it with Adelaide Lanasting leading the way.

Chapter Eleven: Sisters

"**G**ood morning!" I shot up out of my hammock, nearly falling out onto the floor in my fright. The cheerful knocking continued as I righted myself, breathing heavily as I smiled. Zakariah's voice wafted through the thin wood as he pounded a lively rhythm on the door.

"Wakey wakey! Come on, Addie! The sun is shining, and it feels so good!"

Laughing quietly, I hopped to the floor and answered to find Zakariah smiling brightly behind in the doorway. His curls were disheveled, and a lopsided grin was smeared across his face.

"Well, good morning," I yawned, rubbing the sleep from my eyes. "You gave me a scare just then. Ever heard of a gentle awakening?"

"What's that?" he joked, shrugging as he spoke. I shook my head as he relaxed. "I thought you might want to be up in time for lunch, but I think you needed the sleep." Taking a glance up at him, I nodded.

"I don't usually sleep this late. The last few days have just taken a toll on me."

"Which is completely understandable," Zakariah agreed. "And you need rest and nourishment. Do you want to get some food?"

"Yes," I replied enthusiastically, already shrugging into my jacket.

We ate quickly, eager to make something of the remainder of the day. To be sure I was welcomed properly, I would not be left alone unless I asked to be. I had no desire to be by myself, so today, I would spend my time with Zakariah. In order to find my niche in the

Village, each position would be showcased to me, so I could decide where I wanted to work. I already knew I would be blacksmithing soon whether or not the Village already had a working forge.

Zakariah took me to his shop, a small structure built only about eight feet off the ground. The space was open but crowded with supplies and projects. One wall held pottery that had yet to be fired, a second was dedicated to pottery that needed to be glazed, and a third displayed finished pieces. The potter's wheel sat in one corner facing a set of windows, and a table laden with jars, brushes, and half-painted pottery.

I wandered around the shop, studying the pieces that he had made. Just as Caleb, Zakariah was incredibly skilled in his craft. A glint of blue caught my eye, and I lifted a cloth to find a stack of stained-glass windows. The scene depicted a river cutting through an emerald green forest.

"Do you make these as well?" I quizzed, gently lifting the first panel to admire the second.

"I do," Zakariah confirmed. "I don't have much time for it right now, but I enjoy it." I nodded, understanding. Seeing as there was a much higher demand for kitchen ceramics, the window pieces he made remained in his shop. They reminded me of the vivid colors found in the windows of the Temple, though the artworks did not praise a cruel goddess.

Most of the pieces depicted scenes of nature, plants and animals immortalized in the panes of glass. I was drawn to a scene of a deer in the forest. The buck's sprawling antlers had golden leaves stuck on the prongs. The striking similarity to the buck I had seen in the woods compelled me to believe it may not be a coincidence.

"They're beautiful, Zakariah," I complimented. I looked up to find his cheeks flushed red. He muttered his thanks as he slipped an apron over his head and tied it behind his back. He handed me one as well, and I quickly put it on. It felt strange to me being made of fabric, as I was accustomed to my heavy leather apron for metalworking. With that we began our work.

He set me to what he called reclamation. I took old, broken, or misshapen pieces of pottery and placed them in a large vat of water, working them until they became soft, usable clay once again. I continually stole glances at his work. His hands were large and muscular, just as Caleb's were, yet he shaped the thin clay with a gentle touch.

"I have a question. If you don't want to talk about it, I understand, but I'm curious," Zakariah began as he expertly shaped a bowl on his pottery wheel. "You were engaged to the Chosen?"

"I was," I confirmed. "We met when I was around fifteen. He was about two years older. I was smitten from the start, but he didn't really take interest until I was seventeen or so."

"I noticed your neck." Zakariah gestured to his own neck, his fingers caked with clay and dripping wet. I touched the skin, my fingers cold and clammy from the muck I worked.

"Oh, from the necklace," I realized. I turned my eyes back to the sludgy water in the bucket before me. "That was probably brash of me. After I was Chosen, I tore my engagement necklace off and threw it at him. We'd already had an argument the day before about the Choosing and such. He had the chance to save me, but he wouldn't." I let my hands go limp in the murky water. "I honestly should have seen it coming."

A tear slipped down my cheek and joined the mixture of clay and water. I quickly wiped it away and shrugged, digging my hands back into the pieces of clay. "It's for the best." I felt a hand on my shoulder, and I turned as Zakariah stood before me. He took a towel from where he'd tossed it over his shoulder and dried my hands with it. The pressure of his hands gripping mine through the fabric was comforting. I could feel the taut strength, but he took care to touch me softly.

"I'm sorry, Addie," he apologized. "I shouldn't have pried like that."

"No, I probably needed to talk about it." I let my arms rest against my legs, drawing in deep, even breaths. "It feels good to say it out loud."

"Good," Zakariah nodded. "Thank you for trusting me. And for helping me with my work." I smiled as he offered me his hand. I glanced out the window to find the light fading. It was nearly time for the evening meal.

"Thank you for listening."

AS I HELPED TWIST FRAMES into shape for Zakariah, a commotion arose outside. Footsteps ran past the shop, and excited shouts sounded. "New arrival!" Someone had arrived from Anyra, and I very well may know them.

I dropped the metal I was working and moved for the door. I hardly registered Zakariah's voice as he called my name, asking if I was alright. It was Gwen. It had to be Gwen. The world seemed to fall away as I clambered down the rope ladder and moved toward the center of the Village. My heavy footfalls were muted in my ears. The wind rustling in the leaves fell silent as I ran. Gwen had to be here. She had to be safe. Finally, I saw her.

"Gwen!" She didn't have time to return my cry before I had grabbed her, holding her tightly to my chest. "You're here!" She fell into me, her tiny body trembling with tears and laughter so intermixed that I couldn't tell which was which. I nearly lifted her off the ground as she clutched to me.

"I'm ok," she promised me. Tears began falling from my own eyes as I loosened my grip. Finally, I looked up to see Xander smiling at us, somehow appearing large and small at the same time.

"Did they give you any trouble?" I asked, extending my hand to my future brother-in-law. He grasped it firmly before he spoke.

"None," he promised. "They think we're searching along with everyone else. I'm sure they'll hardly notice we're gone with how absorbed they are in finding you."

"Good. Hopefully, they'll never find us."

"Addie, Sebastian is a wreck," Gwen divulged. "He appeared before the people. It looks as though he hasn't eaten or slept since you disappeared."

"I'm sure he's losing his mind with how angry he is at me," I brushed it off, shaking my head. "He knows how I feel about the Totem. He should have expected me to run honestly." Without warning, Gwen crumpled to the ground, Xander just barely catching her before she fell. "Gwen!"

"Adelaide, is she alright?" Calvin asked as he ran up to the scene.

"She's alright," Xander promised. "She's still weak from the punishment. She just needs food and rest."

"And she shall have it," Calvin promised. "Come, the healer's lodge is this way." He called for Katharine to come as Xander trailed behind him. Gwen seemed so fragile in his arms. I followed behind to help like a child unsure of how to be of service.

"Addie, she'll be ok," Zakariah called. I turned to him. "Katharine is the lead nurse on victims like her. She's in good hands." I nodded, relaxing into his touch.

"What should I do for her?" I asked. Zakariah smiled.

"You're her sister. Just be you."

I spent the remainder of the day and well into the next becoming integrated into this new society. I watched with wonder as Gwen's condition improved with great speed. I was passed from person to person, each one teaching me something new and different. I learned gardening from Calvin, government from Edrei, medicine from Katharine, and so much more from so many more people. I absorbed the information like a sponge, but I longed for my forge. I wanted to craft, twist metal into delicate, beautiful shapes.

Eventually, I told Edrei of my blacksmith skills, and she brought me to the meager forge. They had built their makeshift smithy roughly half a mile from the main camp, ensuring that any rogue fire could be put out before it reached the Village. As we approached, I could hear the clang of a hammer falling on metal. It came into sight, and I peered through the leaves to see the blacksmith. The man working the forge was young, covered in soot, and unsure of what he was doing. What was more than that was the fact that I recognized him.

"Landon!" I cried at the sight of him. The young man looked up, revealing stunning copper eyes. I had seen those eyes in the face of his sister, Valerie, every day for years. I hadn't seen him in over a year, but I had attributed it to his dedication to his studies. The realization dawned on me that this is how Valerie and Caleb knew of this society.

"Adelaide?" he asked, scrutinizing me from under a shock of blond hair turned black with ash. He had his sleeves rolled up to the elbow, and burn scars marred his skin.

"So, this is where you've been?" I asked, smiling broadly. He left his workbench, removing the long leather apron he wore. "Where are your gloves!?"

"I can't use my fingers with them on!" he argued playfully, pulling me into a tight hug. "How are Valerie and Caleb?"

"They're great as far as I know. They're the ones who sent me here. I was chosen to be the Gift, and there was no way we were letting that happen. They should be joining us soon."

"Oh, that's fantastic news!" he agreed. Edrei chuckled as she watched the reunion of friends.

"I did not realize it was Landon's Valerie you spoke of. Yes, she and her husband have been sending people to us for nearly three years now. Landon was one of the first."

As if on cue, Joshuah approached our group, informing Edrei of two new arrivals from Anyra, a husband and wife. Landon and I grinned at each other before racing toward the village, dodging trees and stumbling on the rugged terrain. We found the pair in the center of the encampment, surrounded by Villagers. They smiled and chatted with people as if they'd known them for years. Perhaps they had.

"Valerie!" Landon screeched, nearly tackling his sister in an embrace. I didn't know how long it had been since they'd seen one another. Laughing, I went to Caleb, jokingly mimicking Landon's cry as I hugged my surrogate brother. After a moment, Landon released Valerie for me to hug, and he went to Caleb.

"What's been happening?" I asked. "Did they suspect you?"

"Not for a second. We went to the Temple at dawn to report you missing," Valerie explained, putting heavy sarcasm on the last few words. "We led a search party, but in the opposite direction of this Village. We're hoping they won't find us."

"Yes, so am I," I agreed.

Edrei, Landon, and I settled Caleb and Valerie into a bungalow, larger and more permanent than my own. They hadn't brought many possessions with them from Anyra, only clothes and a few valuable items. They told me of the events that had transpired in Anyra during my absence. High Priestess Rhoda had practically lost her mind when she heard the news, and she set anyone willing on the search for me.

"You should have seen Sebastian, Addie, he was white as ghost!" Caleb laughed. "He looked like he was going to soil himself!"

"I think he may have," Valerie added. As Caleb and Landon began hanging the curtains, Valerie pulled me closer as we folded and put away the few clothing items they'd packed. "He did look remorseful, Addie," she assured me. "He was wearing your necklace along with his own. It's as if you're already dead to him."

"Because I am in his mind, and I may as well be. I'll never set foot in that city again, and if I ever see his face, so help me, I'll smash it in," I said, drawing a giggle from her.

"I know, but I can't simply believe you're entirely alright. You two had your ups and downs, but you did love each other deep down. Losing him must be as easy for you as it is for him."

"Valerie, I don't know if he did love me, not really," I argued, dropping a shirt into the drawer. "He didn't say it back to me after we had that argument. I tried to make amends, I brought him lunch, I calmed down, I told him I loved him, and nothing. He gave me nothing in reply. I've been wondering if it even would have worked had I not been chosen."

"I was beginning to wonder that myself after you told us about that," Valerie revealed. At this point, Caleb and Landon had overheard our discussion, and I nodded that it was alright. Caleb was just as involved in this as Valerie, and I didn't mind allowing Landon to hear it. Though it stung, Sebastian was now a part of my past. Having the future I had envisioned for years dashed to pieces was an incredibly terrifying thing.

"He wronged you, Addie, there's no doubt about that, but it brought you here. It got you out of Anyra and into a new life. A safe life where you can start over," Caleb assured me. He pulled me under his arm, my protector since the age of four, and I let out a heavy sigh. "Sebastian didn't appreciate you when he had the chance."

I wiped a tear from my eye and smiled up at my friends. They had been the best support system I could ever have hoped for. Through it all, Caleb and Valerie had been by my side, and I could sense Landon beginning to take on that role as well. As children, he had tagged along with Valerie, Caleb, Gwendolyn and I, our constant shadow.

He was always a welcome presence. Now in this new home, we could be that way again.

"Now, we need to cheer up," Valerie claimed, patting my shoulder gently. "We have some happy news for you." I furrowed my brow as Valerie moved to slip her arm around her husband's waist. She could hardly keep the grin off her face.

"What is it?" I asked. I spotted tears glinting in Caleb's eyes, though his cheeks twitched with the smile he fought to keep at bay. After a terse pause, Valerie could contain it no longer.

"I'm pregnant!"

"What!?" Landon shrieked. He beat me to the couple, hugging them fiercely once more. I, on the other hand, could hardly breathe, my jaw slack and eyes wide.

"What?" I echoed much softer than Landon.

"I'm going to be an uncle!" he cried, overjoyed. I took a brief pause of disbelief before running in to hug my friends. I looked between Valerie's eyes and her stomach, hardly able to process the fact that there was a tiny new life inside of her. The ultimate creation. Something one could never forge with their hands. Rather, this beautiful thing was forged by love.

"You're joking," I accused her, my cheeks stinging with how wide I smiled.

"Absolutely not," Caleb laughed, grinning broadly. From the time we were children, Caleb wanted to be a father. Now that dream was finally coming true. Should their child be a girl, I knew they would never allow her to be chosen as the Gift. Sooner or later, our patchwork family would have found its way to this Village.

A wordless cry escaped my lips as I rushed in to hug the pair, hardly able to believe it. They clutched me. It had been so long since I had felt such joy. I doubt I'd feel anything as such until I discovered I would have my own child.

SOON ENOUGH, VALERIE and I had taken over the forge, building it up into something much greater than the small fire Landon was running before our arrival. He had never been as interested in it as me and Valerie, but he had done the best with what he had been given. Within days, we were forging everything from carving knives to engagement necklaces. Edrei had commissioned us to forge as many weapons as we could, crafting new spears and swords in case of an attack.

Caleb had begun working with Zakariah, as both of them were skilled in pottery and glasswork. They made a wide array of items, creating each piece for a specific purpose. For now, they were creating household kitchenware like plates and pitchers, but I knew Caleb could create incredibly intricate stained-glass windows and statuettes twisted into beautiful imagery. I had seen that Zakariah was at a similar skill level.

I met with Zakariah at the community's lunch one day, and he excitedly led me into the workshop where he and Caleb worked. As if he were a child proudly showing his artwork to a parent, he showed me his workbench and the pet project he'd been creating. A gorgeous stained-glass window rested on the bench, the light of the afternoon sun setting the colors alight. The pattern was bright and colorful with incredibly intricate handiwork. The image was a bloodred flower with delicately woven leaves surrounding it, each petal somehow shaded as if it were a painting. My hand drifted out to touch the artwork but stopped before my skin met the surface.

"Zakariah, this is gorgeous," I complimented, tearing my eyes away to look into his face.

"Thanks," he grinned proudly, nearly bouncing with excitement. "I'm not sure where it will go yet, but I know it will be good."

"I think you ought to frame it so it can be moved. Surely these bungalows won't last forever," I argued.

"Maybe," he ceded, studying his handiwork. I nodded, picturing the artwork displayed in a home as it should be. "Maybe I'll live in an actual house one day, and we can install it there."

"We?" I quizzed playfully, smiling as I met his eyes. A deep blush crept into his cheeks, but his smile didn't fade. He shrugged, nodding as I giggled.

"We," he confirmed. We were barred from any further discussion as Caleb returned from lunch, ready to begin his work again. I caught Zakariah's eye before leaving, and he smiled sheepishly before turning to begin his work once more. After bidding the pair of them goodbye, I slipped out the door and down the rope ladder.

Chapter Twelve: Expanding

"Adelaide, may I speak with you?" Edrei asked, approaching as I made for my bungalow and some much-needed sleep. I had somehow completed twelve projects in one day, and the toll of the work was creeping into my arms.

"Of course, Edrei," I replied. I turned to give her my full attention, and she motioned for me to follow. We began walking as we talked.

"Firstly, how have you been enjoying your time with us? Is everything comfortable?"

"Oh, incredibly so. I feel more at home here than I have in Anyra all my life."

"Good," Edrei smiled, "I was hoping you would be happy during your stay." She lifted the drape, allowing me into her bungalow. "In a way, that's what I wanted to talk to you about. The duration of your stay."

Instantly, my stomach dropped to my feet, fear creeping into my chest as I turned to her. I thought this place was permanent, and just as my former home of Anyra, I feared it would be ripped away.

"What do you mean? I thought this would be my home now?"

"In a sense," Edrei placated. She motioned for me to take a seat at the table, and I followed her gesture, nearly falling into the chair. "The people, the community are your home as long as you will stay. But this location cannot be permanent for us."

A great sigh of relief escaped my chest as I understood. Edrei smiled warmly, her eyes apologetic for the small scare. I smiled in return, already beginning to agree.

"Yes, it's too close to Anyra, we could be found," I nodded, turning my full attention to her. "Where shall we go? Deeper into the wood?" I watched as Edrei dragged her chair over to the small pantry and stepped onto it to reach the highest shelf. "The Temple claimed Anyra was the only civilization left, but I don't trust Rhoda as far as I can throw her."

"The Temple does nothing but lie," Edrei remarked. She stepped off of the chair holding a folded piece of parchment she'd fished out of the pantry. "Anyra is far from the only civilization left standing. I'm living proof of it."

The parchment crinkled in her hands, and she unfolded it and spread it on the table, spanning almost half the surface. It was a map. My eyes immediately found Anyra next to the sea and the vast forest it neighbored. These were familiar. Roughly twenty miles outside of Anyra, the Village had been marked onto the paper, obviously much fresher ink than the rest.

The rest of the map stunned me into silence. I counted to myself, taking note of the names and sizes of the drawings. At least thirty other cities and countries were marked on the map, one only a few days journey away from Anyra. I found myself leaning forward, mesmerized. My world had grown nearly fifty times its original size.

"We're not alone."

"Not by a long shot," Edrei agreed. I looked up to find her grinning, proud and joyful. The Anyrans thought themselves special, that they were the ordained people of the Totem. Little did they know that the world was getting on fine without them.

"There's so many of us though. We can't just waltz up to some unsuspecting kingdom and knock on their gates!" I reasoned.

"And we won't. I'm showing you this for many reasons, but the main one is this: Ramona read your future, but she saw nothing but fire and change. What that change is, we don't know. So I'm asking you now to help us. You are the one who will save Anyra, rip it from the Temple's grasp." I stared up at Edrei, dumbfounded as she spoke.

"I will not be around to guide and protect these runaways forever. I want you to take over the position. I will train you, help you. And you don't have to answer immediately."

"I accept," I interrupted her. Her eyebrows flew up in surprise, but deep in her eyes, I could see that she had known my answer from the start. She began to smile as I gazed up at her. "I don't know what the future holds. Only days ago, I thought I didn't have one. But what life I have, I will use to protect my people. Those that reject the Temple. We'll burn it down one day, Edrei, I promise you that."

She did not speak. I hadn't realized I had stood from my chair in my passionate acceptance of the post, but now Edrei and I stood eye to eye. My leader came around the table and placed firm, gentle arms around me in a hug. And instantly, I felt right. This was my calling, to save the Anyrans from Rhoda and the Temple that had mongered over them for nearly a thousand years. We would stand and say 'no more'.

"Good," Edrei said as she withdrew. "Thank you, Adelaide. I have an idea for our course of action. Shall we discuss?" I smiled as we took our seats across from one another, the map between us.

"Absolutely."

Edrei placed her hands on the parchment, pointing out a city on the other side of the very forest where we resided. The woodland spanned hundreds of miles, and the Village was marked nearly a quarter of the way through, closer to Anyra. Directly opposite of the Anyran valley, on the other side of the vast expanse of trees, lay a landlocked city, roughly the same size as Anyra.

"We're going to Kantrin." I looked up to see an odd twinkle in Edrei's eye. "My home." I understood. Edrei had come to Anyra by accident, but her return to her homeland would be no mistake.

THE CURTAIN FLUTTERED behind me as I ducked out of Edrei's bungalow, reentering the village square. As evening drew nearer, people milled about and began settling in for the evening meal. I breathed the fresh, autumn air and confidently strode forward. Edrei had tasked me with a recruitment mission.

I made my way through the space, nodding as I passed by my new peers. The vast majority of them were either several years older than I or several younger. Mostly the people that fled to this encampment were parents with young children, sons and daughters liable to one day become the Chosen or the Gift. Their protective instincts would not allow them to feed their daughters to the volcano or enslave their sons to the Temple.

Such a family was that of twin daughters Willow and Orchid. Neither had been chosen this year, but until they were wed, there was no guarantee they were safe. Having arrived soon before me, both girls but Willow in particular had taken a shine to me.

"Addie!" Willow cried as they cantered up to me. I smiled, pausing to speak with them.

"Hi, girls. What have you been up to?" I looked between the two of them. It was hard to believe the girls were sisters let alone twins. Willow was larger with massive curls of brown hair. Her skin was dotted with freckles, and her teeth were just a bit too large for her mouth.

Orchid couldn't have been more the opposite. Smaller and thinner than her sister, she had straight yellow hair and fair skin. Her large blue eyes were intelligent and sharp, but her tongue was not silver like her sister's. However, I was sure she would grow into a great scholar one day.

"Great! Addie, look at this!" Willow fished something out of her pocket as her sister smiled, quiet and content. Willow produced a small piece of metal twisted into the shape of a flower. The design was simple, but beautiful for a beginner crafter as herself. "Landon helped me make that."

"It's fantastic, Willow!" I commended her, turning the piece in my hands. It was certainly rough, but it was definitely a great first project for the girl. "You have potential Willow. Perhaps I could begin training you?"

"Really!?" she gasped, practically vibrating with excitement. I laughed as I handed the flower back to her.

"Really," I assured her. "It's about time I had an apprentice, and I think you'll do nicely." She nodded, grinning with the thought of it. I turned my attention to her sister. I had to be sure the shyer, quieter Orchid was given the attention she needed.

"And what have you been up to today, Orchid?"

"I went with Willow to the forge. I read while they were working. It's about the history of Anyra," she recited, smiling softly. My brow furrowed as she pulled a leather-bound journal from her bag.

"Really? Where did you get these?" I asked. Never had I seen an Anyran history book, only the scrolls the Temple cherry-picked.

"Papa gave them to me. And his Papa gave them to him. He says the books were written for generations, from the very creation of Anyra." I drew closer, intrigued. It was possible that these records were the only accurate depiction of Anyra's history. "Each person kept a detailed diary of Anyra's history. But I didn't start at the beginning. I started with Gramp's book."

"That sounds very fascinating," I nodded, incredibly curious about what the books may contain. "Listen, Orchid. I'd like to learn some more about Anyra's history. If you read anything that seems odd, especially if it's about the Temple or the Totem, will you tell me?" My hand drifted forward, and I gently placed it on the small girl's shoulder.

To my surprise, she screamed as my fingers met the bare skin on her shoulder, seeing as she wore a sleeveless tunic. She fell backwards away from me, sitting hard on the dirt. My eyes widened as Willow moved to catch her sister, cradling her to see if she was alright.

"Orchid, what happened!?" I asked, diving to the ground beside her. Willow held her sister's head in her lap, but I refrained from touching her again. "Is she alright?"

"Yes, she just has a thing with people touching her. She doesn't like skin to skin contact," Willow answered as if the reaction were common.

"Skin to skin?" I echoed. Before I could inquire further, Orchid came to.

"Harbinger!" she screamed, shooting up to a sitting position. "Adelaide!" With that, I understood.

"Orchid, are you alright? Can you hear me?" I asked. My every instinct told me to reach out and hold the girl, but I refrained.

"Yes, I'm fine," she agreed, rubbing her eyes as if just waking from a nap. "I'm sorry I frightened you."

"I'm sorry for causing that," I argued. "What did you see?"

"A vision, I get them sometimes. I was you, I saw through your eyes. It was hot, like at the bonfire, and I was wearing a black dress. I don't know why."

"It only happens when strangers touch her skin with theirs. For some reason, she's alright with family," Willow explained further. Her protective gaze never left her sister's shivering form.

"Orchid," I addressed her. Her bright eyes turned to look at me. "I think you're a Seer."

"That's not possible," she scoffed, moving to rise.

"Ramona is a Seer, and she read me just a few days ago. Her reaction was nearly the same. She saw me with fire, too." Orchid paused, beginning to believe.

"I don't know," she murmured.

"I'm certain. Ramona can help you, Orchid, teach you how to use it and control it." Slowly, she began to nod.

"Alright. Where is she?"

"I can take you to her bungalow." Willow helped pick her sister up from the ground, and I led them through the Village toward the Elder Seer's abode. It may have taken time from my mission, but it was more than worth it to help the girl learn about herself and her abilities. I rapped gently on the door, the twins behind me.

"Ramona? It's Addie, are you home?"

"Yes, darling!" she called the excitement in her voice nearly palpable. The door creaked on its hinges as it opened. "I was just putting the kettle on in case you'd like some tea."

"I hope you have a few extra mugs at hand," I smiled. I stepped aside, gesturing to the young girls behind me. "Have you met the twins?"

"Only very briefly," Ramona grinned, thrilled by the extra company. "Willow and Orchid, correct?" Willow nodded proudly as Orchid stifled a yawn. Her accidental reading had obviously taken a toll on her.

"We've come to a bit of a realization," I confessed as Ramona ushered us inside. She sat us at the table, placing a teacup before each of us. None of the pieces in her set matched, but I found it rather charming. She had a small pot of honey set out in the center of the table, prepared for company.

"Oh?" Ramona asked as she set the teapot in the center of the table. Willow reached across and poured both herself and her sister a cup. I deftly filled my own cup, distracted by the matter at hand. "Is everything alright?"

"I think so," Orchid answered. I was a little surprised but proud that she had spoken up unprompted. "Addie touched my shoulder, and I had a vision. It's happened for so long that I never paid much mind to it. But I think I'm a Seer."

"Another Seer!" Ramona gasped, spilling half her cup onto the table. Quickly, I stood and snatched a towel off of a shelf to clear the spill. "What did you see in your vision?"

"It was short. I just saw Addie wearing a black dress surrounded by fire," she explained. Willow patted her shoulder, nervous that her sister would faint again.

"When she came to, she said something about the Harbinger," I added as I sat back down. "It sounded fairly similar to some of the things you said when you read me."

"There is no doubt that you are a Seer, my dear," Ramona nodded. "Most don't develop the gift until they reach sixteen or older. How old are you, Orchid?"

"Thirteen," she stammered. Ramona's eyes widened.

"Your gift must be strong. I didn't have a full vision until I was twenty-three."

"Oh," Orchid murmured, her eyes widening with fear. Willow squeezed her shoulder, having never taken her eyes off her sister the entire time. Her tea was growing cold, but truly all of ours was cooling rapidly. Not one of us had taken as much as a sip.

"I can help you, Orchid," Ramona promised. "Your gift is an exceptional one. You need not fear." Both of the twins seemed to relax at this assurance, and Willow reached for her tea. "Thank you for bringing this to my attention. I've never met another Seer." Orchid smiled as I lifted my cup in celebration.

"Perhaps you'll have a guild one day," I hoped. The other three sitting around the table raised their mismatched cups in agreement, and we enjoyed our lukewarm tea.

I KNOCKED GENTLY ON Caleb and Valerie's bungalow door. A shuffle came from within, and seconds later, Caleb's face appeared as he opened the door. He smiled, his eyes brighter and more alert than I'd seen them in ages. It was as if a weight had been lifted from him once he was away from the city.

"Hi, Addie," he grinned. No doubt the thought of his unborn child was still on his mind. I could see the excitement in his smile. "You looked tired. Are you alright?"

"Yeah, I'm alright," I assured him as he allowed me inside. Valerie sat in the corner, a book in hand. I doubt she'd even heard me come in with how absorbed she was in the literature. She popped a blueberry into her mouth from a bowl beside her, then her hand drifted down to her stomach. I smiled.

"Busy day?" Caleb continued.

"That's an understatement." I laughed as I took a seat. Valerie lifted her head and smiled before diving back into the written word. I tilted my head to look at the spine. It was one of my uncle's works. I tapped her knee to draw her full attention. "I need to tell you what happened today."

"What is it? Are you ok!?" Valerie asked, suddenly urgent. She slammed the book down on the floor, nearly overturning the bowl as she did. I steadied it as she stared at me wide-eyed.

"Everything's fine!" I assured her. "Just a lot to fill you in on."

"Tell us," Caleb urged me.

"Here we go," I murmured, settling in. "Firstly, do you know the twin girls that arrived last week? One of them is a Seer. She and Ramona have had visions of me wielding fire. So that means something, but neither of them knows what.

"Secondly, I had a meeting with Edrei today. She has an idea for our next course of action, and she asked me to help. We came up with a plan."

"Oh?" Valerie inquired, leaning closer. Both were intrigued by my tale.

"She and I agree that we need to leave. We need to pick everything up and get farther from Anyra. We're getting too big, the Temple is bound to take notice of us eventually."

"I've been worried about that for some time now. We have had families leaving nearly in droves," Caleb agreed, and I nodded as well.

"Edrei has a map that she brought with her when she came to Anyra as a child. A map of the entire world, and Anyra is far from the only place with people."

"I knew it!" Valerie mumbled.

"There is a city at the other end of the forest where Edrei came from. We may be able to go to them. She tasked me with putting together a reconnaissance team."

"Who-who are you going to ask?" Valerie asked. She glanced nervously to Caleb as her hand drifted to her stomach. It had not yet started to grow.

"Neither of you two," I assured her. I placed a reassuring hand on her knee. "You have something much bigger to take care of. That's what I wanted to ask. I don't know many people here, but you seem to, and Landon certainly does."

"Ok, good," Caleb sighed, relieved. I could never ask them to do such a thing for me as to risk their child. "Do you have anyone in mind yet?"

"A few. It will be me and Edrei of course. We want probably three or four others. I was thinking Zakariah for starts." Both my friends nodded in agreement.

"He's definitely a good choice. Strong, task-driven, determined."

"He can have a short attention span sometimes," Valerie smiled, giggling.

"But he'll be sharp as a razor when you need him to be," Caleb finished. "Who else?"

"That's where I need help. I don't know many others in the Village. Who do you think would be a good fit for the task?"

"I think you ought to take Calvin and Katharine," Caleb recommended. "They may be a bit older, but they're wiser for it."

"And Katharine is a healer. That could be useful," Valerie agreed. I nodded making mental note. She had cared for Gwen upon her arrival, so I was certain she'd have no problem tending to a wound should one of us be injured on the journey.

"Do you think five is enough? Myself, Edrei, Zakariah, Calvin, and Katharine?" I asked, looking between my two friends. They didn't take long mulling it over.

"I think you'll have a wonderful team with you," Valerie smiled.

Chapter Thirteen: Spellbound

Sebastian shot out of bed, the sheets damp and clinging to his skin from the sweat that drenched him. Another nightmare. They had plagued his every night since the Choosing. A heavy pounding sounded at his door. The all too familiar fall of the garnet staff on the door.

Sebastian haphazardly clambered out of bed to the door, wrenching it open to find the knob of the staff inches from his face. It would have easily broken his nose, but he didn't so much as flinch. Rhoda let the staff rest at her side and looked him up and down.

"You'll want to dress in warm clothing," she advised him. Silently, Sebastian pulled clothes over the shorts he had worn to bed, a heavy sweater scratching at his skin as he pulled it on. Rhoda stood outside the door, studying her staff as she waited.

"I am upset your Gift ran away," she commented as Sebastian pulled a pair of heavy boots onto his feet. "I wanted that new staff. She was an excellent blacksmith." Sebastian did not speak. His jaw was set and his brows lowered in his emotionless display. He would no longer entertain her small talk. She looked him up and down once more and shrugged before moving.

Curiosity ran rampant in Sebastian's mind as he followed Rhoda out the back of the Temple and toward the trail. He knew not why she had roused him in the middle of the night, but he would not give her the satisfaction of explaining herself. He trailed behind her, the chill of the night creeping into his bones. It didn't seem to affect Rhoda.

"Do you have Adelaide's necklace?" Rhoda called over her shoulder. In response, Sebastian hooked both chains with his thumb and lifted them for her to see. She gave nothing more than a fleeting glance. "Good."

The two began to climb the volcano, following a smaller, much less frequently used path that shot off from the main road. The road he would carry Adelaide up to kill her. That is, if they could find her. Every search party had returned empty-handed with not so much as a footprint from Adelaide.

The pit of worry lurched in Sebastian's stomach. It had not left him since the Choosing. He had lost everything, her love, her hand, and now Adelaide herself. She had slipped through his fingers like sand, but he knew it didn't have to be that way. If only he had said yes. If only he had married her when he had the chance.

Sebastian nearly bumped into Rhoda who had abruptly stopped. Lost in thought, he hadn't realized where they were. The path had led them around to the back of the volcano where a circular platform stood surrounded by lamps. Two clicks of the staff brought the lanterns to life. Rhoda turned toward Sebastian and held out her hand expectantly.

"What more do you want from me?" Sebastian asked, his voice gruff as this was the first time he had spoken since his rude awakening. Rhoda gave no response. Rather, she reached forward and snatched the necklaces from around his neck. The metal chain dug into the back of his neck, and Sebastian fell to his knees in the center of the circle.

"These will do nicely." Rhoda lifted the two necklaces above her head, the metal glinting in the light of the half moon. Finally, fear bubbled up in Sebastian's chest. She was going to cast a spell on him. Or a curse.

Rhoda began to move, marching around the circle as she chanted in a meaningless language. Sebastian sat silently watching her, but the spell began to take effect as she moved, slamming the garnet staff on the ground. Sebastian watched as shards of gemstone skittered across the ground, one landing directly in front of him. For a moment, he could see his reflection in the piece of garnet, red and warped. His vision began to grow cloudy around the edges, pain creeping into his chest. He fought, trying to ward off the spell as a horse attempting to buck off their rider. He failed.

Rhoda grinned as he writhed on the ground, broken cries echoing out of him. He was powerless to resist her. As her chanting grew quieter, Sebastian grew still. He sat on his knees, hunched over with his forehead to the ground. No sound came from him now, and he was eerily still. She smiled.

"Chosen," she called him. The young man's body wrenched itself upright as if pulled by a string. His gaze swung left, then right, then settled on Rhoda. She slung the two necklaces back over his neck then pulled him to his feet by his collar.

"Bring the Gift back," she commanded. "And do not fail me."

Chapter Fourteen: Trailblazers

I trudged through the cool grass, damp with the early morning dew. Almost the entire Village was asleep in the chill of the morning hours. The sun had begun to peek over the horizon, but it was far out of sight with the miles of trees between the Village and the horizon where the sun was waking from its slumber.

"Good morning, Edrei," I greeted her as I ducked into her bungalow. She sat at the table where she had placed a pot of tea in the center and four cups neatly beside it. She had a fifth cup in her hand, delicate tendrils of steam floating upward to kiss her skin awake. I would not have been surprised to find she was already on her second or third cup.

"Good morning, Adelaide," she replied. "Would you like some tea? I thought we may need the energy for the journey."

"Oh, I definitely will," I nodded, reaching for a teacup.

"Not a morning person?" Edrei chuckled.

"If the sun isn't up, I shouldn't be either."

"I concur!" a voice yawned. I turned to see Zakariah entering the abode, his curls wild and massive on his head. I giggled as he sleepily reached for a mug. I filled it for him, seeing how he was hardly awake. He nodded his thanks before gulping down a mouthful. "Why did we have to do this so early?"

"I am not sure how long the journey will take us. I don't want us to have to sleep in the woods for many nights," Edrei explained.

"But you made the journey as a child, didn't you?" I asked. "It can't be too far."

"It's farther than my story makes it seem. When I was roughly four years old, my brother and I ran away from home. I don't remember why, but it certainly wasn't a good reason. We got lost in the woods, but an Anyran hunter found us and brought us home."

"You have a brother?" Zakariah gasped, reaching to refill his teacup.

"Had. He passed away from an illness when I was ten and he was twelve." We shared a terse moment of reverence for her loss, but the conversation quickly moved on.

"Do you think we'll find your parents?" I asked.

"I have no idea," Edrei answered. She nodded to Katharine and Calvin as they entered together and offered them each a mug of tea. "That is not the purpose of this expedition."

We continued talking for a few more moments, the conversation remaining light until the morning air had turned golden and Edrei deemed the light sufficient. Finally, we took our seats and looked to Edrei. Edrei, however, looked to me. Smiling slightly as I remembered my role, I stood.

"Thank you all for volunteering for this expedition. You are all aware of where we are going and the purpose of this journey. We have no idea what Kantrin may hold. They do not speak the same language as us, nor do they know we are coming. We do not know if they will be hostile toward us.

"They may recognize Edrei as one of their own and welcome us. They may attack. We also do not know what perils we may face in the wood. We expect the journey to take roughly three days. Knowing that, does anyone wish to withdraw? There is no shame in doing so."

No one moved. I caught Zakariah's eye to find him smiling up at me as I addressed the group. Each of them was determined to find a new land. They had family to protect from the clutches of the Anyran Temple. Each of us five were determined to find a new home for our refugees.

"Fantastic," I smiled. "In that case, let us be off."

"Off on an adventure!" Zakariah agreed. We stood and embarked on foot for the long, tedious journey ahead.

MY EYES BEGAN TO DRIFT slowly lower, my body weary from a full day of walking. The blisters from my first trek had just begun to heal, and they complained as new ones had begun to form. My body screamed for rest as my shoulders sagged under the weight of my pack.

"Addie!" I jolted as Zakariah pulled me closer to him. I found the rough bark of a tree mere inches from my face. I'd nearly walked straight into a tree in my exhaustion. "Are you alright?" he asked as the group turned to look at me.

I nodded, shaking the sleep from my eyes. "I'm alright. Thank you, Zakariah." I looked up at Edrei, who seemed to show no signs of such exhaustion. The rest of us however were heavy with fatigue.

"We camp here for the night," she announced, a small smile lacing her lips. I allowed a sigh of relief to escape my lungs, and we set about camping for the night. Each of us had a bedroll, a swath of fabric for a tent, and enough food to last a week. Once I had shed my pack, I began building the fire, and Zakariah brought me armfuls of wood to burn.

Once the blaze was beginning to lick at the first bits of firewood, Zakariah and I pitched our tents. I had brought extra lengths of rope, and I slung up a makeshift hammock between two trees. I slung my tent over a second rope above the hammock, providing shelter should a fluke rain shower pass. As I stepped back to admire my shoddy work, I heard Zakariah chuckling. I turned with an outraged smile on my lips as he stifled laughter. He waved me off, trying to turn away.

"What's so funny?" I asked, crossing my arms and jutting my hip to the side.

"I'm going to laugh at you when you fall in the middle of the night," Zakariah giggled, draping his own tent over a low branch.

"I'm not going to be sorry tomorrow morning when you're sore from sleeping on the ground," I fired back, taking up a stick to poke at the fire.

"I'm not going to be sorry when you're sore from falling!" Zakariah chuckled as he sawed at a branch with his pocket knife. I shook my makeshift poker at him, a grin across my face.

"Fight me!" I demanded, giggles undermining my threats. With a yank, Zakariah broke the small branch away, leaves and all, and brandished it at me like a sword.

"To the death!" he cried dramatically, springing forward to smack my smoldering stick with his sword of greenery. I laughed as we lunged and parried haphazardly, but that quickly faded when I spotted trails of smoke ribboning up from his branch.

"Zakariah, it's on fire!" I cried, throwing my own feigned sword into the blaze. The goofy smirk was immediately gone from Zakariah's face as I leapt forward.

"What?" he asked, the question barely leaving his lips before I smacked the branch out of his hand and into the fire. The flames consumed it almost instantly, smoldering away before our eyes. Zakariah and I remained silent for a moment, before Edrei stood up from her seat on the ground.

"Are you two alright?" she demanded. "That was foolish! You could have been hurt."

"Yes, I'm sorry, Edrei," I agreed, bowing my head. I looked down at my hands and found them unharmed. I'd only touched the smoldering leaves briefly, not long enough for them to cause any damage.

"It's not her fault, I was the one acting like a fool," Zakariah argued. Calvin's chuckles distracted us three as we looked to where he sat on the other side of the campfire.

"Oh, let'em go, Edrei," he commented. "They were having a bit of fun. No harm done." Edrei nodded, allowing her shoulders to relax.

"Yes, it was a bit of fun," she nodded. "I apologize you two. You deserve some fun." With that, we all sat down for our evening meal, roasting wild mushrooms over the flames and tearing chunks of dried rabbit and chicken from larger chunks of jerky. Our small camp was filled with joy and laughter as we told stories in turn, keeping ourselves entertained until sleep won out.

I WAS ROUSED FROM THAT sleep as light slanted through the trees into my eyes. The sun had just begun to rise, and I smiled. My makeshift hammock had held throughout the night. Zakariah would be sorry and sore when he found out. I peeked around my tent and heard his soft snores from his tent on the ground close to me. The other three were still asleep, though I knew we would be rising to take the journey up again soon.

Moving slowly, I swung my legs to the ground and stretched, my back popping and clicking as I woke my body. I turned to begin dismantling my tent and hammock, but movement in the forest caught my eye. My heart plummeted into my stomach, and I drew my knife from its sheath on my rucksack. The forest was beginning to wake as well, so it very well may have been a bird or squirrel.

Cautiously, I crept into the trees, ready to scream for the others should some threat appear. Would another bear or other wretched creature attack? Could an Anyran search party have come this far? I peered into the trees, searching for some motion.

I relaxed as a massive buck daintily stepped through the trees, his antlers brushing against low branches. I let out a sigh of relief, lowering the knife to my side. The deer swung his head toward me, gazing at me with large, brown eyes. My brow furrowed as I looked back at him.

"Hello?" I quizzed. Surely, this couldn't be the same buck I had met almost a week prior on my journey to the Village. I stepped closer, and the buck turned to face me. Again, I was struck with how intelligent he appeared. Most deer would have run off at the first sight of a human.

The buck blinked slowly at me, closing his eyes for a moment, then opening them once again. It almost seemed to be a nod of greeting. I remembered the strange way Quinton had acted as he was possessed by the spirit of my mother. Could this buck be something more than a woodland creature?

"Adelaide?" Katharine's voice called from behind me, and the buck instantly darted away. He was not frightened of me, but he was unnerved by even the gentle Katharine. Why me? I didn't have time to ponder for long.

"Yes?" I replied, turning back to our encampment. In the few moments I'd been away, the rest of our group had awoken. Zakariah sat on the ground, his hair mussed and fluffy on his head as he rubbed his eyes. Edrei and Calvin had set about preparing breakfast. She had already set out the hardy, stoneware tea set.

"What were you doing?" Katharine asked as she rolled up her tent.

"I thought I saw someone out there," I answered, still shaken from the odd encounter. "But it was just a deer."

"Catch!" Calvin tossed me an apple from the pack on the ground, and I smiled as I caught it. He threw one to Zakariah, but his sleepy reflexes weren't quite ready. The fruit bounced off of his chest, and he grunted as he fell back onto his bedroll. "Wake up, lad! We've ground to cover!"

I knelt to pick the fruit up as Zakariah groaned, his arm slung over his eyes. I chuckled as he lurched forward a second time. I offered the apple, and he deftly accepted it, yawning as he shined it on his shirt. The fruit gave a wet crunch as he bit into it, and I followed suit. The sweet flavor burst across my tongue, waking my senses and ridding me of any lingering sleep.

"We should strive to leave as soon as possible," Edrei recommended as she poured five cups of strong tea. I handed Zakariah a cup then lifted my own to my lips. The warm tea did well to counteract the crisp fruit. Edrei's love of tea was certainly not unfounded. Zakariah moved to sip his tea, but drew away with a gasp as it burnt his tongue.

Quickly, we finished our breakfast and packed our things, attempting to leave the small clearing as we found it. While I doubted any Anyrans had ventured this far, it would be best to leave as little trace as possible. The journey ahead was long and harrowing, but it would be more than worth it.

Chapter Fifteen: The Stag

Sebastian's body steadily grew weaker, yet his footsteps followed one after the other on his seemingly endless trek through the forest. He was unwavering in his quest, the spell proving incredibly powerful. He moved deftly through the woods, narrowly avoiding bumping against trees or stumbling over shrubs. As he passed through, the forest grew eerily quiet.

The birds, rabbits, and squirrels that Adelaide had seen in abundance during her own journey were nowhere to be found. In some strange way, they could sense the dark magic infecting the Chosen's body, hiding away as if he were a storm that would sweep through the land. Even the wind was silent, fearful of the darkness much more powerful than the air. Only one creature dared venture closer to the stumbling figure.

Sebastian's unfocused eyes did not truly see the massive buck standing directly in his path. He only saw an object in his path. Nothing was worth halting his journey toward the Gift. He would only swerve around an obstacle, never stopping or slowing. The buck huffed and pawed at the loose soil below his hooves. He tossed his antlers, remembering how it had frightened Sebastian during their first encounter.

Yet now Sebastian showed no such fear. Not even a wink of recognition flickered in his eyes, only the cold, emotionless determination. He was no longer Sebastian. Only a human carcass animated by one dark goal. His only mission was permeated with the stench of death.

The buck followed closely behind him, huffing and kicking in a futile effort to wake him from his stupor. Sebastian began to slow, his feet dragging on the ground as he trudged on. The buck grew weary, and he knew the young man must be as well. Yet both of them refused to waver from their tasks. It was only when his feet failed him and Sebastian collapsed to the forest floor that he finally was allowed to rest.

The buck stopped, exhaustion causing his long, slender legs to ache. He sniffed at Sebastian's head, ensuring that he would survive. The young man slept deeply, his body exhausted. He would remain where he lay for several hours before his body would be able to move again. The buck knew what his next task would be.

The stag wandered deeper into the forest, heading slightly north of Sebastian's original path headed due east. He only had to walk a few moments before he could hear the sounds of life carried to him on the wind. The Village and its Anyran inhabitants stood before him. Now to wait.

Eventually, a young couple ventured out from the Village hand in hand. Adelaide's sister Gwen and her lover, no less. Surprised but heartened, the buck stood from where he rested and slowly approached the couple as they moved. It didn't take long for them to spot him, and he crept delicately through the brush, making it seem as though he was unaware of their interest in him.

Their voices met his ears in hushed tones, uncertain yet curious. Gwen wanted to go back, but the buck needed them to trudge onward. The stag swung his head back around, gazing directly into her eyes, familiar yet so new. Silently, she nodded, and they moved as one. The leaves and twigs crunched underfoot as they made their way forward.

Finally, Sebastian came into view, but it took the couple a few moments to realize he was there. Gwen was enthralled with the stag, and her lover was curious not only about the deer, but also his own companion. Huffing, the buck dropped his head and snuffed at Sebastian's hair. With a cry of surprise, they finally realized the man was there.

Xander muttered under his breath and forgot the stealth he had been employing up until that point. He darted forward, hurrying to help the young man collapsed on the forest floor. Yet the buck didn't run off into the woods, spooked by the fast motion. Instead, he turned back to the girl, and she absentmindedly laid a hand on his back. He could sense the pain and weakness still present in her body, though he knew not why she suffered.

Xander, exercising impressive strength, hoisted Sebastian onto his shoulders, and he began to trudge back toward the camp. The girl tapped on the deer's back three times, hardly registering that she had done so, then darted to clear a path for her lover. The buck stayed behind, watching as they moved toward the camp.

The girl's voice rose high and clear as she called to those in their encampment, begging for help. They recognized the unconscious priest, and theories immediately sprung forth to explain his presence in the woods. Perhaps he'd had a change of heart and turned from the Temple for himself or for Adelaide. The buck's heart sank, knowing that their hopes would be dashed the second he woke.

Chapter Sixteen: Mistaken

"Caleb! Valerie! Someone, help!" Gwen came crashing through the bracken, heaving for breath as both the redhead and his wife ran to her aid.

"Gwen, what's wrong? Are you hurt?" Unable to answer, she pointed back just as Xander followed much slower, as he carried a great deal of extra weight.

"Oh, dear Totem," Caleb muttered, instantly recognizing the man slung across Xander's shoulders. "Is he dead?" He pulled the Chosen off of Xander who sunk to his knees gasping for breath.

"No... we found him... collapsed in the woods."

"He must have fled!" Gwen said, finally regaining her breath enough to speak. A grin laced her lips despite the fatigue plaguing her body. "He came to his senses."

"Or he found us to bring Addie back," Caleb commented as he held the young man in his arms like a child. He was frighteningly lightweight for a man his age. "Let's get him to Ramona."

Quickly, they moved through the Village, leaving a trail of questions behind them as people took notice, interrupting the still and quiet of the evening. Ramona heard the commotion and came outside to see what the ruckus was about. Her eyes widened as Caleb approached the healer's bungalow. Without Katharine, she would be the best suited for the job. She quickly moved to ready her medical supplies.

"What happened?" she demanded, gesturing for Caleb to lay him on the low medical cot. She pulled a pair of long, linen gloves over her hands, rolling them all the way up her arms. With these, she could touch his skin in order to tend to any wounds or medical needs without being overtaken by visions. Though her abilities as a Seer were strong, her passion had lain in medicine. She was adept enough to care for the wounds, but she wished Katharine were here, able to use her healing magic and knowledge outweighing Ramona's own.

"They found him in the woods, collapsed," Caleb answered.

"We don't know how long he was there," Xander offered, standing slightly back from the bed. "He was facedown as if he fell while walking and just didn't get up."

"That is probably what happened," Ramona confirmed, examining his eyes and mouth. "He needs water and some form of broth or soup. He's exhausted, like he's been walking for days without rest."

"He probably has been," Gwen commented before turning to fetch the items Ramona requested. Xander turned to help along with Valerie, leaving Caleb and Ramona alone with the patient.

"Gwen thinks he fled, but I don't think that's the case," Caleb told the Elder, crouching to look into the Chosen's face. "I think there's something a bit more sinister going on."

"There is. He's under some sort of spell." Ramona lifted his eyelid and nodded for Caleb to look. Sebastian's pupils were enormous, nearly erasing the pale blue of his eyes. From just a few feet away, his eyes would look nearly entirely black.

"We'll keep someone on guard."

"DO YOU THINK HE'LL ever wake?" Gwen asked, looking up at Ramona. She was pouring tiny spoonfuls of warm broth into Sebastian's mouth, trying to give him some nourishment in his unconscious state. "And what will he do when he does?"

"I'm not certain." Ramona laid her hand on Gwen's back, careful to avoid her shoulders which were bare. The small bungalow was overly warm with the heat from the fire. "I don't know exactly what kind of spell he is under, only that he is under one. It's most likely to force him to find and retrieve Adelaide."

Gwen's brow knit with concern as she spooned another sip into Sebastian's mouth, and he swallowed instinctively. "Do you think he's going to kill her?"

"No, Rhoda wouldn't allow that. He may hurt her in his attempt to get her back to Anyra, but she will not die. Rhoda needs her alive."

"You don't think they would have just chosen a different Gift?"

Ramona shook her head solemnly. "There were times when Gifts tried to escape their death before, but they never made it past Anyra's borders. They were held in the dungeons below the Temple until the day came for them to be sacrificed." Gwen took a small cup of water and dribbled it into Sebastian's mouth. "Your sister is the first Gift to successfully flee Anyra."

Gwen smiled as she continued feeding the Chosen. "Even on Choosing Day, some part of me knew she'd escape." The bowl finally empty, she set it to the side and stood to look into Ramona's eyes. "I couldn't be more grateful for it all. We're safe now." A tear slipped down her cheek as she laid her hand over her stomach, the pain still lurching in her guts as her insides continued to tear themselves to shreds. Although the worst of it had passed, a different pain blossomed inside her.

"It's not your fault, darling," Ramona assured her. "But I'm sorry it happened."

A yelp of surprise rang from Gwen's throat as Sebastian sat bolt upright in the cot, not a sound falling from his lips. Clumsily, he rose from the makeshift bed as the two women screamed for help. Landon stumbled inside, but not soon enough to stop Sebastian as he grabbed Gwen by her thin, pale arms.

"Don't," Gwen warned, struggling to raise her palm to stop Landon from tearing the cursed Sebastian off of her. "We need to know what he's doing."

Sebastian took sharp, quick sniffs like a bloodhound, seemingly trying to discern whether he held Adelaide or not. Gwen reasoned that the spell must be a bit confused, as she was Adelaide's sister which made her similar to the target. At least similar enough to confuse him a little bit.

"You found me, Sebastian," she said, lowering her voice slightly in a rather poor imitation of her elder sister. "I'll go back with you, just don't hurt anyone else."

Even the crackling of the fire seemed to cease as everyone in the hovel held their breath. The ruse was far-fetched, but would he fall for it? Slowly, he released one of her arms and turned toward the door. It had partially worked.

"I don't think he can tell if I'm Addie or not," she reasoned. "I think he's still tracking her, but he wants to take me just in case." Gwen allowed herself to be led through the door and out into the morning sunlight. If Edrei's estimations were correct, their group should be halfway to Kantrin by now. "I'll go with him so I can warn Addie when we find her."

"Gwen!" She turned at the sound of her name, and Xander came barreling toward them. "Let her go! Don't touch her, you disgusting mongrel!"

"Xander, don't!" Her lover had already reached them but stopped with his fisted poised to strike.

"Are you alright, Gwen?" he demanded, his voice terse and his brow lowered.

"I'm fine. I'm going with him to find Addie. He can't tell whether or not I'm her."

"Then I'm coming, too." He lowered his fist but continued glowering at Sebastian. The Chosen simply stared straight ahead with dull, empty eyes. It was as though the spell had scooped him out of his own body and filled it with something else.

"Deary, wait!" Ramona called. She caught up to them holding a rucksack which she handed to Xander. "Provisions. Heaven knows how long your journey will be. Stay safe."

"We will, I'll be sure of it," Xander promised, shrugging the pack onto his back. They faced no further hindrance as Sebastian took staggering steps toward the eastern border of the Village. Gwen and Xander knew Kantrin was at least two days away, but who knew when they would be able to get the cursed Chosen to stop for rest.

Chapter Seventeen: Kantrin

After almost three days and two nights of travelling, the city of Kantrin came into view. We approached from the west, though the entrance to the city proper stood facing the south. The buildings were blocked by a wall stretching around the entire civilization, tall and tan. I assumed it had been built with mud and many hours of labor.

The tops of the tallest buildings were visible above the barrier, all at varying heights. A single spire shot skyward from the center of the city. None of the walls carried any color, most of them the same beige as the wall surrounding the city. The shingled roofs sported a brilliant array of colors from brilliant, royal purple to striking, pumpkin orange.

The tall spire, however, was incredibly colorful, the walls painted with beautiful artworks. I assumed this was where their government was housed. The rounded walls were a blood red, the roof the same deep blue of the sea back in Anyra. The borders around the windows were painted so brightly we could see them from the hundreds of feet away where we stood. Each was decorated with a pattern of vines and branches in deep, emerald green, adorned with purple flowers.

The sounds of the city floated over the wall, people bustling about and the clangs of construction. This was a thriving, breathing society. Anyra was not alone in this world. I drifted forward, lightly tracing my fingers over the smooth stone. Dust came away on my fingers. The wall must be kept well in order to maintain its integrity.

I marveled at something made without Anyran hands. Something untainted by the Totem.

"Adelaide," Edrei called, drawing me from my wonder. She fought to maintain her composure, but I could see the light of excitement in her eyes. "Let's go. That's just the beginning."

I smiled, following behind her as Zakariah sidled up beside me. He took my hand, giving it a squeeze.

"I'm sure you feel the same as me," he said in a hushed voice, keeping the conversation between the two of us. "It's not Anyra. It's entirely new. And it's alive!"

"I know!" I agreed, hardly able to contain my excitement. "It's incredible. The world is so much bigger than we have ever known. And now we get to see it ourselves."

"I can't wait," Zakariah breathed. It was only when he gave my hand a second squeeze that I realized he was still holding it. My heart stopped, and I stared at the ground ahead. How had I not realized it? Yet I didn't wrench my hand out of his grip. My heart tremored at the thought of being betrayed again. Yet something in me knew Zakariah wouldn't fall into the same trap Sebastian had.

As we rounded the corner, the gates came into view. The intricate, gold structures glinted in the sunlight, and a guard stood to either side. What threat was there that the city must be guarded as such? The gates were shut at the moment, but they seemed easy enough to open.

As we came closer, our group fell into formation without needing to communicate. Edrei took the lead, with me falling slightly behind her on her right side. Zakariah trailed closely behind me, essentially our muscle should something go wrong. Katharine and Calvin walked shoulder to shoulder directly behind us. We drew no weapons.

We came close enough to draw the guards' attention, and I was finally able to get a good look at them. They were dark skinned, as I assumed most if not all of the people of Kantrin to be. They wore gold armor, spears topped with wicked sharp steel held firmly in hand. Their helms were adorned with sprawling, antler-like decoration, and their visors were pushed up to reveal their faces.

"Hello," Edrei began as we approached, her tone calm and even. "My name is Edrei, and I am here to entreat your leader." The two men furrowed their heavy brows and exchanged a glance. "We mean you no harm. We come to ask for help."

The guard on the left raised a placating hand, his palm out and stance relaxed. Both spears remained pointing skyward, and no fear bubbled up in my chest. Words fell from the guard's lips, but the language was meaningless to our ignorant ears. His tone seemed questioning, but we could not understand. I exchanged a glance with Edrei. I could practically see the cogs churning in her mind as she searched for a solution. I took a step forward.

"Adelaide," I introduced myself, placing a hand on my chest. I then extended it, gesturing to each man in turn. They began to understand. The man who had extended his hand in kindness took a step forth.

"Galom," he said, his voice deep and accented. The other guard stepped forward, following suit.

"Abir," he introduced himself. Gingerly, I extended my hand in friendship, hoping he would understand. Abir smiled broadly and clasped it in his own. I feared he would crush my fingers with the strength in his hands. I could see how Edrei certainly was one of these people.

Each member of our group stepped forward and announced their name, greeting the guards with warm faces. Once the introductions were made came the challenge of communicating out intent. However, the men seemed to be hung up on one thing. Galom pointed to Edrei, his eyebrows furrowed.

"Edrei?" he asked, seemingly clarifying. Edrei nodded, glancing at me as we both grasped for a way to communicate without words. Galom's eyes grew wide, turning to Abir. "San eesen com et tru?"

"Don, san eesen," Abir nodded. They both turned back toward her and bowed their heads.

"Kantira Edrei," the pair said as one, seemingly reverent. For the first time I had seen, Edrei was dumbfounded. Before we knew what was happening, Abir was pulling the gates open, and Galom beckoned for us to follow. Confused, we complied. We entered the gates, the city opening around us.

Once again, I found Zakariah at my side, and I appreciated his presence in this unfamiliar place. As we passed through the town toward the blue-capped spire, we passed through the bustle of people in the city. They wore clothes woven with intricate patterns, colors decorating every piece of fabric in contrast to the plain beige buildings.

As we passed, people took notice. Just as Edrei and the two guards, the people had beautiful, dark skin, smooth and unblemished. Their hair was dark and thick, worn in many different styles. Men and women alike wore their hair at varying lengths. Some were shaved close to the scalp as Edrei's. Others wore it in curls or large bushy styles, and some had it twisted into braids that hung as low as their knees.

They stared at me and my fellow Anyrans. Our skin was much fairer than anyone we'd seen in Kantrin as of yet. My own was a warm olive color, but it could vary anywhere from paper white as Gwendolyn or caramel gold like Zakariah beside me. My long, thick tresses seemed thin in comparison to the voluminous curls of the Kantrinians.

Their stares, however, were not hateful or disgusted, nor were our wide-eyed gazes in return. Simply a discovery and appreciation of differences. As we moved, life began to return to normal, people going back about their business. These were not the prying eyes of the Anyrans staring down their Gift as I passed.

Laughter met my ears, and I turned to find a small child bounding up to our troupe, a broad grin on his face. He had to be no older than two years of age, and a woman I assumed to be his mother followed closely behind. He toddled right up to me, grinning as if he had known me all his life.

"Randa!" he cried, pointing up at me. I knelt down to his level, desperate to understand. He quickly answered. His tiny fist snagged a handful of hair, pulling me down closer to him. "Randa!" I quickly deduced that his favorite color was red, as my hair carried red tones.

"Domma, mara domma," his mother fretted pulling her son away. I laughed as she untangled his hand from my hair, wincing as he tugged at my scalp.

"It's alright," I assured her, knowing she couldn't understand me. Yet simply based on my body language, she seemed to get it. The child continued grasping for my hair, and I could tell that a tantrum was about to erupt. I realized that I could quell that. I held up a hand and dove into my bag, retrieving a jar of strawberries.

As I offered them to the mother, hoping the child would enjoy the red snack, she furrowed her brows at me. Apparently, Kantrin was deprived of strawberries. I took one out and took a bite, showing that they were safe. The child was practically drooling, staring at the red berries with wide eyes. Nodding, I held out the jar, and the mother accepted.

"Traunsah," she nodded. I turned to Galom and Abir, and they leapt to my aid, immediately knowing what I needed.

"Sunnar," they chorused.

"Sunnar," I repeated, hoping I pronounced it correctly. The woman and her child went on their way, and we continued toward the castle.

"That was really nice of you," Zakariah commended me as we walked.

"It was nothing, I could tell the child was upset. I had something to please him," I shrugged. Zakariah shook his head.

"But strawberries are your favorite."

"I think they're going to be his too," I agreed, throwing a glance over my shoulder. I caught sight of the mother and child, and red was already smeared across his face as he chomped happily on the berries.

As we moved through the city, the base of the spire came into view. What we hadn't seen was that it was flanked by two shorter towers. I wasn't certain the purpose of any of the three, but obviously they meant something. Whether it be persistence, ingenuity, or sheer will to reach the sky, Kantrin stood strong and resolute.

The structure that the tower sprouted from was a magnificent palace, the only building in the city thus far with painted walls rather than cream colored like the others. It sported brilliant colors similar to the clothes of the people we had passed. Similar to the gates into the city, two guards stood to either side of the grand doors of the castle.

These were the only defensive measures taken to protect whatever stood within. That is aside from the moat, but something gave me the inkling that protecting Kantrin was a rare problem to face. These did not seem to be a war faring people.

The guards stood aside with only a few words, a sense of urgency and excitement in the tone of the brief conversation. The five of us Anyran refugees were perplexed, but unable to do anything else in this strange land, we remained quiet and patient. We followed promptly, curious and cautious and craving a new home.

We were each mesmerized as we were led down the corridors deeper into the palace. The walls were crowded with decoration, filled to bursting with tapestries, paintings, skulls, and hides. The floor was lined with statues, depicting scenes of people and animals alike. One statue in particular caught my eye.

I drifted, as if caught in a trance, toward a statue of a young woman. Her arms were stretched above her head, as if reaching up to grasp something. Her face was twisted in anguish, eyes wide and tearful even immortalized in stone. Flames licked at her feet, the dress she wore beginning to disintegrate. The image was all too familiar. I looked to the placard below the girl's resemblance and found words I could understand.

"Sterrin Esme, ta priemin Gift do Anyra." I could hardly breathe, my hands beginning to shake as I reached out to touch the words. The world remembered us. Though I couldn't read all of the inscription, I picked out enough to understand. Before Anyra shut itself away, this nation at least mourned the loss of the first gift. Esme. I hadn't known her name until now.

"Addie?" Zakariah asked, his voice ringing distant and hollow in my ears. I heard the drip of water as tears fell onto the stone floor. "Addie, what's wrong?!" He dove to his knees beside me, placing an arm around my shoulders as I simply stared up at the image of the girl. Without tearing my eyes from her face, I pointed to the words, and Zakariah gasped.

"They know," he breathed.

"Know what?" Calvin inquired. I felt the air move as he leaned in to look, and the others gathered as well. Katharine gave a sharp inhale as she fell to her knees beside me. Edrei gripped my shoulder, her strong hands desperate to hold something.

"Kantrin paid its respects to the first Gift," Edrei announced. "Then Anyra shut itself away."

"Anyra?" Abir asked, drawing our attention. "Cand tru eesen et Edrei?" I could tell he was questioning. How could Edrei be Anyran? Galom seemed to understand. He pointed to the rest of us, each in turn.

"Tront eesen do Anyra?" Seemingly for the first time, I began to understand. I nodded, gesturing to my four Anyran companions and myself.

"We are from Anyra. We fled." I pointed up at the statue, then to myself. "I was the Gift. I will not die as she did."

"You. Gift?" Galom asked, his voice wavering as he struggled with the language. He pointed to the statue, ensuring that I understood. I was surprised to hear any Anyran come from his lips at all. Surprised, I nodded.

"Kantro ohn Theodore see you," he continued. "Now."

"Kantro? Theodore?" I repeated. Their Anyran vocabulary exhausted, they bid us follow once more. Somehow even more confused, we followed. This time it was I that found Zakariah's hand and clutched it desperately in my own. I had no idea what was going to happen or who we were about to meet.

The guards took us to a large, open chamber, the walls bare except for the multitude of windows allowing sunlight to pour in. At the far end against the wall sat four thrones on a pedestal. Yet only the center two were occupied. The two Kantrinian men stopped short in the entrance and bowed deeply.

"Kantro Eitan, Kantra Halleil," the two said in unison. A man and woman sat in the thrones, the man reaching across to hold the woman's hand. Strangely, they were not wearing the same colorful garb as the people we had met. Rather, they wore pure white, the woman's dress reminiscent of my own wedding gown left forgotten in Valerie and Caleb's abandoned home. It was long and sleek, hugging her figure with easy elegance.

The man wore a looser fitting shirt, embroidered with cream and ivory patterns, and pants made of the same material. They both wore turban-like head coverings, so their hair was not seen. Unlike the rest of their clothing, these were bright red, covered in jewels and precious metal. I assumed it was their culture's version of a crown worn by rulers.

"Galom, Abir. Reisen," the man commanded, his voice deep and authoritative. I also detected a hint of sadness, the soft kindness hiding behind his kingly status.

"Eesen dontarones do Anyra."

"Anyra?" the woman quizzed, leaning forward in her chair. "Abir, corra san Theodore."

"Domma, Kantra," the guard responded, bowing deeply before nearly sprinting from the room.

"What is going on?" Zakariah whispered. He was stunned into silence as the king rose from his throne.

"Welcome, visitors from Anyra," he said, speaking Anyran with a thick accent. A chuckle fell from his lips, and the queen giggled as well as my jaw dropped. I'm certain my comrades were as shocked as I. "My name is Eitan, and this is my wife Halleil."

"Kantro, siendo massa," Galom interjected. He gestured to Edrei, and the king nodded. He had obviously taken note of the fact that she appeared more Kantrinian than Anyran. "Doy perrevir de tru eesen Kantira Edrei."

With that sentence, the king's face fell in disbelief. Halleil rose from her throne, drifting forward as if in a trance. She wore nearly the exact same expression of disbelief. Now that they had drawn closer, I could see faint wrinkles of age in their faces. I had seen the same worry lines in Uncle Quinton's skin.

"Edrei?" the queen asked, placing a hand on her husband's shoulder. I turned to my leader, my eyebrows furrowed in confusion. She turned back to me with her jaw set. She had deduced the same truth that I had. We *had* found her parents. What was more was that we discovered that Edrei was not only a leader, but what appeared to be this society's equivalent of a princess. She turned back to the rulers.

"You had a daughter named Edrei? That disappeared when she was four?" Edrei asked the couple, always so straight to business. They nodded, hardly able to speak. I hoped they understood correctly. "And a son named Jadiel that went missing at the same time? He was around seven?"

"Yes," the woman answered, "our children both disappeared nearly thirty years ago." This was the first the woman had spoken in Anyran, and I was struck by how similar she sounded to her daughter. Both of them carried strong, deep voices for women, yet they were no less beautiful.

"Then I suppose it is true. I must be your daughter," Edrei breathed. I could see tears gathering in the corners of her eyes as the woman reached out for her. She almost seemed to revert to the four-year-old child she was when they'd last seen one another.

"Where did you go? Why did you leave?" Halleil asked. Edrei seemed nearly to collapse as the woman's hands cradled her face. The maternal figure she must have desperately wanted for so long finally in her life.

"I don't know. Jadiel pulled me out of bed, and we ran," she gasped. The tears began to fall, and no more words were needed. Without needing to communicate, the group of us Anyrans drifted back away from the tearful reunion of parents and daughter. This was an incredibly tender moment, and I did not want to intervene.

As we crept silently back toward the door, Abir appeared from the hallway. He took my arm and placed an open hand over his mouth. I took this as a signal for quiet. I nodded as he led our group into the hall. It felt as though something took over me with our leader absent.

"Katharine, I need you to stay here, be here for Edrei when she is ready," I instructed. "Calvin, Zakariah, with me." The two men nodded, as we followed Abir farther into the castle, though toward what I was unsure. We approached a large set of wooden doors, grated windows high above my head. Through them I caught a glimpse of a high ceiling and dozens of bookshelves. Perhaps this was a library.

Abir raised his spear to lift a heavy knocker, allowing it to fall and cause an echoing boom. Almost instantly, the door began to creak open. Voices speaking the Kantrin language drifted to us, excited and frenzied. I caught a few words that I recognized: Anyra, Edrei, and Kantira. News was spreading fast.

"Commen," Abir beckoned, waving for us to follow. "Tre eesen Theo. Theo!"

"Domma!" a voice cried. A tall, lean man rounded the corner, a stack of books in his arms. Even though I could hardly see his face, I could see the that he had the olive complexion of an Anyran. "The Anyrans! Traunsa, Abir."

"Sunnar," Abir smiled, a word I recognized. As Theo set down the books, he clasped Abir's shoulder in gratitude before turning to beam at the three of us. His hair was so dark it was nearly black, his wild curls falling into his eyes. Large glasses filled his face, making his eyes seem larger than life.

"My Anyrans," he greeted us. "It's wonderful to see you. I haven't seen another Anyran face in nearly seventeen years." A faint twinge of familiarity tugged at my brain as he clasped each of our hands in turn. "My name is Theodore Corander. You all are?"

"Wait, Corander?" I asked. I realized the familiarity. "Sebastian's father?" His face fell in shock and shame.

"Yes. I wanted him to be here with me, his mother as well. But she disagreed with my views and wouldn't come."

"He thought you abandoned him. She lied," I breathed. After my brief moment of shock, I stepped forward and extended my hand. "I was his betrothed. My name is Adelaide Lanasting, it's wonderful to finally meet you."

"Was?" Theo quizzed. "Is he alright?"

"No, he is the Chosen of the Temple. And I was supposed to be this year's Gift."

"No! I was so afraid of that," Theo groaned, placing his fists to his head. "I wanted to save him from such a fate. I was the Chosen when I was his age. I knew what horrors lived in the Temple, but it seemed that none would listen."

"They will now," I assured him. I reached out to place a hand on my would-be father-in-law's shoulder. "We represent a large group of Anyrans that have fled from Rhoda's fist and staff." Slowly, Theo began to nod.

"There may be yet hope for my son. How many of you are here?"

"Five of us are here in Kantrin," Zakariah answered, "but many more reside in an encampment roughly thirty miles outside of the Anyran border."

"Oh, yes, I'm so sorry," I shook my head remembering. In my surprise at meeting Sebastian's father, I had forgotten to introduce my comrades. A soft smile tugged at Zakariah's mouth. "This is Zakariah and Calvin. Two others, Katharine and Edrei are here as well."

"I heard of the return of our lost Kantira," Theo nodded, beginning to smile once again. "I'm certain the Kantro and Kantra are more than thrilled."

"I keep hearing those words, I still don't quite know what they mean," Calvin interjected. I was surprised he had waited so long to speak up. Usually, his mouth got the better of him.

"The closest translation would be king and queen in our tongue, though they're not exactly the same," Theo explained. I nodded, having assumed that was what the titles meant. "They're more like governors or even landlords in a sense."

"How did you get here from Anyra?" Zakariah asked.

"I packed as much as I could carry and walked. It took nearly two weeks. A Kantrineir patrol found me collapsed in the woods, dying of thirst and exhaustion. They nursed me to health, and I've devoted my life since then to studying their language and teaching them ours."

"That's incredible, Theodore," I commended him. "But I have some questions."

"Of course, I would expect no less. Come!" He beckoned us to follow as he turned, excitedly marching back into the shelves of books. We trailed behind him through the labyrinth of knowledge to a small desk near the back wall. Windows filled the wall the desk stood against, allowing a view of the city. I could see the Kantrineir people bustling excitedly about. I assumed the news of their lost princess returning home was beginning to spread through the city like wildfire.

Theodore's desk was overflowing with books and papers, the scribbled words illegible whether they were in Anyran or the Kantrin language. I assumed Theodore could read them, however. Theo unburied chairs from the stacks and piles of books, and we settled into them. I sat in the center, Zakariah to my left and Calvin to my right. The chair legs scraped against the stone floor as Zakariah moved his chair closer to mine. Theo turned his desk chair around to face us and sat down, looking expectantly between the three of our faces.

"Well, what questions do you have?" I turned to my two comrades, but neither of them seemed to have anything on their minds. Rather, they probably had so many questions that they couldn't choose any singular one to ask. I, on the other hand, had one glaring question burning in my mind.

"Why didn't Kantrin or anyone else come to Anyra's aid?" I demanded, sitting forward to rest my arms on my thighs. My hair fell over my shoulders like a curtain, but I didn't care to brush it off. "Obviously they knew what was happening, and they knew it was wrong. Why haven't they made contact, tried to help or get those who disagreed out?"

"I thought you may ask that," Theo nodded. He stood and plucked a large, white book off a high shelf. "Anyra has defenses none of its citizens may ever know of. The High Priest or Priestess and possibly anyone in the Temple as a whole wields dark magic."

"What?!" Zakariah burst out. Out of the corner of my eye I saw Calvin nodding as if he had known this all his life. I realized that perhaps he had.

"You knew?" I breathed, staring at the older man in disbelief.

"How do you think Katharine healed your sister?" Calvin asked in response, his usual sarcastic tone replaced with a deep sadness. "The Temple has wielded magic since its creation."

"How did you know about that? Why didn't you tell anyone?" Zakariah begged, leaning closer to me to crane his neck at Calvin.

"My great grandfather's brother was the High Priest decades ago," Calvin confessed. His face was stern as ever, the light in his eyes had dimmed in shame. This was most likely the first time he had divulged this fact. "My father wanted me to take the position when he retired. He was training me to take over, but his aunt proved herself much more ambitious. I never wanted the role. That's all Rhoda ever wanted."

"Rhoda is your great aunt?" Zakariah questioned, still in utter disbelief.

"You knew about the magic? And Katharine can wield it?" I followed up. "Why didn't you tell anyone? You could have led a revolt and overthrown the Temple with that knowledge alone!"

"If that shocked you, just you wait. I'd tell you to sit down if you weren't already." It was almost comforting to hear the sarcastic tone return to Calvin's demeanor. "The Totem isn't real. She never has been." Rather than needing a seat, I leapt up from mine.

"What!?" I screeched, unable to contain the shock this time. "She's not real!?"

"And she never was," Calvin repeated, his brows furrowed in anger.

"The Totem isn't real," Zakariah breathed, letting his head fall into his hands.

"Calvin, why didn't you tell anyone?" I asked, facing him once again in order to stare into his eyes. "There would have been uproar, rioting in the streets. The Temple would have been razed to the ground!"

"If I had told anyone, they would have killed Katharine."

Zakariah and I both fell silent. I glanced at Calvin's neck and realized that the necklace there signified his bond to her. They certainly did not make that relationship public, but if he was willing to endure that for her, I had no doubt of Calvin's love.

"They cast a spell on me. If I spoke to anyone in Anyra about it, they would know. That's how they spy one everyone. Every priest or priestess under the Temple has a spell cast upon them. Rhoda would know everything. If they speak ill of the Temple, if they are unfaithful to the Totem, if they're planning to leave or rebel. The priests and priestesses swear their lives to the Temple."

"What of the rest of the citizens? Do they cast this spell on everyone?" Zakariah chimed, nearly stealing the words from my tongue.

"They receive a modified version of that spell when they are born. Every child that is blessed by the Temple is not truly blessed, but cursed. The spell is how the Temple knows if a girl commits adultery to the Totem. It's in effect until they leave Anyra's borders unless they receive a blessing over their journey like the hunters. If someone leaves without this blessing, they may only return if they are escorted into the city by a priest or priestess or the Chosen of the Temple."

"What happens if they try to return without that?" I asked. The theory had already begun formulating. Like every other child born in Anyra, myself, my sister, and my parents had been blessed by the Temple at birth. My mother's shipwreck was almost certainly the Temple's doing.

"They simply can't. It's like there's a force keeping them out."

My suspicions confirmed. Unable to reenter Anyran waters, my mother's ship had been dashed against the rocks, and she had drowned. The Temple truly had taken everything from me. For the triplet funeral, we didn't even have bodies to bury. Nothing but memories and lives taken too soon. My sister and I orphaned all thanks to a false goddess and the Temple that worshipped her.

"That's why no one came to Anyra's aid. They feared the magic the Temple would use against them. Rhoda could wipe out armies with a click of her staff," Theo explained. "She's insanely powerful."

"Then why do they continue the giving of Gifts? If there is no Totem requiring a virgin sacrifice, why do they keep throwing innocent girls into a volcano?"

"Magic comes at a price, especially dark magic. Dark magic feeds on life." Theo offered the answer. He held open the book, showing an illustration of the volcano. Depicted within was not magma, but a swirling pool of blue. "The souls of the Gifts are trapped, feeding the Temple's magic. Like the oil in a lamp, their lifeforce allows the sorcerers to practice their craft without consequence to themselves."

"The selfish bastards," I growled bristling with anger. Zakariah put his head in his hands, sweat beading on his brow.

"The Totem isn't real," he murmured, his voice terse. "Elizabeth died for nothing but to feed Rhoda and her magic." I glanced over to find tears smarting in his eyes, and I clasped his hand. He willingly gripped mine in return, the pain of the loss of his sister dredged back up.

"We will end it, Zakariah," I promised him. He nodded, wiping tears away with his shirtsleeves. "I don't care what it takes. I'll tear the Temple apart brick by brick if I must. They'll pay."

"They will, I'll be beside you tearing it down," Zakariah promised. When he raised his head, a fire had been lit in his eyes. "We'll avenge them all. Every Gift, every Chosen, all of them. That demon will pay."

Theodore smiled, a sadness in his eyes. "I have no doubt."

Chapter Eighteen: Alliance

"We are honored to have such unusual visitors," Halleil assured me. She lifted a silver goblet to her lips and sipped the blackberry wine within. "Anyra has been silent for so long. Before Theodore came along, we thought you may have died out."

"It is very much alive," Katharine assured her. "And unchanged."

"For now," Eitan smiled. He had not stopped beaming since the dinner had begun. He sat on the opposite side of the table from me, Edrei and Halleil to his right and Theodore to his left. Both of the rulers continually glanced at Edrei as if they feared she would disappear. On the Anyran side of the table, Zakariah sat to my right and Katharine and Calvin to my left.

The food was like nothing I had ever tasted. A roasted bird similar to a turkey but much larger took up the center table, and I was told that it was called a cassowary. The only thing I could liken the flavor to was wild hen, but something in its preparation gave it a delightful heat. Vegetables I had never seen sat in gilded bowls down the center of the table to either side of the bird, most roasted or pan seared.

Each new flavor was incredible. Spices I couldn't name flavored every dish. Halfway through the meal, Halleil warned me to slow down, for dessert would be coming afterward. If the dinner food was this amazing, I could only imagine what the sweets would be like.

The conversation continued as the plates were taken away and replaced with bowls of a soft, dark substance. What looked like whipped cream had been dolloped on top, and a decadent, rich aroma wafted into my nose. Seeing as our hosts had already begun to eat, I took up my spoon and helped myself to a bite.

The dessert was somehow cold and warm at once, the flavor filling my mouth with a beautiful, bitter sweetness. The cream added the perfect amount of freshness to the rich treat. I practically melted into my chair, and Edrei laughed.

"I take it you like it?" she asked jokingly. My mouth full, I nodded vigorously. Struck with an idea, I gripped Zakariah's arm.

"This with strawberries!" I suggested. He laughed as I shoveled another spoonful into my mouth then fell back into my chair with a hum of delight. The Kantro and Kantra laughed, smiling as warmly as the dessert itself.

"That is called black sapote," Eitan told me. "We will send some back with you to share with your people."

"Thank you so much!" I said after swallowing another bite. "Gwen is going to love this."

Once the dessert was cleared away, the table seemed to stretch far in between the Kantrineirs and us Anyrans. It was strange seeing Edrei on their side rather than ours. Yet she seemed to fit so easily with them. Hopefully, with some careful discussion, we could come to a beautiful partnership.

"We understand that there is an uprising in Anyra," Eitan began the discussion. "A sect of your people has broken away from your Temple and vowed to deny your goddess."

"Yes, precisely," I nodded, and my companions nodded their agreement as well. "The giving of Gifts must come to an end. We have learned that the goddess the Temple worships is false. There is no such thing as the Totem." Edrei's eyes narrowed, her suspicions confirmed.

"And the Temple knows this, or...?" Halleil inquired.

"According to Theodore, the High Priestess and the higher ranking priests and priestess below her are well aware that the Totem is a hoax," Zakariah explained. "The Gifts are not sacrificed to the Totem, but rather to feed the magic the Temple wields." Theo nodded when the rulers looked his way, assuring them that this was the truth.

"The refugees in the forest don't know this, but they will," Edrei added. "When we return, we will tell them of the magic used against them."

"We?" Eitan questioned, his eyebrows furrowing in horror and confusion as he looked at his daughter. "You are returning? You finally come home, and you are leaving again?"

"For now," Edrei assured him, laying a gentle hand on his arm. "I wish to propose an alliance." She looked into her parents' eyes, then across the table at us. A smile danced behind her eyes, certain that her plan would work. In an instant, I knew where she was going with this idea. I smiled in response.

"I concur," I agreed.

"Aye, the first in Anyran history," Calvin chimed in, raising his goblet to his lips. "At least memorable Anyran history."

"What we ask of you is a great deal, so we understand that you will want to take time in consideration," Edrei prefaced. "We ask shelter for our refugees. We will go to our Village, gather the people that have fled Anyra's borders, and return here. The Temple cannot find us as far as we are aware."

"They place spells on every child blessed by the Temple that alert the High Priestess," Calvin offered. "But those spells are broken when they leave Anyran land. Our Villagers are safe and undetectable by Rhoda's magic."

The Kantro and Kantra were silent for a moment, Eitan's lips pressed tightly together. They exchanged a glance, no doubt daunted by the enormity of the request. This was an entire village of people to house and feed on top of the large population already inhabiting

Kantrin. I steeled my heart, preparing to gracefully accept their refusal.

"We'll take them," Halleil said. I felt the blood rise hot in my cheeks, my jaw dropping open. Edrei broke into a grin as I shook my head then matched her smile.

"You're certain?" I asked, wanting to be absolutely sure that this safe haven was guaranteed.

"Of course," the Kantro assured me, leaning back in his chair. "Our ancestors were allied with Anyra before the rise of the Temple and its false Totem. Our people never forgot Anyra and its tragedies. We have an opportunity to help your people. It is not a question of if, but of when."

"This is fantastic news," Katharine grinned. I turned to see her face alight with joy, her hand grasping Calvin's. Rather than looking to our saviors, he gazed at her face, grinning.

"How soon can you return with your people?" I locked eyes with Edrei across the table.

"It'll take us about two days' time to get back, a few days to pack, and probably four or five to move the whole group here," I reasoned. Zakariah began tapping the table, muttering calculations under his breath. He was already working out how to pack and move everything.

"We shall send a group with you with carts and horses to speed your journey," Halleil promised. Again, my eyes widened, astounded by their generosity. "And if it is easier, you do not have to arrive all at once. You can send multiple waves of people. Hopefully you can emancipate more from within Anyra's borders, particularly those at risk of becoming the Temple's Gifts and Chosen."

"The Anyrans' stay here in Kantrin will not be permanent," Edrei assured them as well. "This is a temporary escape while we work out how to overthrow the Temple."

"And overthrow it we will," I grinned. The image of the unholy structure burnt to the ground filled my mind, the Totem's black statue shattered to pieces on the marble floor, Rhoda amid the ashes. In some sick way, it brought me joy.

"And we know that such an endeavor could take you a great while," Eitan assured us. "However long you need, you will be welcome."

"Thank you so much," I said, bowing my head in gratitude. My comrades quickly followed suit, and Edrei smiled between her parents. Though the plan had not been solidified, I assumed that she would remain here in Kantrin when the Anyrans were able to return to the homeland. A pang of sadness pierced my heart, anticipating how I would miss her.

"You are very welcome," Halleil smiled. She lifted her goblet, raising it to us. "A toast to our guests. To your health and prosperity in your endeavors. To our newly forged alliance."

"Down with the Temple!" Edrei added as we all took up our wine.

"Down with the Temple!" we chorused. Blackberry wine spilled onto my sleeve as we raucously clashed our goblets, staining the fabric dark purple. Yet nothing could wipe the hopeful grin from my face.

Conversation exploded around me, and we continued our pleasant evening together long after the food and wine were gone. Though there were no windows in the dining hall, I knew the sun had long set.

"Adelaide?" Theodore called as we began to trickle back to our guest bedrooms for some well-deserved rest. "Could I have a moment?" I waved Zakariah onward before turning back to Theodore.

"Of course," I nodded. I folded my hands in front of me, giving Theo my full attention. In the dim candlelight, he truly bore a striking resemblance to his son, sporting wide, saddened eyes and an angular face.

"I wanted to ask you about Sebastian," Theo continued. I nodded, having suspected as much. Still, my stomach clenched at the sound of his name. I could almost feel his smooth skin under my rough fingertips, taste the lingering sweetness of his kiss on my lips. I shuddered at the thought, a pain in my chest.

"I am sorry we had to meet like this, after all that happened between me and him," I apologized. Theodore gestured to my neck.

"I noticed the scrapes on your neck. You said you were Sebastian's betrothed?" Again, I nodded.

"Yes, he asked me to be his bride about four months after he became the Chosen. He and I had been romantic for nearly two years at that point. But he seemed... *different.* Once he became the Chosen, it seemed to take more and more of him away from me." I found myself clutching my arms, discomfort settling in my gut.

"The day before the Choosing, I asked him to marry me that night rather than in a month's time as we had planned. I didn't want to risk being chosen as the Gift. But he refused. The next day after I was chosen, I ripped the engagement necklace off and threw it back to him." A sense of deep guilt wracked my body and mind as I confessed all this to Theodore, the man who would have been my father-in-law, and the one I thought I would never meet.

"I'm sorry, Theodore," I apologized, my voice hoarse and choked with emotion. He shook his head, tears clinging to his thick glasses.

"No, you have no need to apologize," he assured me. He took the glasses off his face and began wiping the lenses with the hem of his shirt. "I know what it is like to be the Chosen, I know what they're doing to him. But that is no excuse for him to neglect and mistreat you as he did." Deftly, I shook my head, unsure of what to say.

"He always hoped you would return somehow," I finally croaked. "Perhaps one day you will be able to see him again." Theodore forced a smile, the profound sorrow permeating throughout his entire body. He seemed to sag under the weight as though he carried anvils in each hand.

"I certainly hope," he nodded. "Thank you, Adelaide. I know this must be extremely difficult for you."

"I won't lie, it's been hard. I feel like I've lost everything I've ever known. But I'm lucky to have found people that make me feel at home again."

"As am I," Theodore agreed. "Now you need some rest. Goodnight, Adelaide."

"Goodnight, Theodore." I turned, feeling slightly lost in the unfamiliar palace. Deep in my chest, I knew my feet would carry me where, or rather to whom, I needed.

Chapter Nineteen: Omens

A knock sounded at my door as I pulled my boots on and began lacing them. I stumbled as I rose, already knowing who stood behind the door. Smiling, I opened it to see Edrei. My face fell slightly, having hoped to see Zakariah's grin behind the door.

"Good morning, Edrei," I greeted her, smiling once again.

"Adelaide," she smiled warmly. "Did you sleep well?"

"Definitely," I replied, gesturing for her to enter. She did so, and I took notice of her motions. From the day I'd met her, the way she carried herself was simply regal. Her posture was impeccable, her shoulders square, and her chin held high. Knowing her origins, it made sense now. "I slept easier knowing we're getting away."

"I concur. Although, I am sorry to say I have troubling news." My stomach immediately dropped to my feet. I felt my cheeks grow cold.

"What is it?" I demanded. Edrei beckoned me to follow.

"Three Anyrans arrived at the gates this morning, begging to see you. Two I recognized, your sister and her lover," Edrei told me, her voice even.

"What are they doing here? How did they find us? Is Gwen all right!?" Edrei stopped in the stone hallway, taking my shoulder in her hand. She furrowed her brow as she touched me, laying the back of her hand on my cheek.

"Are you well, Adelaide? Your skin is burning," she asked.

"I'm fine," I brushed her off, pushing her hand away. "Who was the third Anyran? Is Gwen safe?"

"They are all three safe. They are in the throne room. Gwen and Xander were obviously frightened, but the third is confusing. We don't know who he is. Gwen does, but she will not tell us. It's better for you to see for yourself."

We sailed into the throne room, and I stopped dead in my tracks. Three Anyrans sat on the floor with their knees folded under themselves like children, facing the four empty thrones. Gwen and Xander sat huddled together, keeping away from the third newcomer. Sebastian had arrived with Gwen and Xander in tow, most likely as hostages. His arm was outstretched, and he kept a death grip on Gwen's arm. Heat rose to my cheeks as I saw him. To the side of the room, Eitan and Halleil stood talking with Calvin and Katharine.

"Gwen, are you two all right?" I asked, and she whipped around at the sound of my voice.

"Addie! We're fine!" she replied quickly. I nodded grimly. I saw Edrei dab sweat from her brow as I marched forward. Sebastian hadn't moved which surprised me. The group that had been talking turned to watch as I made my way toward my former betrothed. He never so much as twitched. I snatched the back of his collar and pulled him back to look at me.

"What are you doing here?" I demanded. Sebastian seemed to look through me as if I weren't there. His eyes had become dark and clouded, as if he were ill. He stared lifelessly up at me, his expression hollow and emotionless. "Sebastian?"

"We found him in the woods," Xander piped up to explain. "He hasn't said a word. He was collapsed from dehydration, but he'll only drink the bare minimum."

"He's under a spell, Adelaide," Calvin revealed, moving toward us. "We believe he was sent by Rhoda to find you."

"Well, here I am," I shrugged, looking down at him once again. "What now?" As if to answer, Sebastian finally released Gwen's arm and reached up to grab me around my neck, pulling me down toward him. A wordless shriek escaped my chest as I tumbled forward, somersaulting over Sebastian. My back popped audibly as it hit the marble floor. My comrades immediately sprang into action, ripping him away from me. I scrambled to my feet, fists clenched and prepared to swing should he attack again.

"Calm yourself, lad! Wake up!" Calvin implored him. Quickly, he got a hold of the Chosen's arms, pinning them behind his back which nearly immobilized him. Xander stood beside him at the ready should he break free. And he would certainly try. Like an animal, Sebastian wrestled against his captors, throwing his weight back and forth in an attempt to break free. His cold, dead eyes never left my face.

Edrei's arm wrapped around my shoulder as I backed away, and I felt Gwen clinging to my waist. I pulled her into me, holding her close with one arm as if that would protect her. My other hand drifted to my throat, gently rubbing away the choking sensation that lingered there. The one comfort lay in the fact that he only wanted me. I truly believed Sebastian would not harm anyone should they simply stay out of his path. Most chillingly of all was that he was stone cold silent. Not a sound left his lips. He uttered not so much as a word or even a groan of effort as he violently rent himself against Calvin's grip. Luckily, it held.

"What did Rhoda do to him?" I demanded.

"Let's get him somewhere secure," Calvin suggested, his voice strained with the effort. Two guards rushed forward to take Sebastian away. "Then we can talk."

"Wait!" cried a new voice. I turned to see Theodore sprinting into the room. "My son! Release him!"

"We can't, Theodore, he'll hurt Adelaide," Halleil placated him.

"He'd never do that," Theo argued. He took his son by his shoulders, searching his face. "Sebastian, it's me, your father." Tears streamed down his face into the scraggly beard on his chin. Seeing the two of them side by side, the resemblance was uncanny. They shared the voluminous black curls, both of them messy and fluffy at the moment.

"Theo, he's under a spell. He can't see or hear you," Calvin tried to explain. He placed a gentle hand on Theo's shoulder, but the man gave no response. He stared longingly into the eyes of his son, begging to be seen. It had been seventeen years since he'd gotten this chance, and he would not give it up easily.

"Can you lift it?" he begged, not even glancing back at the sorcerer.

"Our magic isn't strong enough to break Rhoda's spell," Calvin said regretfully. At long last, Theo tore his eyes away from Sebastian, gaping at Calvin in horror.

"Will he be like this for the rest of his life?" he gasped, the tears never stopping.

"No, it will be lifted when he completes his mission. Which is why he can't be left unattended."

Halleil spoke in Kantrineir, and the guards holding Sebastian moved, dragging him out of the throne room. Theo matched their steps, refusing to let Sebastian out of his sight. Though I doubted it, a spark of hope yearned that a father's love would be enough to free him of Rhoda's magic.

"Where are you taking him?" I asked, surprised by the pang in my heart. It had been over two weeks since my choosing, yet I was still used to caring for him. Some deep part of me always would. Compounding that ache though was watching Theodore's reaction as he finally saw his child once again, but his son could not reciprocate.

"To the dungeon. He will be comfortable and secure, my child," Eitan assured me. I nodded.

"Where is Zakariah? We need him to be part of this discussion. We must decide what to do with Sebastian."

SEBASTIAN STILL HAD yet to make a sound. He simply stood pressed against the bars of his cell, staring intently at me. A pit had formed in my stomach as I stared back at him. It was as if he no longer was himself. His soul seemed to have been rent from his body, and now his animated corpse would follow me to the bitter end. Gwen had not left my side, holding onto my arm with both hands. It was our childhood all over again.

Theodore stayed as close to Sebastian as he could, whispering and muttering, begging his son to wake. I watched, my heart following, as Theo slowly crumpled to the ground by Sebastian's feet. He sobbed quietly, his shoulders shaking. Zakariah stepped forward and crouched beside the stricken man, placing a comforting hand on his shoulder.

"How did this happen?" Zakariah asked, his brow furrowed at the captive. "What kind of magic did Rhoda use on him?"

"Very dark magic. That's what the Temple has always used," Calvin explained.

"Is he secure?" Katharine asked, turning to the Kantro and Kantra.

"Of course," Halleil answered. "We've doubled the guard on him, and they will rotate every two hours." She nodded to the guards, one of them a familiar face. Galom, the guard that had escorted us into the city, stood beside the locked cell doors. "But he could not escape from the cell. No one man could tear through those bars."

Calvin looked up at her, finally drawing his eyes from Sebastian. "Thank you. I do want to warn you though, this magic is complex. Rhoda's spells could give him the strength of a hundred men. Let's just hope it hasn't."

"If so, a hundred guards will be at the ready," Eitan concurred.

"Fantastic, thank you," Katharine replied.

"Anything for your safety," Eitan nodded, turning to give me a warm smile. My unease was still festering in my gut, the cold grip of fear clenching my heart in a strong fist. Though it was not my own safety I fretted for. It was Sebastian and his distraught father. He missed his one chance to reconnect with the father he believed had abandoned him.

The small hope of regaining the man I had loved sparked inside me. But I knew I would never fully trust him again. He had chosen to kill me whether he was under a spell or not. Nothing could mend that. My gaze fell to Zakariah, comforting the father of my murderer. A different pang resonated in my chest. Something familiar and new. I smiled softly as Zakariah met my eyes.

ONCE MORE, WE WERE seated around the dining hall, goblets of drink set in front of us. My mug steamed from a dark elixir inside. It smelled deeply of earthy notes and smooth, dark richness. A small pitcher of sweetened cream had been set beside it for me to add to my own taste. I was told it was called coffee. It was horribly bitter without the cream, but once I had added a few sips, the mixture became a lighter brown and was smooth and sweet.

Zakariah sat beside me with his own cup of coffee. He had added a considerably greater amount of cream than I, but he seemed to be enjoying it. His hand was below the table, resting heavy and secure on my thigh. I welcomed the touch, although some strange part of me felt as though I was betraying my former love that had himself betrayed me. I forged on though. I leaned back in my chair with coffee in one hand and the other resting atop Zakariah's.

"What are we to do about Sebastian?" Edrei asked, looking between each of us in turn. I looked to Calvin and Katharine who appeared to be well versed in magic of this sort.

"I'm fairly certain even our magic combined won't able to lift something of this stature. Rhoda's magic is much more powerful than ours," Calvin announced. I stared wide-eyed into my goblet, wracking my brains for an answer. "However, I think Katharine and I can divert it." I turned to him once again, my expression unchanged.

"What do you mean?" Edrei asked.

"The spell will not break until his mission is accomplished," Katharine turned to gesture to me. "Return to Anyra with you, Adelaide. What we will do is transfer the spell. So rather than returning with you, he will return with something *from* you."

"Such as?" I prompted.

"Anything, a shirt, a necklace, a shoe. Something of you," Katharine clarified. I reached into my pocket, producing the crude wooden figure I'd made the night of my escape. It was meant to be a fox, but it was warped and ragged. One ear was considerably larger than the other, and its teeth were crooked.

"Would this work? I carved it just last week."

"Perfectly," Calvin answered. He took it in his hands, studying it. "This should be a simple process."

"Should be?" Halleil prompted.

"Magic is a dangerous beast, even the light magic we employ. The simplest spells can go awry even for the most skilled masters. And it comes at a price," Calvin explained. "Which is why the Temple requires the sacrifice of the Gifts, to fuel the Temple's magic. Without a sacrifice of some sort, it will come back on the spell caster."

"Do you have a way to avoid that?" Halleil asked. Calvin and Katharine exchanged a wary glance.

"Yes, we do," Katharine assured her.

"There is absolutely no way for you to free my son?" Theodore asked again, hoping that they would give a different answer than before. Katharine's face fell, her forehead creasing with sympathy.

"None that we can perform," she shook her head no. Teardrops splashed into Theodore's goblet, his chest beginning to heave.

"But once his mission is over, the spell will break. Once he delivers his quarry, he will be himself once more," Calvin stated. Some part of me wondered how many spells had been placed upon him. If he truly wanted to get married the night before the Choosing, or if Rhoda had him in her grasp. A tear fell into my own coffee as well.

I WATCHED UTTERLY FASCINATED as I stood beside Zakariah, Gwen pressed into my side. I didn't know whether she wanted protection or was attempting to protect me. Katharine and Calvin knelt in front of the cell, the wooden carving on the ground between them. What they did was like no magic I had ever imagined. This was not like the stories Old Delilah told us as children, no sparkles or flashes of light as they cast spells in poetry like the wizards in her tales.

Rather, the pair of sorcerers sat quietly, staring intently at the items on the floor. They had taken a lock of hair from me and one from Sebastian as well, and they placed them on either side of the carving. Off to the side of their spell casting, they had placed a large bowl of water. They had mixed a handful of sand into the liquid then torn flower petals into the mixture so that they floated atop the water. Katharine had explained that this would act as the 'fuel' for the spell.

Katharine and Calvin muttered under their breath, though they didn't speak in unison. The words were as meaningless as the Kantrin language to my ignorant ears, but I knew that whatever they were saying was powerful. Their hands hovered over the hair and carving, touching the items in turn. They would lay their hands on my hair then on the wood figure over and over, occasionally reaching over to place their fingers on the lock of hair from Sebastian. They moved in perfect unison, but their speech overlapped into a garbled stream of meaningless words.

Sebastian was the thing about this that truly terrified me. He stood pressed against the bars of the cell, eyes glazed, staring straight through me. A strain of cold fear ran through my core as I locked eyes with him. He hadn't spoken a word, nothing of his personality showing through the spell. I hated to think what Rhoda would do when he came back empty-handed. Katharine broke the silence and my staring match with Sebastian.

"That should be it then," she announced, drawing my gaze. Visibly, nothing had changed aside from Sebastian's intense gaze. It was now locked onto my carving, his muscles tense as if readying himself to pounce. I could have sworn that he didn't even blink. Calvin rose from the floor, the figurine in hand. He moved it from one hand to the other, and we all watched Sebastian's gaze follow it. He didn't even take a glance at me.

Cautiously, Calvin stepped forward and offered the wooden shape to him, and Sebastian snatched it from his hands. He clutched it tightly to himself as if it were something precious rather than just a rough scrap of wood from the forest. Now that he held his prize, his gaze shifted again. Now he stared blankly ahead at nothing in particular. The sorcerer nodded as he stepped away from the bars.

"He's harmless now. Kantro, could we unlock the cell and escort him to the gates? He can find his way back to Anyra easily from there."

"Will he not simply lead his Temple and their army back here?" Eitan asked.

"This spell is a strange one," Katharine placated. She snapped her fingers in front of Sebastian's face, but he didn't so much as flinch. "He will remember nothing from the moment the spell was cast until the moment it is lifted. Rhoda will either have to lift it herself, or it will break on its own once his mission is complete. When the prize is in Rhoda's grasp, he will be himself once more."

"He will be alright though?" I asked. Somehow, I still cared for Sebastian despite all he had done to me. Katharine's expression of sympathy assured me that such compassion was understandable. She nodded, and I did so as well in reply.

Eitan spoke in Kantrineir, and Galom stepped forth from his place by the ruler's side. He unlocked the cell, and Sebastian stepped out. He began walking, but Galom took him firmly by the arm. Sebastian would wander the dungeons until he found his way out. It would be better to lead him there quickly. Galom steered him toward the steps, no doubt to guide him upstairs with Theodore trailing slightly behind.

"We will supply him with enough food and water for the journey. Whether or not he will use it is up to him," Halleil assured us.

"Thank you," I nodded.

"I will go with him," Theodore called over his shoulder.

"Theo, are you certain?" Eitan replied, reaching to grasp the scholar's wrist as he began ascending after his son. "The Anyrans may be hostile toward you."

"He is my son," Theo replied, a fire behind his eyes. "I'll not abandon him again."

"Very well," Eitan nodded. "We will supply you with everything you need for the journey."

"Thank you, my Kantro," Theo nodded before rushing back up the stairs. A sense of calm washed over me, knowing that Sebastian would be under his father's watchful care. For the first time in seventeen years, Theodore had the opportunity to care for and guide his son. He would not miss it.

Finally, their echoing footsteps faded into the walls, leaving us in silence. As I inhaled, the putrid scent of burnt hair met my nose. I turned to Katharine who still sat on the floor. Both she and Calvin were staring intently at the two locks of hair. My own reddish strand was smoking, sizzling on the ground as flames slowly burnt it away, leaving a pile of charred ashes.

"Did you do that?" I asked, perplexed. Without drawing his gaze from the smoldering hair, Calvin shook his head. "Then how did it happen?" Fear began to well up in my heart, and Gwen pushed herself into my side, hugging me tightly around my middle.

"Adelaide, this is a very bad omen," Katharine warned me, fear choking her voice. "This is an omen of death and destruction." A whimper escaped from Gwen's throat as she buried her face in me. I held her tightly to me, swallowing my own fear for her sake.

"It's just an omen. It doesn't mean anything for certain. And that's exactly why I'm here. To avoid the death of my sacrifice that the omen is warning of." I stood tall, squaring my shoulders. "The Totem can't kill me. She never held any power. She's dead."

"But Rhoda can," Calvin argued, drawing his gaze off what was now nothing more than a pile of gray ash on the dungeon floor. "You have no idea the power she wields."

"And she has no idea how strong I am to fight back," I replied. "We'll rally the people. At least half of Anyra will fight at my side, if not more. We'll throw *her* into that damned volcano."

Katharine and Calvin exchanged another glance, Katharine's lips pursed. "Just be wary, Adelaide. Rhoda is beyond us." She took a long gaze at her husband, fear in her eyes. "All of us."

I nodded again, not letting the fear pull me to the floor where it wanted me. "Her magic and her false goddess can't kill me."

Chapter Twenty: All Things

We remained in Kantrin for another day and night, allowing all of us time to recover from the encounter with Sebastian. Gwen and Xander recounted how they had found Sebastian unconscious in the woods, and how Gwen had confused him upon his waking. The two of them were utterly exhausted, as Sebastian had refused rest throughout the night, forcing them to walk until they arrived.

Halleil and Edrei escorted them to a suite and provided them with bread, cheese, and cured meat to sustain them. They remained there for several hours, sleeping off the exhaustion and pain. Gwen had already been weakened by the Punishment, then to be forced to walk for a full day and night was too much for her.

Uncertain what to do with myself, I found myself in the library, surrounded by books that I could not read. I wandered to the back of the massive space and sat down at Theodore's desk. Papers were scattered across its surface, and an inkwell had been knocked over, covering nearly the entire desktop in black. The stains were still damp. I assume this happened when Theo discovered his son was in Kantrin.

I sifted through the pages, hardly able to read anything Theo had written whether it be in Anyran or Kantrineir. One of the few things I could decipher was Sebastian's name written several times. Even so many years later, he could never stop thinking of his son. Perhaps if Theo had stayed in Anyra, things would have ended differently. But at this point, I wasn't sure if I wanted them to change.

"Adelaide." I tore my eyes from the pages to see Halleil approaching me, her shoulders square but her expression soft and kind. I smiled as I met her eyes.

"My Kantra," I greeted her, bowing my head. I had quickly picked up the traditional greeting from Theodore and the guards. She waved her hand as if brushing the gesture aside.

"There is no need for that, my dear, I am not your Kantra. I'm here as a friend," she chastised me kindly. She came to stand beside me and let her fingers glide over the desktop, but not allowing her skin to touch the still wet ink. "And Theo was a friend as well."

"I fear for him. Rhoda, the Temple," I fretted. "Who knows what they'll do to him. If they'll believe him or not."

"I was worried about that as well," Halleil nodded, turning toward me. "I don't think we'll be seeing Theodore again." I watched as a tear slipped from her eye and down her cheek. I shook my head in reply. "He was a good friend to us. We learned so much from him."

"How were you able to communicate when he first arrived here?" The question had been itching in the back of my mind from the moment we realized some of Kantrin's people could speak my mother tongue. "The Anyrans didn't even know other civilizations exist, let alone other languages."

"There was a tome in our library with some very old writings in your language," Halleil began. "Or at least what it used to be. Your dialect has changed since this tome was written, but it was close enough to translate." She drifted over to a bookcase, searching the spines for the title she needed.

Only now did I notice that the Kantra's dress was not her typical white. Now, she wore a darker cream-colored gown with red embroidery. The fit was more form-fitting than her normal wear, suggesting this was an older dress. It dawned on me that white must be their color of mourning. For nearly thirty years, she and her husband had mourned the loss of their two children. Now that Edrei had returned, she began wearing her royal red once again.

"Here it is." The Kantra pulled a small, leather-bound book from a high shelf, dust raining down around her. She found a spot where the ink had dried and settled it on the desk before me, flicking through the pages. The book was more a journal that an actual scholarly book or fictional novel as my uncle had loved. The left side was written in Kantrineir, and the right in Anyran. I assumed they read the same thing, allowing anyone who spoke one language to learn the other.

"This is amazing," I breathed, searching for the few words of Kantrineir that I had picked up in our short visit and flicking back and forth trying to find each Anyran word's counterpart. "Who wrote it?"

"Here." Halleil turned back to the front cover, and inside was a name: Harlan the Third. No true last name, and no indication of a family history. "This is all we know of the author."

"Fascinating. I wonder how he learned both languages."

"I suppose we'll never know," Halleil shrugged sadly. "But I am grateful for it." I closed the dusty cover and handed the journal back to the Kantra.

"As am I. I can never repay you for the kindness you've shown me and my sister, not even to mention Anyra as a whole."

"Of course. We are more than happy to give aid where we can. You are part of Tomano just as we are." Halleil smiled. "And you brought our daughter back to us. Nothing can ever repay that debt."

I tilted my head at the word she used. This was the first time she had let a Kantrineir word slip into her Anyran speech. She chuckled at my perplexed expression. "I don't recognize that word. What is Tomano?"

"Anyra has its false Totem. We believe in Tomano. Theodore told me that the closest translation in Anyran would be 'all things'. We all come from one spirit, and you in Anyra are no different. How could we turn away you, who we see as an extension of ourselves?"

I nodded, beginning to understand this. With the truth of the Totem still reeling in my mind, I had hardly stopped to consider that other faiths would exist beyond what I had always known. The idea that every person came from one entity suggested that we were all somehow linked to one another. I felt a sense of comfort in my chest as I thought of my parents, gone but still connected.

"I like that. We are all a part of Tomano." Halleil nodded in response, and I continued. "It's certainly better than Anyra. But I don't want to completely abandon my home. We hope to build a new Anyra one day, where the Temple and their false goddess do not reign," I stated. "I would hope to have you and Kantrin as our first allies."

"We would have it no other way, Adelaide." I made to bow to her, but she stopped me. "Now, don't do that," she chided me. "You are a friend, not my subject." She opened her arms and drew me into a hug, almost before I realized what she was doing. Though I placed gentle hands on her back, she held me tightly to herself.

Something in me stirred, a longing for the motherly affection that had been denied to me from my early childhood. Delilah did her best, but she was a poor substitute at best for my own mother. Halleil also failed to meet that exact quality of my own mother, yet somehow, she fulfilled the deep need in me for reassurance. Her arms were strong yet kind just as her rule over Kantrin.

"Thank you," I whispered.

"Always, Adelaide," Halleil assured me.

Chapter Twenty-One: Homebound

I sat astride a beautiful red-brown mare, her saddlebags filled with provisions for our journey. Gwen sat in the saddle behind me, clinging to me as she always had. She had begun to gain weight, her love of food thrilled by the new cuisine she had sampled in Kantrin. A sneaking suspicion that a tiny life was growing in her belly pestered me, but I let it rest for the time being. If she was pregnant, Xander would take care of her with myself as both sister and aunt ready to help.

After saying our final farewells to our Kantrineir friends, we set off at a considerably faster pace than the one with which we'd arrived. The horses were well-trained and sure-footed, allowing us quick passage. Few words were spoken as we rode, focused only on getting back to our people. Zakariah stayed close by my side, his black stallion nickering to my steed every once and again. It seemed they were friends or perhaps a breeding pair.

Xander rode on the saddle behind Zakariah, looking tense and uncomfortable. He continually stole glances at Gwen, who always returned them with a smile or a word of reassurance. Edrei rode in front, her shining brown steed much larger than the rest of the horses. He was a trailblazer, meant to lead the way and forge our trail.

We moved at such a pace that we reached our Village just after sundown, and we were greeted with excitement. Edrei called an emergency meeting, and we told them of all we had seen and learned. I was ecstatic that we had found our safe haven, somewhere to regroup as we prepared to reclaim our homeland.

"My people!" Edrei cried, smiling broadly. "I am glad to inform you that our journey has been successful. Our small group traveled to Kantrin, my homeland, and we have found allies within its walls!"

A cheer rose up from the Village, surprisingly loud considering we numbered below two hundred people. I smiled, clenching Gwen's hand in my right and Zakariah's in my left. Something continually tugged at the back of my mind. Perhaps it was Sebastian and the strange state in which he had been, or the fact that my sacrifice should take place in just four days. The omen Katharine had warned me of hung dark and dreadful over my head. Perhaps it was all of these small and large things making me feel sickly.

"In two days' time, the first wave will set out. The elderly and families with small children," Edrei continued. "Three days after that, the second wave will go, any and all girls of Gift age and their families. Two days later, anyone that remains will leave. Take care to pack what is necessary, enough food and water for everyone. We expect the journey to take five days with so many, though it only took a small number of us one day on horseback." Edrei nodded to me, and I took my cue. Releasing my companions' hands, I stepped forth.

"And what is more, my people, is that we have made an empowering yet chilling discovery," I addressed them. "One Anyran already resided in Kantrin, living among the people. Theodore Corander, the father of the current Chosen, has lived there since he fled Anyra seventeen years ago. He was exiled when he discovered something many of us have suspected." I took a breath, and the people seemed to hold theirs, anticipating the news I would share.

"The Totem does not exist!" I proclaimed, allowing a smile to tug at my face. "She never has! The Temple uses the fiction of her to control the people of Anyra, mongering over them with fear. The true power lies in the High Priestess, who wields dark magic." The crowd broke into mutterings of fear and disbelief.

"We are safe beyond Anyra's borders," I assured them, quieting them once more. "But we don't know for how long. That is why we must make haste. Take only what you need. Kantrin will house and provide for us until the day comes when we can overthrow the Temple." I jumped as Xander stepped up beside me, his fear transformed to rage and power.

"Down with the Totem!" he cried, raising a fist in the air.

"Down with the Totem!" the people echoed, raising fists and voices alike. I grinned as the anthem was repeated over and over, even joining in myself. Edrei stood quietly to the side, grinning at the empowered Anyrans. No longer were we enslaved by fear, crippled by a Temple that craved control and power, worshipping a false goddess. No longer.

"DOWN WITH THE TOTEM!"

Chapter Twenty-Two: Father

Theodore hadn't slept in what felt like days, never letting the son he had thought he would never see again out of his sight. Though he was almost uncertain if this was his son after all. Sebastian was hollow, emotionless, focused only on the task at hand. Nothing would stop him. Diligently, Theodore followed Sebastian's footfalls, keeping him safe.

When the Chosen grew weary, Theo fed and watered him, warned him of pitfalls, kept him from bumping into trees. At several points, a large ten-point buck seemed to be watching them from the wood, but he paid little heed. All that mattered was Sebastian.

At long last, Anyra came into view. The wretched volcano that housed the hundreds of restless spirits loomed over the city, flanked by two smaller mountains. From the place on the hill overlooking Anyra, Theodore could see everything. All the shops and houses, the Temple and its corrupted inhabitants. The home he never wanted to lay eyes on again.

Sebastian was unperturbed by the beautiful scene as the sun began to rise behind them, the light dazzling on the ocean. He trod on, unwavering in his quest. Theodore followed three steps behind, eyes trained on the dirty, overspent form of his son. The father had hoped the spell would break when they reentered Anyra's borders, but it did not. Rather, a horrible dizziness came over him.

"Sebastian!" the man called, but his son could not hear. As Theodore's vision darkened on the edges and his stomach threatened to expel its little contents, he clapped a hand on his son's shoulder, following him into the city proper. The spell was working, trying to keep him out. But he had the Chosen to guide him.

As the pair made their way through Anyra, the city began to awaken around them. Life went on as normal despite the missing Gift. Theodore reminded himself that he must not let on what he knew about Kantrin or the Anyran refugees that would reside there. He would take on the persona of an imbecile, a hermit that had lived off the land for the past seventeen years.

As the pair neared the Temple, Theodore shed his glasses and tossed them aside, ridding himself of any evidence that he had lived in civilization. Sebastian mounted the steps, and Theodore's aching feet followed. Always three steps behind. The young man still remained silent as he entered the Temple and took a second set of stairs into the Sanctuary. There stood his goal.

"Who is this?" Rhoda demanded, turning at the sound of footsteps. "Where is the Gift!?" Theodore flinched at the immediate display of rage. The same rage and abuse he had seen during his tenure as the Chosen, though Rhoda's behavior seemed to have worsened in the past thirty years. Sebastian shoved the wooden figure from Adelaide into the High Priestesses hands, and immediately crumpled onto the marble floor.

"What is this!?" she shrieked as Theodore dove to his knees beside his son, gathering him into his lap.

"Sebastian!" he cried, desperate to hear his son's voice. "Are you alright, my boy?" Finally, he was cognizant again, his eyes light and intelligent once more. He looked around the room as if uncertain how he had arrived there before his gaze settled on his father.

"Who...?" he murmured, utterly perplexed.

"I'm your father, Sebastian," he promised, tears beginning to fall from his eyes once again. "It's me."

"You came," Sebastian muttered in wonder, remembering his wedding invitation. He had prayed to the Totem to bring his father back to see him marry Adelaide. He had gotten only one of the things he begged for.

"Chosen!" Rhoda screamed, shoving Theodore aside with her staff. She held up the wooden figure in Sebastian's face. "What is this? Where is the Gift!?"

"I don't know," Sebastian replied, scrambling away from her with his feet. Theodore witnessed the exchange utterly horrified. "The last thing I remember is you taking the necklaces." His hands drifted up to his chest, finding both chains there unaltered.

"Imbecile!" Rhoda roared, raising her staff to land a blow. Sebastian ducked, slinging his arms over his head instinctively. The staff never met its mark. Theodore stepped between the beast and her target, catching the staff with an open hand.

"You will not harm him," he said, suddenly filled with strength. Rhoda only smirked in response.

"You have no idea," she remarked as she withdrew. Sebastian knew what was coming.

"Papa, move!"

A heavy, guttural shout emanated from Theodore's chest as Rhoda's dagger found its place between his ribs, blood spurting from the wound. Sebastian froze for a moment as time seemed to slow. Red stained the floor as it gushed out around the dagger, and Theo's skin quickly became pale. Finally, Theodore began to fall backward, and it was the son's turn to catch his father.

"No, no, no," Sebastian fretted, shaking like a leaf about to fall. Rhoda wiped the blood off of her blade on the inside of her robes before twisting the knob back onto the staff. "Papa!" Sebastian raised his head to look at Rhoda, asking one thing and one thing only of her. He knew magic was capable of good and miraculous things. Rhoda, however, he was uncertain. "Please, save him."

"Clean this mess up," came her only response. As she departed for her chambers, Theodore reached up to hold his son's tearstained face.

"I love you, my boy," he gasped, hardly able to choke out the words.

"I love you," Sebastian replied, clutching his father desperately to himself. He was too late. The light had already left Theodore's unfocused eyes, his hands falling limply away from Sebastian. Blood soaked into their already filthy clothes, filling the Sanctuary with the metallic scent so dense you could nearly taste it. The son's screams and bellows echoed on the cold marble walls.

Chapter Twenty-Three: Morning

The hazy morning light drifted through the window, waking me from a restless sleep. Just three more days and I was meant to be thrown into the mouth of the monster. The first sideways slants of sunlight were beginning to filter through the trees. Three days. Tomorrow the first wave of refugees would be off.

As I lay in my hammock, swinging gently in the morning breeze, a thought came to me. Hundreds of people resided in Anyra's borders, and so many of them disagreed with the Temple. Many of them must be girls of age or simply those tired of living under the Temple's control. They had no clue that there was a way out.

I sat up in the hammock, thinking of Gwendolyn, the twins, Zakariah's sister, my own aunt Sylvia. There were girls still at risk, even if we did escape the Temple's clutches. If I lived, another girl may die. The pillow and blanket flopped to the wooden floor as I tumbled out of the hammock and quickly dressed and pulled on my boots. I braided my hair loosely down my back. It had grown fuller in the time I'd been away.

I snagged a rope dangling outside the platform and slid down it, my callused hands hardly registering the pain of the rope burn. I did not reach the ground, rather ending my descent halfway down and stepping onto the landing of Caleb and Valerie's bungalow. I pounded on the door, forgetting that Caleb was a late riser typically.

"Addie, what's going on? The sun is hardly up," he groaned as he came to the door, his carrot-orange hair sticking up every which way and his eyes bleary.

"We have to go back to Anyra," I stated, pressing my palms together as he stopped abruptly while rubbing the sleep from his eyes. The silence hung tersely between us.

"Are you sleepwalking?" he demanded, pulling me away from the edge. "That's absolute madness, Rhoda would take you."

"You were one of Edrei's messengers, you sent people here when you knew they could be trusted. There must be so many people that would be left behind in Anyra when we leave. They never got the chance to escape, we have to give them that chance."

Caleb paused, his tired mind slowly coming to and realizing the truth of what I was saying. He most likely was running through the people he and Valerie had known, perhaps a mental list of those they would have saved. In saving myself, I may have doomed them.

"Damn, you're right," Caleb breathed, his eyes wide as he stared at me. "How can we get them out?" I blanched, my mouth opening and closing like a fish out of water. Whatever we did, it had to be under the Temple's nose. Rhoda could not know we were smuggling people out.

"I'm going to call a meeting. Where's Valerie?" I asked.

"At the forge, helping Landon pack." I nodded and turned back to the rope.

"Ramona's in twenty minutes?" Caleb nodded, turning back to properly dress for the day, and I slid the rest of the way to the ground. I broke into a sprint toward the forge, smiling and waving hello to the few Villagers milling about. The Village was waking, preparing for the long journey ahead. I could hear Valerie and Landon's faint voices as I approached, my chest beginning to ache with the strain of running.

"Addie, are you alright?" Valerie asked, rolling tools into a sheet of leather for the journey.

"Had an epiphany. Meeting at Ramona's in twenty," I huffed, trying to catch my breath. "We have to rescue the people in Anyra who aren't loyal to the Temple." Valerie nodded, her brow furrowing in worry.

"Landon, keep packing the forge, I'll be back to help once we've figured this out." Her brother nodded as she began walking toward the Village once again, and I walked with her.

"How are you feeling? Will you be alright on the journey?" I quizzed, glancing down at her stomach. There was very little change now, but I knew soon enough her belly would be swollen with the baby.

"I've been having pretty bad morning sickness, but it passes after a while. And the journey will be fine. There are a few other women with child in the Village, and Katharine spoke with us about a wagon."

"Good, I'm glad it's going alright," I nodded.

"I'm not worried, Addie." I looked up to see her smiling softly. "You shouldn't be either. The baby will be perfect." I nodded in agreement, allowing her words to sink into my fretting mind.

"You're right. It's all going to be alright."

"As for the people, I'm sure we can get them out. They can go with the second or third wave. Edrei had many more spies than only me and Caleb. Some of them have sent more Anyrans or returned themselves." I continued my nodding, trying to let her convince me. Something in me told me it wouldn't be as easy as we hoped.

We stopped at Zakariah's bungalow and I pounded on the door. Like Caleb, Zakariah was a late sleeper, and I very obviously woke him from his slumber. Valerie laughed as we heard him clatter to the floor inside. The door flew open to reveal a sleepy and confused Zakariah.

"What is it?" he asked, his morning breath making my nose crinkle. I smiled at his fluffy hair and half-closed eyes. He wore no shirt, so he had wrapped himself in his blanket, though for decency or warmth I was uncertain. "Everything alright?"

"Meet at Ramona's in fifteen minutes, alright?" I told him, laying a hand on his shoulder. A shiver ran through his body as he continued to wake up. He nodded and turned to dress as Valerie and I continued on.

"What about you?" Valerie added as we made our way to Edrei's home. "How are you holding up with it all?" I hesitated, trying to find the right words.

"Better than I expected. I feel like I'm doing something right, like I'm honoring my parents and Sylvia." Valerie nodded, prompting me to continue. "And, I mean, look at all the support I have. I never expected this, Edrei, Zakariah, the Village as a whole. I feel like I'm actually home."

"Good, you should feel at home, these people are genuine and true," Valerie agreed. "They're much kinder than Anyra seems to be often. I never noticed the fear running through the Anyrans until I came here."

"I hadn't either. But we can end that." I raised a gentle fist to rap on the wall beside Edrei's curtained doorway.

"Come in," the Kantira's voice called. The beads clicked against one another as Valerie and I brushed past them. I started at the sight inside. Edrei's home was now baren whereas before it was filled with books and scrolls. She had packed exceptionally quickly. "Adelaide, Valerie, good to see you both." She placed her pack on the ground beside the door and stood before us. "How are you feeling?" Edrei gestured to Valerie's stomach, and the mother-to-be smiled warmly once more.

"Feeling well. And you?"

"Ready to go back," Edrei smiled. She seemed almost giddy with excitement, ready to return to her homeland once again.

"Edrei, we've realized a problem," I blurted, my worry unable to be contained any longer, and her face fell. "The people still in Anyra, many of them would join us if they knew of our existence. We have to get them out before we go. Who knows what could happen in our absence?" Edrei's brow furrowed and she crossed her arms, placing her fingers on her chin in deep thought.

"You're absolutely right," she agreed. "I propose a meeting at Ramona's to discuss our options."

"Already underway," I nodded. "Caleb, Zakariah, and ourselves will be in attendance in ten minutes. I thought we could ask Calvin and Katharine to come as well."

"Yes, good work, Adelaide," she commended me. "Let's be on our way."

As we made our way to Ramona's home, we stopped at Calvin and Katharine's home, requesting that they join us. Readily, they agreed, and we moved along.

Chapter Twenty-Four: Nightmare

As the sheets tangled around Sebastian's legs, damp with cold sweat, he was almost relieved that sleep eluded him. When the darkness did swallow him, a second set of dead, hollow eyes had joined Adelaide's staring down at him over the lip of the volcano. Beside her charred, burnt husk of a corpse was the shambling, undead form of his father.

The soft, kind features of Theodore had shriveled away, his skin gray and ashy as rot overtook him. Dirt crumbled off of him, smarting in Sebastian's eyes as it fell in his face and hair. His eyes were sunken, glazed over and white behind his shattered glasses. His hair fell out in clumps, and his skin hung off of him in shreds.

Theodore had only been in Sebastian's adult life for mere moments before his death, but those had been enough to right seventeen years of wrongs. Sebastian knew in an instant that Theodore had not chosen to leave him, and if he had been able to, he would have taken young Sebastian with him.

Now, just as his betrothed and his mother before, Theodore was dead. What's worse was that Rhoda had forced Sebastian to carry his father's lifeless body out of the Temple in the dead of night, unseen by the other priests and priestesses. He had buried his father at the foot of the volcano in an unmarked grave. The spot looked out over the sea rather than toward Anyra.

He selected a place beneath an oak tree, close to where he had buried Adelaide's uncle. In the tree's bark, he carved Theodore's initials, so lightly marked that they were barely there. If he ever got the chance, he would tell Addie or her sister Gwen where the men were buried. Perhaps one day they would get proper funerals.

Where he dangled from a fragile rope in the volcano, Sebastian had given up his futile screaming. Even in the dream he had learned that the phantoms above him either could not hear him or simply didn't care. The exact events of the nightmare changed with each occurrence. Occasionally, Sebastian would attempt to climb out of the mouth of the monster, but always he could not reach the lip.

When Adelaide reached down for the rope, she seemed to somehow burn through it, her body having absorbed the scorching heat of the lava that would kill her. If his father reached down, it would rot under his touch, the decay spreading to any flesh or fiber and causing it to crumble. Every time, Sebastian would feel his stomach drop as the rope went slack, and he began to plummet downward toward his death.

Rather than risk seeing the apparitions again, Sebastian would keep himself awake. He sat at his desk for long hours, often waiting to greet the sun as it rose and threw sunbeams over the sea outside his window. To stave off the sleep and exhaustion that dogged him, he would write. Scrolls upon scrolls were filled with his delirious, sleep-deprived scrawling.

Sebastian had begun writing his life's story, detailing everything he could remember from the faintest of his childhood memories to every moment he'd spent in the Temple. It sickened him to think that there was at least one span of several days that was blank in his mind. When Rhoda had cast the spell on him, it was as though his soul had parted from his body, and he couldn't recall anything from the days he spent on Rhoda's mission.

A great deal of what Sebastian wrote was addressed to Adelaide, a form of apology and explanation for all that had happened. Some deep, sickened part of him had known that she would be chosen as the sacrifice, but he believed he could save her from that fate if he remained loyal and obedient to Rhoda and the Totem. Now, he questioned if the Totem was truly there at all.

As his quill scratched against the paper, penning out yet another apology to his lover, a scorching hand fell heavily on his shoulder. Over time, Sebastian's instincts had changed, so rather than crying out in pain, he remained silent and stiffened like a board. He turned, expecting to see Rhoda wielding her magic for some fun with her favorite plaything, but a different sight met Sebastian's eyes.

He nearly cried out now as he rose from his seat, backing toward the door in fright. He instantly recognized the features of his betrothed staring at him with glowing, bloodred eyes, but now the rest of her skin was black as if it had been turned to obsidian. Cracks marred her skin, glowing red-hot with the lava that had replaced her blood. Her hair billowed out around her head, redder than it normally would be, but now also glowing with flames.

"Addie," Sebastian gasped, his chest heaving as she turned toward him, her magmatic eyes never leaving his. Somehow, she was reminiscent of the statue of the Totem in the Sanctuary, her features beautiful but hardened and cruel. "What is going on?"

Unlike in his dreams, her lips parted, and a harsh, rasping voice met his ears. The voice was not hers, though it was similar. Even her vocal cords seemed to have turned to stone.

"You did this." She marched closer, and Sebastian could feel the heat coming off of her in waves, bathing him in the sickening warmth and causing sweat to bead on his brow.

"I know, Addie, I'm so sorry." Bravely, he stepped closer to her. It had been over three weeks since her disappearance, and his heart longed for her. He had been near her during his time under the spell, but hadn't been able to glimpse her face or hear her voice. "I did this, and I will never forgive myself."

As he stepped nearer, the fear disappeared. Pain was no cause for fear now in Sebastian's mind, simply a fact of his existence. Life is pain, and pain is almost all life has to offer. Almost. The one thing that remained to bring him joy and love, he had hurt beyond repair. The pain would be more than worth it to hold her once again.

He noticed that she seemed to be wearing the same clothing that the Totem wore in her depictions: two pieces of black cloth tied over her chest and around her waist as a skirt. Both had been burned and worn away so she was nearly indecent, though the cold posed no problem for her.

Her shoulders and brow relaxed as he crept closer to her, the heat threatening to make him expel the little contents of his stomach. Her eyes were wide and curious as she stared up at him. Sebastian could tell that she was hesitant, but he would not miss his chance again. He placed a gentle hand on her waist, wincing as the scorching heat of her skin met his palm. She hardly seemed to notice his pain, and he pushed it aside.

"I love you, Adelaide," he promised her. Tears streamed down his face, and he could feel his chest aching as the physical and emotional pain mingled in his body and soul. She did not speak. Rather, she raised her hands to gently take his face in her hands, and Sebastian could feel blisters forming wherever she touched him. Again, he shoved the pain down and away. She was so much more than worth it.

With some sickening mixture of pain and pleasure, her lips met his, scorching the sensitive, cracked skin, but he forced himself to kiss her back. His arms tightened around her, clinging to her desperately as if he could make her revert to her normal self. His shirt melted into his chest, ravaging his entire body with pain and heat. He didn't even flinch when her hands slid down to his neck and began choking him.

Chapter Twenty-Five: Confession

"Ramona?" I called, knocking gently on the doorframe. Seconds later, the door opened, Ramona appearing in the door frazzled but happy all the same.

"Hello!" she greeted us, quickly twisting her hair into a bun. "Come in, Caleb told me what is happening." We entered, and found Caleb already sitting at the table with a cup of tea and a large teapot before him. He raised a hand to wave, and Valerie took the seat beside him.

Edrei sat across from them, and Calvin and Katharine took a third side of the square table, but I stayed standing. I glanced out the window and spotted Zakariah approaching as he futilely attempted to tame his curls. I smiled and opened the door before he knocked.

"Hi," he greeted me smiling, but his face fell when he remembered why he was here. "What's the situation?"

"Adelaide came to a dire realization," Edrei began as Zakariah and I took up our place on the fourth and final side of the square. "There are still dozens of people left in Anyra that would join us, should they have the chance. However, they do not know of us and our mission to escape the Temple and its rule. We need to somehow free them without the Temple or Rhoda taking notice."

"Several of our spies sent more refugees, and most returned themselves," Valerie added, "but yes, many more remain unaware of us. But we don't have a way of contacting them. We can't get back in without a priest or the Chosen."

"The spell holding people out is weak," Calvin chimed in. "We can get through it fairly easily. We simply have to open a kind of 'doorway' in the barrier."

"What do you need in order to do that?" Edrei asked, looking between the two sorcerers. They looked to one another, both going over the magic in their minds. I had dozens of questions about the magic they wielded, but I held my tongue.

"Olive oil, a willow branch, and about five minutes," Katharine answered after a moment. I recognized the items as traditional wedding or housewarming gifts, used to bless the front doorway of a home. It made sense they would need these items to magically open a doorway back into our homeland.

"I'll fetch them as soon as we're done here," Edrei promised. She then turned to Caleb and Valerie. "How many people were you planning on sending to us before you had to leave? Do you have a list of those that were good candidates?"

"Yes, we weren't able to reach all of them before we left, but I know there had to have been more that we didn't know," Caleb answered. A part of me was still bewildered that they kept this from me for so long. I reached for the tea in front of me and drank in gulps, my mind racing as I tried to think of a way to reach everyone in Anyra that would turn from the Temple. Hopefully the tea would speed my mind.

"Is there any way we could give some form of a signal? A way for those that would join us to know it is time to flee without Rhoda noticing?" Zakariah mused, stirring honey into his own teacup before sipping it himself. He gasped as the liquid touched his lips, still too hot to drink just yet.

"We don't have to tell everyone," I mumbled, beginning to realize the strength we had.

"What do you mean? How else would they know to escape?" Zakariah asked, furrowing his brow at me. I set my cup down too quickly, and tea sloshed onto my hand. I hardly noticed.

"We don't have to tell every single person," I grinned. "We just have to tell enough, then instruct them to tell their friends and family, those that also hate the Temple. We just plant the seeds, and they'll do the rest."

"That could work," Edrei nodded, a matching smile beginning to creep across her face. "Ramona, are you able to See anything about this mission?"

The Elder Seer had removed her gloves, stretching out her hands in front of herself. We all leaned in closer, waiting with baited breath for her premonition. Slowly, she shook her head, but she looked up at me.

"Adelaide, may I read you again? I feel there may be more to glean from your future." Immediately, I nodded and offered her my hands. Her fingers were icy as I took them, and her eyes rolled back into her head.

"So much fire," she muttered, her eyes flicking back and forth beneath her lids. My stomach clenched as I waited to hear more. Zakariah laid a heavy hand on my thigh in support, and I leaned into him. Though I hardly knew what her visions entailed, they frightened me.

Her eyebrows rose after Zakariah laid his hand on me, and her mutterings changed. "Legacy... a garden... the end and the beginning." Though ominous, these words seemed more optimistic. Perhaps she was somehow reading both Zakariah and I at once, or even our combined future. A legacy of what?

At long last, she released me and opened her eyes once more. She looked around the table at each of us staring expectantly at her. Slowly, she shook her head.

"I saw little difference from the first reading of you." I nodded, hoping for some good news. A childish part of me had hoped she would tell me that I would not die in three days' time. Not even a Seer could be so certain of what the future may hold.

"Whatever happens, it will be alright. What matters now is helping the survivors in Anyra," I assured her, and Edrei nodded her agreement.

"Ramona and Valerie, continue packing," Edrei instructed. "The rest of you, meet at the Western border of the Village at dusk. We'll get them out." I nodded, a grim smile on my lips. I had fully accepted the idea that I would never return to Anyra. Now I would be creeping back into the city's borders in the dead of night.

"Adelaide, you remain here as well," she corrected as if reading my thoughts. "You'll be leaving with the first wave tomorrow." My jaw fell slightly open in shock, but I shook it away.

"With all due respect, Edrei, I can't do that," I argued. "I fear that I'll only put our people and the people of Kantrin in danger. At the moment, the Temple and Rhoda are only hunting me, not the refugees. I could very well be putting their life and safety in jeopardy even as we speak."

"That's why we need to be with you, Adelaide, to protect you," Edrei said in return, lowering her eyebrows at me as she spoke. She crossed her arms over her chest, but I would not back down.

"Yes, the children, the ill, and the elderly are going to protect me against Rhoda's dark magic," I snapped, and Edrei's eyebrows shot up in surprise. "We know Rhoda can track me. I'm honestly surprised she hasn't captured me by now. Until she does, I'm going to do all I can to protect *you*. To protect *our* people." Edrei shook her head at my insubordination, but the tiniest of smiles laced her lips. She had expected me to resist.

Eventually she sighed. "I can't change your mind, can I?" I shook my head solemnly. "Alright, but please at least allow us to help you where we can."

I nodded, smiling once more. "And allow me to help you where I can," I replied.

NO SLEEP CAME TO ME as I watched the light fading from brilliant yellow to the glimmering gold of late evening outside my window. I had a few hours yet before we must leave for Anyra, and Edrei had suggested we each rest while we could. We had spent the remainder of the morning preparing tents for the Anyrans we expected. The temporary structures provided enough shelter should it rain, but they could quickly be broken down and carried along to Kantrin.

After lunch, Edrei forced us to at least try to nap, but I had never been able to sleep during the day even as a child. Only when I was extremely exhausted could I sleep while the sun was awake. Now even as the sun settled for its rest, I could not.

I could almost sense Anyra to the west, like a trap set to spring the second I stepped inside. Yet somehow, I knew I had to go back. As much as I dreaded what could be a fatal homecoming, something was calling me back. Perhaps we would reclaim Anyra in my lifetime, and my children would get to grow up where I did. In a brighter, kinder Anyra than I knew now. We could make it this way.

I lay watching the last drops of sunlight filter through the trees and listening to the hoot of owls calling to one another when a knock sounded at the door. I called for them to enter, and I moved to get up as the door swung open. Zakariah stepped inside, his usual grin absent from his lips. The corner of his mouth pulled into a small smile after he shut the door.

"Hi," he greeted me sheepishly.

"What's going on?" I quizzed. "I thought you'd be asleep, we don't leave for another hour or so."

"I couldn't sleep. I'm worried, Addie." I beckoned him closer, and he sat beside me on the hammock. Our feet hovered just above the floorboards.

"I am, too," I nodded. "I feel like something terrible will happen. Like Rhoda will be waiting for us."

"Oh, I hope not." Zakariah let his head fall into his hands. "I've been away so long, and now with you in danger. Part of me thinks we shouldn't even risk it."

"You don't have to go," I offered.

"No, Addie, I'm not worried about me. I'm worried about you." He turned to face me, gripping the fabric for leverage. "Edrei was right, you shouldn't go. It's too dangerous. If we get captured it's one thing. If you're captured, you die."

"In all fairness, I'd say it's quite likely that Rhoda would kill you too. She's absolutely insane."

"I know," Zakariah groaned, turning back to face forward.

"She killed my uncle," I confessed. I could see Zakariah's eyes widening out of the corner of my eye. "I've hardly had time even to think about it. It's all insane, Zakariah, I just can't believe it all actually happened."

"Do you want to talk about it?" A tear slipped down my cheek and plopped heavily onto my open palm.

"I don't think you'd believe me if I told you." I shook my head and keeled back to lay down once again. After a pause, Zakariah slipped from the hammock. I thought he was leaving, but rather he knelt to be at eye level with me.

"Try me," he challenged, though his eyes were kind and soft. Any tension I held in my muscles eased, my body recognizing the safety I had with him. I allowed a heavy sigh to whoosh from my lungs.

"The day after I was chosen, I visited my uncle," I began. "He hasn't been right since my mother died, his sister. The day my father died, she took his boat and tried to sail away to find a place for us to flee to. She never made it back. He was convinced that her spirit, her... ghost was trapped in the sea and haunted him."

Zakariah nodded, offering his hand for me to hold as my voice became thick with tears. I turned onto my side to face him. "I never believed him until that day. Something went *wrong* in him. He started screaming at me that the Totem was dead and that I needed to run or they'd 'steal the gift' from me.

"The next day, the Temple took him. I got to visit him, but he would only respond to my mother's name, Evelyn. I'm convinced that she possessed him. Then Rhoda executed him for heresy."

"Addie," Zakariah breathed, drawing my gaze. He cradled my head with his free hand, gently swinging the hammock to soothe me. "I'm so sorry."

"Don't apologize, it's Rhoda." I sniffed, wiping the tears from my face. I gulped, my mouth dry as if I'd swallowed sand, and calmed my breath. "We'll avenge them, all of them, eventually." Zakariah nodded, and I glanced at the alarm candle I had made. By pushing nails into a candle, they would clatter on the tin plate below and wake me as the wax melted. There was still time before we had to leave for Anyra.

"We have time," Zakariah shrugged. He glanced at the alarm and nodded.

"Will you stay with me?" I asked. I felt as a child asking her mother to sleep on the floor as she recovered from a nightmare. A soft smile came over Zakariah's lips as he stood.

"Of course." I wriggled closer to one side of the hammock, and Zakariah practically fell into the hammock beside me.

Chapter Twenty-Six: Rescue Mission

When the nail from the candle clattered onto the tin plate below, Zakariah and I rose quickly, any traces of sleep gone in an instant. The fear and excitement that had been waiting below the surface reared its head. Back to Anyra, the seat of the Totem. We pulled on our shoes and laced them tightly to be certain we would have sure footing should we need to run.

We were not the first to arrive at the rendezvous point on the western edge of the Village. Edrei stood with her back to the Village, though Anyra was far out of sight. Her shoulders were square and taut, her muscles seemingly prepped for a battle rather than a stealth mission. The horses from Kantrin were all saddled and rested, though they seemed confused as to why we were setting out in the middle of the night.

"Good evening, Kantira," I greeted her as we came to stand beside her. Her shoulders relaxed as she smiled.

"I am not your ruler, Adelaide," she corrected me.

"No, but you most certainly have my respect. Kantira is your title, though it may not be over me. I will use it to honor you." The Kantrineir shook her head, but argued no further.

"Did either of you get any rest?"

"Not enough," Zakariah answered, rubbing his eyes with his free left hand. His right was occupied holding mine.

"Could you ever get a satisfactory amount of sleep?" I chuckled, and he laughed in return.

"Never." The conversation quickly turned somber as Edrei turned to face me.

"Adelaide, before the others arrive, this is your final chance. I still think it is foolish of you to return to Anyra. Stay here, where it is safer for you." I could see the concern creasing her brow, but I held firm in my decision.

"Thank you, Edrei, but I have to do this. I'm their Gift, but I want to give them freedom rather than my own life." Edrei's dark eyes studied me, and finally she shook her head once more.

"Damn your nobility, Addie. It'll be the death of you, I swear." I smiled, and we both returned to gazing westward as footsteps approached. Caleb joined our lineup, his normally wild red hair combed away from his face. Valerie remained in bed, no doubt worrying herself away from sleep. We had tried to assure her Caleb would not be in danger.

Shortly after, Calvin and Katharine appeared hand-in-hand. The final members of the group and arguably the most important. With a nod of greeting, Edrei handed Katharine a leather bag, and she slung it over her shoulder. I assumed this contained the necessary items for the spell they would cast. My curious mind strained to arrive, eager to see them perform more magic.

"Does anyone have any final concerns?" Edrei asked, looking to each face in turn. No one made a sound, any objection held silently to their chests. My feet practically itched to be off. Edrei nodded. "Good. Onward."

We mounted the horses. Caleb took the smallest horse, Katharine and Calvin shared one, Zakariah and I another, and Edrei rode single as the leader. Our steeds trotted quietly through the woods, careful not to snap twigs or rustle bushes on our way. It was as though they knew we required stealth. The only prominent sounds came as the hoots of owls or the screeches of bats swooping overhead. Though I wasn't certain why, I continually scanned the surrounding forest for the buck I had seen on my first journey through the wood. Part of me thought he may be there, watching over us. I saw nothing.

Now knowing what direction to travel and traveling on horseback rather than foot, it took just over an hour for Anyra to come into sight. Settled down in a valley below, we could see everything from our vantage point.

"Do you know where the barrier begins?" Edrei asked, turning toward the two sorcerers. Katharine shook her head as Calvin studied the landscape.

"We'll know when we feel it," he assured us. We left our horses to graze amongst the trees and began making our way down the hillside. Just as we met the fields of crops marking Anyra's eastern border, Edrei stopped suddenly. Her hand moved to cradle her head as if it were beginning to ache, and she moved backward. As she did, she seemed to recover from the sudden wave of illness.

"I found the barrier," she announced.

"Good," Katharine agreed as she sank to one knee. She began unpacking the bag Edrei had given her, pulling out several long, draping willow branches and a corked bottle.

Curious as to how the barrier felt, I moved toward the field of corn. I put my hands out in front of me as if I could feel it, expecting to press my hands against a cold, invisible wall, but nothing came. My eyebrows furrowed as I looked back at the others. Calvin and Katharine were dousing a bundle of branches with olive oil and hadn't taken notice of me.

"Where is the barrier?" I asked, my voice hushed even though we were still about a mile from the nearest home. Zakariah stepped forward, trudging forward as though with great difficulty. Yet he remained a few feet away from me, his face growing pale as a wave of sickness came over him. He hastily drew a line in the dirt before stepping back.

"There," he answered, the color returning to his face as he took deep, calming breaths. "How did you cross it?"

"Perhaps when I became the Gift the same magic that the priests and priestesses have to come and go freely extended to me. Just like the Chosen," I shrugged, theorizing answers for the strange ability. "Or they took it off of me hoping I'd return."

"All the more reason you should not return," Edrei shot, tearing her eyes from Calvin and Katharine who were sitting facing one another with the oily branch between them. They stared, their mouths moving as they chanted under their breath, the same scene as when they modified the spell cast on Sebastian. As I studied them, I noticed that they each held fistfuls of loose soil in their hands.

As we watched, Katharine stood, taking the branch in her hand, and she moved to stand before the rough line Zakariah had drawn. Muttering her magic words, she drew the branch over the line as if painting it with the oil, then continued to draw an arch in the air.

Once the branch met the ground once again, she dropped it to the ground beside her and pressed her hands out against the barrier. Her palms seemed to press against something solid before it gave way, and she stepped through the invisible archway like a door. She smiled at me as she came to the other side.

"It worked."

I grinned in return as the other members of our troupe followed her through to portal. Something did feel strangely different now as we stood on Anyran soil. I looked to Caleb, my friend's demeanor conflicted. I could see the homesick longing in his eyes. The home where he had grown up and married the love of his life, and the home his child may never see. I clasped his hand in mine, and he smiled down at me.

"We'll change Anyra one day," I promised him, and he nodded.

"We will. But not today," he answered. I looked down at the dirt below my feet. No, not today. But hopefully sooner rather than later.

I turned to Zakariah who was staring to the north of the city at the volcano, flanked by two smaller mountains set behind it. His sister had been fed to that monster. I took his hand as well. As if just now realizing, he quickly wiped the tears from his face.

"It'll change," he said distantly. We began making our way toward Anyra, and our minds became focused on the task at hand. Caleb had given us assignments earlier that afternoon of where each of us were to go. There were several households that Caleb and the other spies had not yet reached with knowledge of the Village. We must tell them now, and have them spread it to those we could trust with the information.

As we reached Anyra, the city had fallen into a deep, silent sleep. We split off in different directions. I made my way to a home just a few streets away from where I had lived with Caleb and Valerie. The scene was somehow simultaneously familiar yet foreign.

I gently rapped on a downstairs window, continually looking over my shoulders for any sign of trouble. A lamp flickered to life inside, and a woman's face appeared in the window. I recognized her, Eliza, the woman that ran my favorite restaurant. Her eyes widened at the sight of me, and she pointed me toward the door.

Silently, I crept along the edge of the house until I reached the front entryway, and Eliza pulled me inside. She put a finger to her lips, seemingly already knowing something I did not. I remained silent as she beckoned me inside. I followed her, padding silently on the wooden floor. Her close-cropped hair reminded me of Edrei's, though Eliza's was fine and so light that it may as well have been white in the silvery moonlight slanting through the windows. She led me down into the cellar by candlelight, and once we had mounted the steps, she began to speak.

"Adelaide, what in the Totem's name are you doing back in Anyra?!" she hissed, throwing a glance over her shoulder. "The sacrifice is meant to be in just two days!"

"I know!" I defended, matching her hushed tone. "I joined a group of refugees. We're fleeing farther from Anyra and wanted to rescue as many as we could."

"Noble. Stupid, but noble." We reached the dirt floor of the cellar, Eliza's candle throwing jagged shadows around the room. I swore I saw eyes peering out from the darkness. "Lights up."

In quick succession, more candles flickered to life in underground room, illuminating a surprisingly large group of people. I recognized the baker along with his husband and their three children, the smallest curled in his arms fast asleep. Several teenage girls around the age of eligibility sat huddled together in the corner, one boasting a swollen belly. I was surprised to see that not one, but two engagement circlets hung around her neck. Many more were present, about thirty people in total crammed into the small space.

"You inspired us, Addie," Eliza explained. As I looked to her, her eyes seemed to glow with excitement and anger in the dim light. "There are dozens of safehouses scattered across Anyra housing upwards of two hundred people. People that want out from under the Temple's control. No more sacrifices."

"No, no more sacrifices," I agreed. "You all are getting out tonight, there is an entire village of people that said no and left Anyra's control. There are six of us here tonight to spread the word of the safe haven."

I heard sniffling, and I turned to find several of the young girls in tears. I began shaking my head, but quickly realized these tears were not fearful or angry. They were tears of hope. The young lady with child stood with some difficulty, her stomach looking as though it were ready to burst. She swallowed hard before she spoke, and I saw that her face was wet with tears.

"Thank you," she said, her voice choked with emotion. I turned to give her my full attention, and she stepped forward. Her movements seemed pained, but her jaw was set with determination. "My husband Thomas was a priest of the Temple, but he tried to leave. Rhoda executed him for insubordination against the Totem because he abandoned the Temple and his service. I would do anything to bring her down. Thank you for leading us." Shakily, she opened her arms, and I gladly accepted her. Her trembling form collapsed into me, and her stomach pressed against mine. I could feel how tense her entire body was, sweat slicking her skin.

"Kaylin, you need to rest, please," another girl called, and when I looked to her, I realized the girls were probably sisters. They shared the same red hair and fair, freckled complexions. I slowly was able to piece together the truth and pulled back to look into Kaylin's face.

"Are you in labor?" I demanded, holding her by her shoulders. A bead of sweat ran down her face and clung to the tip of her nose, her eyes screwed shut in pain.

"She is, but we don't know what to do," her sister answered.

"Oh, for the Totem's sake, why didn't you tell me?!" Eliza cried, breaking the quiet in panic. She rushed forward and felt Kaylin's stomach. The contraction seemed to pass and she relaxed. "It's early, the baby hasn't dropped lower yet."

"Alright, time to move," I decided. "Eliza, take her upstairs." I turned to the sister, and flicked my head toward the steps. "Go with her. The rest of you, prepare and leave before first light. Move following the rise of the moon, either you'll find the Village or the Villagers will find you. No fewer than three to a group, and no more than six. Leave in shifts, but be out by sunrise."

"Thank you, Adelaide," Solomon, the baker's husband said. I shook my head.

"Don't thank me," I corrected. "Just get out of the city safely." I turned and thundered up the steps after the three women. Eliza had outfitted both girls with heavy trousers, hiking boots, and thick jackets. Another contraction had begun, and Kaylin was leaning against a wall with her sister for support.

"Eliza," I hissed, and she turned to me. "The others downstairs will be leaving in shifts, they'll be gone by sunrise. Are there others in Anyra that are trustworthy, that disagree with the Temple?" Before I had even finished the question, Eliza had begun to nod.

"Dozens, and those are only the ones I know of."

"Good. Spread the word of the Village, a safe haven. Tell them to move under the moon's path, only leaving in the secret of night," I instructed her. Out of the corner of my eye, I watched as Kaylin's pain began to ease. We had to move quickly before another contraction began and before they worsened. "By the time the sacrifice comes around, Anyra will be a ghost town."

"Absolutely, thank you so much Adelaide," Eliza said.

"No, you don't need to thank me. Now, Kaylin and...?" I continued, furrowing my brow at the other girl.

"Brenia," the girl answered, "I'm Kaylin's sister."

"Brenia," I nodded. "We have to get Kaylin out of the city before the contractions worsen. Kaylin, I promise you're going to be alright." Hardly able to speak, Kaylin simply nodded, her eyes wide with fear and pain. I slung her arm over my shoulder, and Brenia copied with her other arm. "We're going to walk, quick as we can, alright? Can you do that, Kaylin?"

"I can do it," she answered immediately, although she didn't seem entirely confident in herself. "I can do it."

"Yes, you can," I agreed. Eliza opened the door, and I steered our strange, waddling group toward the forest. Luckily, Edrei had assigned me a house on the edge of town should I need to make a hasty getaway. I made a mental note to thank her for that when we met once more. We had almost made it to the cornfield when Kaylin stumbled.

"Woah, alright, Kaylin how are you feeling?" I asked as Brenia and I kept her upright. "Another contraction?" Between great, heaving breaths, Kaylin nodded. I glanced up at the moon, which was about to reach its apex. We had plenty of time, but the sooner we could reach the meeting point, the better.

"Just a few more steps into the field for cover, then you can rest a moment." Brenia and I marched forward, practically dragging Kaylin with us. Once we were a few feet into the cornfield, I settled Kaylin onto the ground with Brenia sitting behind her. Kaylin leaned back into her sister's chest for support, cradling her stomach.

I stood to keep watch, but the corn was too tall for me to see over. Brenia muttered encouragement into her sister's ear, doing her best to lull her sister into calm and keep her quiet. I caught the girl's eye and silently nodded my thanks. She gave a small smile in return. I listened for footsteps, my hand poised over the dagger in my belt should I hear any sign of trouble. None came.

As soon as the contraction passed, Kaylin released a heavy sigh. She nodded up at me, and I reached down to help her up. Brenia and I resumed our positions on either side of her, ensuring her footing was steady as we began to move once more. Kaylin seemed determined to keep up pace, though her feet were shuffling with the pain and discomfort.

"You're doing incredibly, Kaylin," I commended her in a whisper. "I can't believe we're moving this quickly while you're in labor."

"Me either," she heaved, a small smile of pride flicking over her face. "But how much farther?" I chuckled, but I knew this must be harrowing for her.

"Just through the cornfield."

We made it to the edge, the line Zakariah had made in the dirt faded from the breeze though still visible, as I knew to look for it. We were the first of the rescue group to arrive.

"This is it," I announced, and just as I did, Kaylin gave a short, broken cry. My eyes widened, the sense of safety I'd had gone in an instant. Brenia and I lowered her back into the position from before, settling her with her back leant against her sister.

"We're outside of Anyra's borders?" Brenia asked, her hands gently working Kaylin's shoulders. I nodded, searching for any sign of the others. I hoped beyond hope to see Edrei or Katharine moving through the corn.

"We're out of Anyra," I confirmed. "We'll be safer once we reach the Village. Katharine is a healer, and she should be here any minute." However, it was her husband that arrived first. He had with him three elderly men and women, hobbling along with canes over the rough ground.

"What in the Totem's name is going on here?" he asked as he surveyed the scene.

"This is Kaylin, she's in labor, and her sister Brenia acting as midwife," I said flippantly. I bounced from foot to foot, trying my best not to worry the sisters. "Do you know how to help her? Or when Katharine will be here?"

"Totem's mercy," he swore under his breath. "I know a little, I can ease the pain. The others will be here any minute now." I stood back should one of those in Calvin's group need aid, and Calvin dove to his knees beside the young mother.

"Hello, my name's Calvin, I'm here to help," he promised her. She nodded, hardly able to speak. I had a feeling it wasn't truly the pain causing such a state, but more so the fear crippling her. "I have healing magic. I can cast a spell to ease the pain. Not get rid, but ease. Is that alright?" Kaylin nodded vigorously, her teeth clenched so hard I feared they would break.

A rustling sounded behind me, and I turned toward it preparing to defend the others if I must. Caleb and Zakariah emerged, no others in tow with them. I breathed a sigh of relief.

"Just Edrei and Katharine left," I muttered. Zakariah's eyes had gone as wide as the moon itself, staring at the scene behind me.

"Is she alright? Is she having a baby?!" he hissed, glancing between me and Kaylin.

"Yes, but it will be alright, Katharine and Edrei should be back soon," I nodded, glancing back to see Calvin holding his hand over Kaylin's stomach. The light, sweet scent of raspberry met my nose, and I saw torn up leaves scattered over her swollen belly, and water had been spattered over her shirt as well. Calvin chanted, and her body seemed to relax as he spoke his magic.

Soon enough, Edrei arrived, followed quickly by Katharine who was leading a couple and their two small children. No one had even said a word to Katharine before she saw the situation unfolding before her. She dived down to the ground on Kaylin's other side, across from her husband. I didn't even have to explain for her to take action.

"Good work, everyone," Edrei commended. "We need to move, and now. Adelaide and Caleb, we'll take these people. Zakariah, stay with Katharine and Calvin, help them however they need." We each nodded, eager to return home and leave Anyra far behind.

Silently, we began to move. I loaded two of the three elders onto my horse, the other keeping a hand on the horse's flank for support. Edrei had also given up her horse to the two children and the mother. I saw people trudging toward the Village all around us. Soon enough, I had a parade of Anyrans behind me, heading toward home and safety.

Chapter Twenty-Seven: Comfort

The moon winked between the leaves as I walked, wandering aimlessly in the forest around the Village. It was late, far too late for me to be awake. Yet sleep had eluded me. Fear and worry that I couldn't name prodded me, keeping sleep at bay as I laid awake in my hammock. Finally, I had risen.

A smile crossed my lips as I conjured a happy memory from the day. Kaylin had given birth to a healthy baby girl after sixteen hours of labor. She asked for me by name after her daughter had arrived, and she asked me to hold the child. Nervous as I was, I accepted, and I held the baby girl gingerly in my arms. I felt they were too rough and strong to hold something as precious as this child. Kaylin had named her Adelaide after me. I hardly felt worthy of such an honor.

I traced circles and patterns in the dirt with my boots, trying and failing to tire myself out. The pit in my stomach could not be filled with food or water, could not be walked off or distracted away. I had no idea what could soothe the fear and restlessness. Perhaps my deer would make another appearance and lull me to sleep. A different benevolent creature found me.

As I walked, footsteps began approaching from the direction of the Village. I suspected to see Edrei or perhaps Caleb or Gwen, but I gripped the hilt of my dagger all the same. It would be just like Rhoda to send someone to find me even after Sebastian's failed attempt at capture. With the sacrifice day approaching, she must be growing desperate.

Rather, Zakariah emerged from the brush, his eyes shining by the light of the moon. I softened, relaxing as he smiled kindly at me. We spoke no words, simply gazing at one another. He seemed to understand the turmoil in my mind without my needing to express it. I don't think I could have spoken it aloud if I tried.

He stepped forward, wrapping me tenderly in his arms. I melted into his touch, craving the security and safety of his embrace. Somehow, even though I had known him less than a month, he was invitingly familiar, like coming home after a long journey and falling asleep in one's own bed. He had taken up that role as friend and protector so easily.

My eyes stung with tears as Zakariah pressed his soft, gentle lips to my forehead, his hand running down my hair. I gripped him tightly to me, in desperate need of the rest he brought. He seemed to know exactly what I needed. He kept one arm around me, turning back toward the Village and walking me back. I balled my fist in his shirt as if something would snatch him from me, my only rock.

He walked me back to my tree and followed me up the ladder to my bungalow. When we reached the landing, I dove into him once more, clutching him to myself. Guilt and fear and joy and desire swirled in me, confusing and frightening me beyond my wits. The tears finally spilled out onto my cheeks as Zakariah began to pull away. I pulled him back into myself.

"Please stay," I begged him, my voice hoarse. Those were the first words I had spoken in hours.

"I was hoping you'd say that," he smiled. A new yet familiar light had risen behind his eyes, and I felt the same thing burning in me. I opened the door and pulled him inside after me, needing him near me. He closed the door behind him and turned to face me. I pressed myself into his arms again, and he reciprocated without hesitation.

"I can't stop thinking about fire," I confessed. "With the Seers' visions and the burnt hair. I just..."

"I know, Addie," Zakariah shushed me. "But we'll protect you."

"I can't let anyone else die for me." I looked up at him, my heart pounding in my chest. Though not only fear hummed there. His features were cast in a beautiful, silver light, and the glow of the moon seemed to live in his eyes. "I don't think I'm going to make it back to Kantrin."

"I won't let them hurt you, Adelaide," Zakariah promised me. He took my shoulders in firm hands, though he remained as gentle as always. I allowed my hands to drift up to his face, taking his head in my hands. I hesitated.

"C-can I...?

"Yes," he answered quickly, and our lips met with a fervent desire.

Chapter Twenty-Eight: The Raid

"Adelaide, wake up! Wake up!" The voice was Zakariah's. He was frantic, vigorously shaking me by my shoulders. I shot up in the hammock and searched around with wide eyes, panic rising in my throat.

"What!?" A chill passed over me, but warmth radiated from Zakariah's body beside mine. He stood beside me, halfway dressed and his hair mussed on his head. Usually, sleep hung around him like fog after he woke, but not now. Panic had driven every ounce of drowsiness from him.

"There's shouting outside. Something about Rhoda!" he cried. Terror struck me from his words, any traces of sleep instantly gone.

"Why are they still searching!?" I demanded as I leapt out of the hammock. I searched through the pile on the floor, forced to quickly dress and flee once again.

"Because they're desperate," Zakariah answered. I pulled on my boots and shrugged into my jacket as quickly as I could, tossing a few items into my knapsack. As I turned to rush out the door, screams met our ears, causing Zakariah and I to freeze. Terror shot through me. They were here. Without another word, we darted down the rope ladder as quickly as possible and searched the ground for the source of the screams.

Villagers ran in every direction, gathering what necessities they could as sound rose from the farthest side of the Village. They were not coming directly from Anyra. Somehow, they had found their way here from the south rather than due west where Anyra sat in its shallow valley. And there were screams. The Villagers were in a panic, rushing to flee before the small battalion from the city. They would stop at nothing to get to me. As I searched for my sister and friends, I heard the grating, shrill voice of the High Priestess herself.

Rhoda was with them, screaming at the top of her lungs amidst the chaos. "Where is she!? Where is the Gift!?" I snatched Zakariah's hand in mine. People were everywhere, running and shouting, and the invaders from Anyra were tearing through like bulls in their search. They had no qualms destroying everything in their path. Wood splintered with the blow of their hammers, people screamed as they were snatched and questioned. Most were let go with nothing more than a few bruises.

A pair of twin shrieks met my ears, and I turned to find a priest pinning Willow and Orchid to the forest floor. Orchid was screaming with all her might, hiding her face in her hands. Luckily, she wore long sleeves, so the priest's skin was separated from hers. Willow, however, was feeding the fury right back. She shouted into the man's face, unwilling to cower before him. Every questioning demand he threw was met with fierce backlash as Willow demanded he free her sister.

"Zakariah, the twins!" I told him. As he set his sights on the attack playing out, his jaw became grimly set. He didn't speak. With a growl of rage, he charged forward, barreling into the man and knocking him off the girls. I quickly followed, my feet striking the ground with great force. The priest and Zakariah grappled in the dirt as I pulled Willow and Orchid to their feet.

Brazenly, Willow joined Zakariah, landing a surprising blow to the priest's stomach. Orchid was sobbing, and I pulled her into myself, careful not to touch her skin, as her sister and Zakariah easily overcame their adversary. He was breathing, but a swollen bruise adorned his eye. I could hardly tear my eyes away from the gruesome sight. This shouldn't be happening.

"Girls!" the twins' mother sprinted up, and Orchid dove into her as Zakariah placed a protective arm around Willow. "We have to go, come on now!"

As they ran, I stood once more, searching the crowd. Finally, I found the one I was looking for. I ran silently through the madness, sprinting to where my sister lay motionless on the ground. She was frozen, helpless at the sound of Rhoda's voice. The voice that had tormented her for weeks and most likely would for the rest of her life. I reached her at the exact moment Xander did, our touch waking her from her stupor.

"Addie, what's happening!?" she demanded, clutching me by my shoulders.

"Rhoda is here for me. She's not here for you, once she gets what she wants, she'll be gone." Xander hefted Gwen into his arms, and she cowered into his chest, shuddering with each word from Rhoda as they drew steadily nearer.

"You need to move. Go, get out!" I instructed, pushing the pair away from the carnage.

"But..." Xander argued.

"Just go!" The young man looked down at Gwen as Landon charged toward us, bellowing with the force of the forge.

"Run! Addie, they're coming for you!" Landon stumbled to stop, his chest heaving from his sprint. "We have to go. Now." Xander gently placed Gwen in Landon's arms, his face grim and jaw set. Confused, but lacking the will to argue, Landon took her trembling form gladly.

"Get her to safety," he instructed, as Gwen shook her head.

"Xander, what are you doing?" she begged, tears glistening in her eyes.

"I'm keeping my promise," he explained. He kissed her deeply, their tears mixing on her cheeks. "I love you!"

"Xander, please!" she screamed as he sprinted toward the sounds of Rhoda's cries.

"Alexander, don't!" I shouted. He paid no heed. I moved to run after him, planning to tackle him to the ground, but Zakariah's strong grip on my arms stopped me.

"He's made his choice, we have to go," he begged, trying to pry me away. "Landon, go!"

Landon followed his orders but stopped after a few steps as a horrifying sound met our ears. The noise was hardly human, a guttural shriek accompanied by a deafening blast. Tree branches snapped and leaves shuddered as something flew through the air toward us. My stomach plummeted to my feet as I realized it was a body.

"Xander!" I cried. Some impossible force had blown Xander back, and he rolled like a ragdoll across the ground. He landed at my and Zakariah's feet.

A wordless screech left Gwen's lips, and Landon began his flight anew, carrying her away from the oncoming sorceress, her lover dead at my feet. I nearly gagged at the scent as I fell to my knees. Rhoda's magic had killed him instantly, singeing every strand of hair from his head. His skin was charred and cracked, and thick, dark blood oozed from the wounds. His eyes were black, nothing but burnt, sightless orbs staring up at me. I screamed without meaning to do so.

Zakariah dragged me to my feet, pulling me away until I regained myself and sprinted with him, my hand clutching desperately to his. I heard Rhoda's screams behind me, mingling with the cries of the Villagers once again. She had seen me, and she would stop at nothing until I was in her grasp.

Finally, somewhat recovered from the gruesome sight of Xander's corpse, I took in the scene around me. I sighted Sebastian coming out of Caleb and Zakariah's workshop. Immediately, the anger that had been quelled for nearly a month bubbled up again, doubled now with the death of my would-be brother-in-law and the destruction of my new home. With a gasp, Zakariah let go of my hand as if just now realizing he was holding it.

"There he is," I growled, indicating to Sebastian. My voice was hardly audible in the cacophony surrounding us.

"Sebastian?" Zakariah asked, following my gaze. I nodded grimly. He shook his head, reminding himself of his mission. "Addie, come on, we have to get you out of here." Hesitating, I nodded.

"Let's go." Zakariah and I darted away, running the opposite direction of Rhoda's booming voice. Upon the Anyrans arrival, the Villagers had scattered. They had grabbed what little they could and fled, knowing the safety of the Village had been compromised. I spotted Valerie and Caleb ahead of us, heads ducked to avoid being recognized. I broke away from Zakariah, sprinting to catch up with them.

"Are you two alright?" I demanded, looking them over for injuries.

"We're fine," Caleb assured us. "You have to go! They'll tear the Village apart looking for you!" My shoulders fell as the realization dawned on me. They would do anything; they would kill and maim to get to me. Rhoda already had.

"Almost everyone else is already out, we have to get you to safety," Valerie assured me.

"Then let's go."

"Lass!" I turned to find Calvin and Katharine sprinting toward us. "Why are you still here?"

"I had to get everyone out," I mumbled, my gaze transfixed on the form of Rhoda amidst the trees.

"We'll never get you out in time," Katharine heaved, out of breath from running. She and Calvin shared a tense gaze, seemingly reading one another's thoughts. Perhaps they were.

"I'll buy some time," he promised. "Get her and the rest out, as far as you can!"

"No!" Katharine pulled Calvin back by his jacket, gripping him with ferocity. "You're no match for her!"

"I know," Calvin nodded. The two shared a deep, passionate kiss, knowing it could be their last. Tears began to streak Katharine's cheeks even before they broke apart. He turned, marching toward the High Priestess, hurling insults and spells as he moved. Katharine allowed herself one heaving sob before she shook her head and moved.

"Come on you mite-ridden, slimy old hag!" I heard Calvin shout, but my attention was focused on Katharine. She took a waterskin from her hip and poured it over my head before I could protest. The cold shocked me, and a strangled cry escaped my lips. Before I could demand to know what she was doing, Katharine gripped me by my shoulders, muttering words I would never understand. I had no clue what the spell was for but I trusted her.

"Where is Adelaide?" Rhoda asked, easily drowning out Calvin's slew of curses, both magical and not. "I have something for her." Katharine finished her spell in time to turn and see what was happening. Zakariah pulled me further away, but I kept stealing glances over my shoulder.

"You'll never have her," Calvin growled, hurling his light magic at her. Thick, black smoke swirled around him, concealing his body from Rhoda's attacks. She spoke no words, so I had no clue how her magic worked. She pounded the staff on the ground, and streaks of light flew amidst Calvin's shroud of smoke. She hadn't scored a proper hit since she didn't know where to aim. Still, her confidence was unfazed.

"You know this is futile," she admonished him.

"You think I care?"

With that Rhoda, extended her staff toward him, and a bolt of lightning streaked through the cloudless sky. A strangled cry escaped from Katharine as a metallic taste filled my mouth. I screamed, but no sound came as Calvin crumpled to the ground, as he was not charred and burnt as Xander had been. We stopped cold, our flight forgotten when Calvin fell.

The smoke cleared, and Calvin's form lay on the forest floor. Even from a distance, I could see his chest heaving for breath. Katharine stood, taking fistfuls of dirt in her hands, and more words flew. As she spoke, more of the black smoke escaped her mouth, giving her the appearance of a dragon breathing fire. The tendrils of smog crawled across the ground like hands, and they wrapped themselves around Calvin. By some miracle, he was not dead. The smoke retrieved him, carrying him gently into Katharine's arms.

Rhoda didn't seem to care. After shrugging the brief duel off, she snapped her fingers, and two priests brought forth a prisoner. Had Zakariah not been holding me, I would have run into Rhoda's trap without a second thought. The two priests shoved Old Delilah onto the ground beside Rhoda, though she was not bound in any way. She lifted her head, searching her surroundings for me.

"What are they doing with her?" I asked, my words hardly a whisper.

"Chosen Gift of the Totem!" Rhoda called, not even using my name. I was nothing but a slab of meat to her. "Come back and fulfill your duty to your people. To your surrogate mother, your Old Delilah."

"Adelaide, please!" Delilah burst out, interrupting Rhoda. This drew a glare from the High Priestess, but she paused to hear her words. "Please, just do as they ask! Your people will all die if you keep hiding! The Totem will strike us with famine and disease! She'll never be satiated!"

"She is right!" Rhoda smiled. "You have to the count of ten."

"Till what? The count of ten till what?" I fretted, looking between Zakariah and Katharine as the count began. My words were silent though, and I realized what Katharine's spell had done. She had hidden me, my voice silent and my body shrouded by her magic. I glanced over my shoulder to find Valerie forcefully dragging Caleb away from the scene, moving silently through the brush. The truth dawned on me just as Rhoda reached nine.

I turned back around as the final number left Rhoda's lips, and a flash of silver glinted in the morning sun. Red stained the dirt, and a horrifying, gurgling scream fell from Delilah's lips. Zakariah clapped a hand over my mouth, although he didn't need to mute the scream I wanted to make in response, though it was silent anyway. I watched as Delilah collapsed to the ground, her white hair stained red from the pool of blood below her. I couldn't move. They may have found me had Zakariah not slung me over his shoulder and sprinted deeper into the wood, Katharine using her magic to carry Calvin following closely behind.

I STARED INTO THE CRACKLING fire before me. Just as when we were children, Gwen and Caleb sat on either side of me, tears wetting our cheeks. My breath hitched every now and again, though my face was unchanged. Three taps on my shoulder drew me away from the flame, and I turned to see Zakariah behind me. He offered three small loaves of bread, one for each of us, and I took them gladly.

Edrei sat on the opposite side of the fire. She was no doubt exhausted after taking extensive care to ensure that all the Villagers were present and accounted for. All but one. Delilah and Xander had been retrieved after Rhoda and her Anyrans retreated. Although he was hesitant to leave me, Zakariah had gone with a few others. They returned with shovels gathered from the garden sheds and the two bodies wrapped in torn, muddied sheets salvaged from the destroyed bungalows.

Gwen had wanted to draw the sheets back and look upon their faces one final time. I knew that Xander had almost none of his former features left. Looking at him and trying to kiss his forehead farewell would only have broken her more. We lit torches and held a makeshift funeral. We had buried Xander and Delilah beneath a pair of old oak trees. Katharine had magically carved their names and a few words into the trunks.

Gwen was still sobbing at the loss of her two loves. My suspicion had been confirmed and my heart broken as she selected a much younger oak beside that of Xander. She had asked Katharine to carve into that tree as well. "The child of Alexander Montenay and Gwendolyn Lanasting, gone before she arrived." Gwen and I had sobbed for a great while between those two trees.

Katharine had set up a meager cot for her husband, and he slept peacefully now that she had worked her healing spells. I couldn't begin to know what she had done, how she had performed the magic. But it had worked. His skin was pink with the flush of life. No one would ever have guessed he had been mere inches from death. It was a miracle that he had survived. Though I was certain she must be exhausted, Katharine had also helped those that had sustained injuries during the siege, dressing wounds and even administering sutures and passing out healing salves.

"We must accelerate our plans," Edrei announced. She produced the map which she had managed to save, smoothing it out on the ground. "We can't stay here long. I have no doubt they'll keep searching."

As she spoke, I let my gaze wander over the people around me. These strong and sturdy people of Anyra. Those who took a stand and said no, left all they had known because they knew it was wrong to stay. Pride and fury bloomed in my chest as I looked into each face.

Orchid and Willow had not left their parents, staying connected at all times. As far as I was aware, Orchid had not stopped crying. Valerie was huddled into Caleb's shoulder, both of them resting protective hands over her stomach. I turned to place a kiss on Gwen's forehead.

I reached behind me, and Zakariah's hand quickly found mine. I squeezed and he returned it. I replicated his triple tap, hoping he understood its intent. Ramona sat behind Edrei, also staring into the flames. No doubt she was thinking of her vision from reading me. A gift that carries a gift of her own. I finally understood what she meant.

"Adelaide, you must leave immediately with the first wave of refugees," Edrei rattled off, formulating her plan. I cut her off.

"I can't," I argued, turning my attention to Ramona. I saw pieces of Delilah behind her eyes. I couldn't allow Rhoda and her brutes to harm these people anymore. Without another word, I stood and began my dreadful march toward the ruined Village and Anyra beyond it.

I glanced back at Caleb, and he seemingly read my thoughts through my eyes. Through her protests, he pulled Valerie away. I stormed forward as Zakariah followed after me. He tried to pull me back but couldn't force me to swerve from my path. Edrei understood and remained where she sat. Landon, knowing why I must act, took over holding Gwen in his arms.

"Adelaide please!" Zakariah screamed, darting to stand in front of me. "I can't let you walk into your death!" I smiled at him as a tear spilled down his cheek. I placed a hand on his face, and he closed his eyes at my touch.

"I can't let them hurt you," I replied. He gave a half-hearted chuckle.

"You can't let them hurt *me*, now can you?" He should have been smiling as he said this, the jaunty grin so familiar and comforting. Yet now his face was drawn. His jaw was set in anger and determination, immobile. He would not allow me to walk into the jaws of death.

"No, I can't let them hurt *you,* Zakariah," I confirmed. I quickly dove into him, hugging him close for a brief moment before moving on toward the Village. The broken scream and the thud of Zakariah's knees against the dirt were dull and muffled. I walked alone, screams and sobs fading behind me.

I sobbed as well as I walked away from the people I loved, my sister, my friends, the man that I had quickly come to love. Yet I knew in my heart what must be done. This was my gift to them: life. A chance to get away and make something better. Before I realized it, I found myself entering the ransacked Village. The Anyrans had returned. I assumed they hoped the Villagers would begin trickling back to their home, and me along with them.

"Adelaide!" My ears perked up at the sound of my name. I groaned as I glared toward the source of the voice. Sebastian ran toward me, and I didn't have time to react before he snatched me into his arms.

"Let me go!" I shrieked, thrashing violently to wrestle away from him. I couldn't tell if he was hugging me in relief or trying to capture me. Perhaps it was a strange mixture of the two. "Get off me!" I pitched my head forward, and my forehead connected with Sebastian's nose, causing blood to gush from his nostrils.

"Leave her alone!" Zakariah bellowed. In a flash, he was there, and he tore Sebastian away from me. Pulling back, Zakariah landed a hard blow across Sebastian's face. A side of Sebastian I had never seen before seemed to surface. His face became dull as if he were used to the pain. Gritting his teeth, Sebastian reeled back and returned the blow. The pair began to brawl as I hesitated. I turned toward where the High Priestess stood.

"Rhoda!" I cried, my stomach wrenching with the word. It was as if time froze. Sebastian and Zakariah stopped, and the Anyrans relaxed with the relief of knowing the Totem's bloodlust would be quenched. I walked up to Rhoda who was calm now as opposed to earlier in the day. She didn't even speak a word to me. I was nothing but a piece of meat to be thrown to the dogs.

A single nod from Rhoda, and two priests seized me, forcing me to my knees and wrenching my arms behind my back. My knapsack was torn from my shoulders, followed quickly by my jacket. I felt exposed and vulnerable, the chill of the air prickling my skin. I couldn't contain my cries of pain as they jerked my body into submission.

"Don't you *dare* touch her!" Zakariah shouted, moving to sprint toward me.

"Zakariah, no!" I cast a glance over my shoulder, tears glinting in my eyes. The twisted expression of pain on his face said all, but he said no more. Rather, he gave Sebastian on last shove away from me and darted into the bracken. I heard him crashing through the brush, growing faint and distant. A priest moved to follow, but Rhoda held up a hand. She had her prize. Moments later, an echoing scream sounded in the distance, guttural and grief-stricken.

"We shall find the other traitors after tomorrow's events," she promised, gazing in the direction Zakariah had disappeared. The priest, a tall man with a young face, seemed relieved. I recognized the bruise on his eye, and I realized Zakariah had already bested this particular priest once before.

Sebastian righted himself and approached to stand beside Rhoda. She reached into her robes and drew out several small coils of rope in order to bind me. My eyes grew wide, and I uselessly shook my head. Sebastian accepted them after a moment of hesitation, and he moved behind me.

Sebastian began his wretched process of tying me. I felt like an animal being prepared for slaughter. I suppose in their eyes, I was.

Rather than bind my hands where the priests held them, Sebastian first bound my ankles together so that I couldn't run.

"You're a monster," I growled, my eyes unfocused and my vision swimming. I felt the rough texture of the twine as he wrapped it around my wrists, tying it into a tight knot.

"I don't have a choice, Addie," he defended himself.

"Don't call me that!" I demanded, the sudden rise in volume surprising my captors. He didn't say another word. He moved on to my elbows, tying one end of the rope around each of them so that I could hardly move my arms. The priests wrestled me to my feet, linked so closely together that I struggled to keep my balance. Sebastian knelt down and tied my knees together, pulling the rope as tight as he could. I feared my feet would lose all blood supply.

I felt his hands withdraw and then the warmth and pressure of his all too familiar touch appeared on my waist, surprising me. I jerked away, suddenly fearful of what he may do. I did not know who he was anymore. Unable to move my legs, I fell with a heavy thud to the ground, resting on my side. The sideways image of Zakariah hiding behind a tree stifling his sobs nearly broke my heart.

"Come along, now," Rhoda ordered, calling to all the people she brought. "We have many preparations to make for tomorrow." Two of the priests lifted me from the ground and threw me into the back of Rhoda's carriage, separate from the riding cabin. At least I didn't have to look at Sebastian or Rhoda for the duration of the trip.

After a short but bumpy ride back to Anyra, the cabinet I had been held in was opened. Light flooded in, causing me to flinch as hands pulled me out of the carriage. There was no sound aside from the footsteps on the cold marble as the priests carried me up the steps into the Temple. Rather than up into the Sanctuary, I was taken down a set of stairs to the dungeon and held in a cell below the main floor.

I was tossed onto the cold stone floor, and the iron bars were slammed in my face. They failed to untie me, so I couldn't move other than wriggling so I sat up against the wall. I had nothing aside from a pile of straw in one corner and a bucket in the other. Whether it was for water or excrement, I was unsure. I couldn't sleep during the long hours of the night, and I was haunted by thoughts of the past Gifts that stayed in this cell awaiting their death.

As my eyes adjusted to the darkness, I got a better look at my surroundings. Strands of strawberry blonde hair littered the floor, and my stomach twisted. This was the exact cell that had held Gwen before her punishment. The light of the full moon filtered through the barred window, illuminating the figure of Sebastian.

"Adelaide," he called in a hushed whisper.

"I'm not sleeping, and there's no one else here," I commented. I would not play any games. Sebastian stepped closer to the bars, looking ghastly in the pale moonlight. "What do you want?" He settled himself on the floor, placing a hand on the bars.

"I wanted to apologize," he began.

"Don't bother!" I shot, cutting him off. He flinched at my words. "You're already going to kill me, don't try to make it better. You can't." He paused.

"I know," he ceded. "But I had to say it. I haven't treated you well. The Temple took over everything." I remained speechless. I didn't want his words, his begging for forgiveness. "Rhoda killed my father."

I gasped, another crack forming in my heart. I had known Theodore very briefly, but he was a good man. He had helped us in our time of need. He was not the horrid figure Sebastian's mother had painted him to be.

"I'm starting to see that the Totem and the Temple are not what I thought they were. What I've gone through isn't right," Sebastian rationalized. I glared at him but didn't speak. He was not the one sentenced to a gruesome death. "I was wrong, Addie. The Temple is wrong. I wish things were different."

"Then change them!" I shouted, making him jump with surprise. "Free me, right now, and we can escape. You're not powerless!"

"I *am* powerless," Sebastian argued. "It's too late now. There's no changing it." He stood, but paused for a moment. "You have the right to know," he said, seemingly reminding himself. "Your uncle and my father are buried beneath an oak tree on the western side of the volcano." With that, Sebastian walked away, dragging his feet with grief and remorse. I balked with the information, but I regained my voice quickly.

"Sebastian, stop! You can fix this!" I shrieked. But he mounted the steps and did not return.

Chapter Twenty-Nine: Preparations

I startled awake as heavy footfalls trod down the stairs. It felt as though I had only just fallen asleep, though it was not a restful slumber. My body ached from the cold stone floor, my skin rubbed raw from the binds holding me almost completely still. The priests unlocked my cell, not even acknowledging me.

"What now?" I asked. The two young priests hardly looked at me. "Alright, my beliefs confirmed. I'm nothing more than a piece of meat to be thrown to the dogs, am I? Not to you, not to your Temple." The two boys looked at each other before clasping me under my arms and dragging me out of my cell. "Not to your false Totem." They stopped cold and exchanged a glance. I was unsure of whether they knew that the Totem was a fiction or not. They didn't let it bother them for long.

I would have fought, but the bounds were still so tight that I couldn't move other than to writhe in their grip. As we reached the steps, I attempted to brace my feet against them, but my ankles had become weak and numb from being immobile. Just as the Temple wanted, I was powerless. The priests carried me up the two flights of stairs into the Sanctuary, settling me on the floor at the Totem's feet before retreating out of the room.

I gazed up at the statue, cold and dead just as the Totem herself. The people of Anyra worshipped nothing. I would die for nothing. No, not nothing. I would die for the survivors. For the people like me who said no to the Temple, the ones who fought back. I would die for Caleb, for Valerie and the child she carried. I would die for

Gwendolyn. I would die for Edrei and the generation she would lead. For Willow and Orchid and the history they would write. I would die for Zakariah. And still, I felt something so wrong in my stomach.

I lost the will to fight back as the bonds were cut away from me. I didn't have the strength to run, the blood finally rushing back to my extremities as I collapsed. The sensation of pins and needles pricking at my skin engulfed nearly my entire body, and I cringed as it persisted. For once in my life, the only way to win was to do nothing.

"Good morning, my dear Gift," Rhoda greeted me, her staff clicking as she entered the room. She came to stand between me and the statue, and I stared at her feet. The rough garnet staff came down right before my eyes, and I could see every imperfection in the stone. "It is sacrifice day," the High Priestess crooned. "Are you ready?"

Rhoda's wicked grin came into my field of vision as she leaned down to look into my face. Her eyes were nearly black as coal, dead and lifeless and so much older than they should be. She was a thief, stealing life, stealing time that should not be hers. How old was she truly? How many lifetimes stolen from the innocent girls of Anyra?

"Damn you," I groaned, unable to sling out my arm and punch her as I wished I could. Rather, I had to fight with my words. I stared into those cold eyes, unchanging and merciless. Unfazed, she tutted and shook her head.

"That's no way for a young lady to speak, Adelaide." She stood and tapped her staff twice on the ground. Hands grasped my arms, and they pulled me upright from the floor. Finally able to glance around, I realized that there were no priests in the room. Only myself, Rhoda, and four young priestesses. My breath began to hitch, knowing what they were going to do.

"Don't you dare touch me," I growled, glaring at the girls. They shrunk back in fear. As Rhoda moved again, strange words flew from her lips. It was though a snake had slithered around me, pulling me so tight in its grip that I was paralyzed. Even the tiniest movement was impossible.

"You demon," I accused her. She only nodded. Fearful, the priestesses bowed their heads, refusing to look Rhoda in the eye. She nodded once to each of them, a smug smile on her face. Slowly, I pieced the truth together in my head.

"You write the notes," I breathed. Again, a small nod confirmed it. I looked to the priestesses in the room, and their eyes were filled with fear. She had them all under her thumb, and most likely Sebastian as well.

"Rhoda, how old are you?" She opened her mouth to answer, but I cut her off. "How old are you really? Only Delilah remembered the High Priest before you. How much life have you stolen?"

With that small, wicked smile, Rhoda leaned close to me, her skin stretched over old, calcified bones. Her breath reeked as if she were rotting from the inside out. Perhaps she was. If I had been free to move, I may have gagged. She placed her lips just next to my ear, her breath sending unpleasant shivers down my spine. My skin crawled at her answer.

"One hundred and fifty-seven."

"You're wrong. You shouldn't exist. You've had your talons in this city for far too long," I growled as she drew back.

"And that won't change anytime soon, darling," she assured me. I shuddered at the sick pet name she used. How many Gifts had she used that name on? "And they won't be dressing you," Rhoda told me, nodding to her young priestesses. My eyes grew wide, knowing what Rhoda would do in her cruelty. She slammed the staff twice on the ground, never tearing her evil eyes off me. "He will."

Through the scarlet curtain, Sebastian entered the Sanctuary carrying the thin linen gown worn by all Gifts. Knowing it was futile, I attempted to wrestle out of the spell's hold. Not even a finger twitched. At this point I couldn't even speak. I could see in his eyes that he didn't want this. Yet he bent to the Temple's will. He would undress me as he would have on our wedding night, and I would have undressed him.

He lifted a shaking hand and placed it on my waist, sending what felt like shards of ice through my body. My skin rejected his touch, feeling wrong and violated. I wanted to scream. No sound came. The linen gown slipped from his hands to the floor as he reached forth with the other trembling hand. My tunic slipped over my head, my hair swishing down behind me, the only part of me that was mobile.

"Rhoda," a faint, shaking voice piped up. I strained my eyes to look at the priestess to my right. Her soft, red hair was pulled back into a bun, her white attire too large for her slight frame. "This isn't tradition. The Chosen doesn't dress the Gift, he doesn't see her until he begins the procession."

"Sarah, don't!" another girl hissed. Her eyebrows lowered as she glowered at her sister in faith, her hawklike features sharp and angry. "She is the High Priestess!"

"Yes, you would do well to listen to Cora," Rhoda nodded. A small smile laced her lips, and the girl took a shaky step forth.

"This is wrong!" Sarah argued. "The Chosen doesn't undress the Gift, it's adultery against the Totem!"

Rhoda gave no further response. She stared at the priestess with silent disdain, and Sarah shrunk back in fear. She bowed her head, but she did not apologize. A pang shot through my chest, knowing that no good fate would befall her at Rhoda's hand. I could see her hands trembling. She knew just as well as I did.

"Pity," Rhoda finally said. She slammed her staff into the marble floor, sending miniscule chips of garnet skittering across the Sanctuary. The girl was wrenched forward as if pulled by a rope, and I assumed she was caught in the same paralysis as me. The sound died in my chest as her feet dragged across the floor, her bare skin screeching against the polished surface.

Rhoda caught the girl by her throat, long bony fingers digging into Sarah's freckled skin. I could only see her back, Rhoda's figure obscured from my view. White smoke drifted upward in soft, delicate tendrils. If I could have shut my eyes against the scene, I would have. Sarah kicked and struggled, her body beginning to thrash as though she were caught in a horrific nightmare. Chillingly, no sound escaped her body as more smoke drifted up from the dark magic Rhoda worked on the poor girl. It swirled in delicate, beautiful patterns as if Sarah's soul were caught in the mist.

Finally, Sarah fell to the floor, and she lay still. Rhoda's eyes were closed, her eyebrows relaxed and her cheeks glowing with a flush. My stomach twisted in my gut, though I had no way to express my horror or disgust. Rhoda snapped her fingers, and two of the three remaining priestesses scrambled to remove the body. I was certain they were terrified that they would be next to fall to the Hight Priestess.

"Chosen, continue," Rhoda crooned as though the murder she had committed was some trivial nuisance. Obediently, Sebastian untied the undergarment I wore over my chest and let it fall to the floor.

I sucked in a sharp inhale, bare and exposed against the cold, stale air inside the Temple. It was as if I could feel the Totem looming over me just out of sight, watching her meal being prepared before her. Yet the true Totem stood in front of me in the form of the devilish Rhoda. She had taken that power for herself. I cringed as Sebastian struggled to undo the belt around my waist, but he finally unbuckled it and allowed my trousers to slip down my legs. The splat of a tear landed on the cold marble floor. I hadn't realized I was crying.

This moment should have been magical, feeling Sebastian lift away the things separating our bodies. It should have been warm and pleasant, the feeling of his skin on mine. The ecstasy of becoming one. Now it felt as though we were driven even farther apart, the moment tainted and sick. Thankfully, Sebastian collected the linen gown from the floor and slipped it over my head. Gently, he smoothed the fabric over my body. A sense of security was restored in me, and the fire rekindled.

I felt my body return to me, Rhoda's spell dissipating and the priestess stepped forward to bind me once more. My jaw unlocked, and my tongue came back to life. The only weapons at my disposal were words, and I would hurl them like verbal stones. My eyes narrowed as Sebastian took a step back, his shoulders shaking. Surely, he had the same thoughts as I had about his undressing me, the sick violation he had put me through.

"You're not the first to undress me," I shot. His head whipped up, eyes wide as he stared at my smug face. I smirked at him, depriving him of that pleasure. Something rotten rose in me as I reveled in the satisfaction. He was not the first man to see me bare, to know me and my body. I had shared that with a man I trusted, a man I had quickly grown to love. One who would do anything to save me.

"What?" he muttered, his hands shaking. I took a glance at Rhoda, but her expression was unchanged.

"You will have no virgin sacrifice," I spat, smiling wickedly in satisfaction. "I've rid myself of the purity you prized." Sebastian's watery eyes seemed to beg me to rescind my statements, to know it was a lie. He and I knew full well that it was not. "It was beautiful."

"No!" he screamed, charging toward me. Only then did Rhoda move, fearful of what her precious Chosen would do. She stepped between us, placing her garnet staff in Sebastian's path. "You cheated on me!?"

"No!" I scoffed. "You let me go. I moved on!" Sebastian dissolved into a crumpled heap on the floor, weeping and muttering to himself. A pang of guilt twisted like a knife in my gut. I'd gone too far. Before any more words could be thrown, the priestess dragged me away with no resistance this time.

Chapter Thirty: The Sacrifice

"Let go of me! You can't do this!" My screams fell upon deaf ears. I struggled and fought, but the ropes held strong. It was hopeless. The heat singed my skin as we drew closer to the mouth of the volcano.

"This is an honor!" cried the high priestess. "You should be thanking us! The Totem smiles upon Anyra with mercy."

"No merciful deity would require such a violent gift!" I shot back, trying to sway the few followers Rhoda had left. I feebly kicked one of the priests in the head, but he did not stumble.

"Silence, you insolent child!" Rhoda screamed in response. She then turned and addressed the small crowd below, but the words were drowned by the pounding in my ears. The time had finally come, and there would be no miraculous escape. Knowing my death was imminent, I opened my mouth and wailed. The cry was wordless, an empty vocalization of my plight. At the sound of this last, hollow cry, Sebastian clutched me tighter, ducking his head. I decided to make one last plea.

"Please, Sebastian, you can still change this," I begged. He had been silent throughout our ascent. I had called, but he hadn't had the courage to answer until this moment. What was to be my final moment.

"I don't have a choice, Adelaide," he whispered. I could hear the strain in his voice. "It's my fault, I'm sorry, Addie."

"You're damn right it is," I growled. I craned my neck to see his face and found tears shimmering in his eyes. "I would have been safe. But the Totem was more important than me. You damn fool!"

"Addie..."

"If you're going to throw me in, get it over with!"

"People of Anyra, the Chosen to give this Gift is a man you know well. The Gift comes at a great cost to him, as she was to be his bride in mere days. But he ceded to the Totem's will."

The crowd cheered at Rhoda's closing words. The two young men supporting me along with Sebastian shifted, moving so he alone carried me in his arms. He held me as he would have to carry me across the threshold on our wedding night. He should have carried me to safety, so that the Totem would not have been able to choose me. Now he carried me to my doom. "Go forth, Chosen giver of the Gift. Make your sacrifice."

"Sebastian, do not!" I shrieked into his ear. He turned, sobs hitching in his chest. "Sebastian! Don't do this!" His steps were slow as if I weighed much more than I truly did. "You have a choice! Don't kill me!" A wave of sickening heat washed over me as he approached the mouth of the monster, the light turning his face a shade of rotten orange. He stopped, horrifyingly close to the edge.

"I'm sorry," he breathed. I turned to gaze into his face for the final time. Remorse was there, but the hopelessness nearly made me gag. He had a choice but refused to make the right decision.

"Damn you," I cursed him. He let me fall from his arms, and the heat grew steadily greater. I screamed. I let the howl rip from my chest as the crowd standing on the mountain cheered. My stomach flew up into my throat, and I nearly gagged on it, bile rising in my throat as I fell further. The black interior of the volcano flashed before my eyes, glowing red and orange with a demonic light.

I waited for the searing pain as I plummeted, but it never came. I landed with a splash in the churning magma, but no burns marred my skin. It was as if I were in a warm bath. With a shriek of surprise, I splashed to the edge of the basin, pulling myself out of the lava as quickly as I could, and I clung to the wall like a spider. Yet I was unharmed. Somehow, I was impervious to the heat, yet the lava had burned the ropes enough that I had unwittingly snapped them in my haste.

I swatted at the flames licking the charred, tattered remains of the linen gown I wore. The wretched piece of fabric that Sebastian had wrestled me into it that morning as they prepared for the sacrifice was no longer. "Pure white, for our virgin sacrifice," Rhoda had smiled. Now the simple slip was blackened and fragile, almost the entirety of it burned away so I was barely decent.

A great cry of agony sounded from above me, and I looked up to see Sebastian fallen to his knees at the edge of the opening, the sound ringing out of his chest and echoing off the sloping walls. I knew his throat must be bleeding with the rough quality of the scream. My eyes narrowed up at him. He had done this. He had no right to feel pain for my loss. Yet my anger was overborne by the question on my lips.

"How?" I breathed, gazing at my hands, warm and strong. "This is impossible!" A gust of wind blew past me, and a strange chill passed over my scalp. My free hand flew to my head, and I found it completely bald, the hair singed away by the scorching heat. The rest of me, however, was unscathed. Inexplicably, my body couldn't be harmed by the magma. In a secondary thought, I began to wonder from where the great breeze had originated. There should be no source of wind. Yet a second gust blew my way, this time carrying a message.

"The Gift. Use it."

Sobs distracted me from the voice, and I looked up to find Sebastian crying over the edge. Anger rose in my chest, and the lava rose with it, a great burst of molten rock. Curious, I raised a hand,

263

willing the liquid to move, and it did my bidding. The lava surged upward in a wave and splashed back on itself at my summons. I smiled.

Turning to the wall of the cliff, I began to climb. Luckily, I had been carried up the mountain rather than climbing it myself, so all of my strength remained. Footholds readily presented themselves to me, and I ascended with relative ease. The heat on my back was almost comforting, as if the lava that was meant to kill me would now protect me. It would catch me as gently as bathwater should I fall. With it and my newfound power, I would exact my revenge.

Sebastian had failed to open his eyes and notice my survival until my hand clapped onto the edge of the stone, scaring him into leaping back with a broken cry. I heaved myself over the side and stood as he gazed upon my form in shock and horror. A small smile laced my lips as he scrambled away from me.

"How in the Totem's name..." he breathed, the utter shock of seeing me alive rendering him dumbfounded. Rhoda turned when the crowd fell silent.

"The Gift lives!" she shrieked, her face falling to show the horror in her chest. For the first time in her life, someone had bested her. Her old eyes widened, showing fear for what must have been the first time in years. Her sorcery had no explanation for me. "How does she live?!"

"Your false Totem can't kill me!" I roared. I threw my arms skyward, summoning the lava. I felt the heat tear through me, empowering rather than frightening now, and a great gust of heated wind threw Rhoda backwards. The mountain's contents shot into the sky, filling the clouds with ash. Not knowing my strength, the two neighboring mountains also erupted, the tops blowing off as I summoned the fire within. The crowd of Anyrans below screamed in terror, their voices rising as one. Some ran stumbling down the mountain, while others were transfixed by the unnatural display.

"Adelaide, please! Mercy!" Sebastian cried. He was cowering on his knees, covering his head from the onslaught.

"What was your response when I begged for my life!" I shouted at him. "You had no mercy on me! Why should I be any different?"

"I was wrong! I'm sorry, Addie! I should have fought for you. I should have protected you," he lamented. I stepped forward and took his chin in my hand, wrenching his face up to look me in the eye. He winced away from my touch, the heat from my skin causing red burns in the shape of my fingers to rise.

"You should have listened," I agreed. "And you're too late now." I sent him tumbling down the mountain toward his high Priestess. She lay flat on her back, her head bent at an unnatural angle. When she had fallen backward, she must have landed on her neck and snapped it. Yet somehow, I felt no remorse. Her stolen life finally had come to an end

"You'll burn! You'll burn for me and all the Gifts before me!" I flung my arms toward them, sending the lava down the mountain and toward the city below. The liquid rushed past my legs like a river, the heat a comfort as the screams rose. I nodded as the lava reached the buildings on the outskirts of the town, setting them ablaze almost instantly as they melted into the heat.

"Justice." I glanced back at the lava pouring from the triplet mountains. "Justice! For me and for you, my Sister Gifts!" I tossed my head back and screamed into the sky. Never again. No more innocent girls would die.

Chapter Thirty-One: Witness

"What's going on?" Orchid quizzed, straining to see the events on the mountainside. She stood between Zakariah and Ramona, her hand clasped gently in the older Seer's. Because they shared the power, they could touch without being overcome by visions. No Seer could be read by another. "I thought Addie would get away."

"No, she didn't," Zakariah corrected. She glanced up to see tears streaming down his face. They watched the procession reach the cusp of the volcano, and though they couldn't see her, they knew Addie was bound in rope and about to be thrown to her death. "She's doing this for us. So we could get away."

"But we did! Everyone else would be halfway to Kantrin by now!" Orchid argued. "We have to save her!"

"Orchid, we can't," Ramona argued, voicing what Zakariah didn't have the heart to say. "She's doing this so that she will be the last one, the last Gift sacrificed to a false goddess. We have to let her do that."

"Look!" Willow cried, her arm shooting out toward the volcano. An echoing scream met their ears, muffled from the distance it crossed. Sebastian had done it. He had let her fall over the edge into the magma below. In an instant, Adelaide Lanasting was gone.

A strangled cry of grief ripped itself out of Zakariah's chest, and he dropped to his knees. He tore up fistfuls of the grass, cursing everything he could think to curse, anything he could blame this tragedy on. How could he let her do this? How did he allow her to walk into the very fate she had narrowly escaped? He felt Orchid's gentle hand on his back, careful to touch only the fabric covering his skin.

"She did it for you," Ramona reminded him, her voice thick with tears. "For all of us."

Zakariah knew it was true, that this brave woman died to save those she loved. So that no others had to die in her place. So that Anyra may become a new and better place. Zakariah would one day set foot into an Anyra forever changed by Adelaide's work, but in that moment he could only feel sorrow. He screamed at the ground again, the contents of his stomach threatening to spill themselves with the force of his howl. He pressed a hand to his chest, needing to feel something against the hole of emptiness opening there.

Another echoing cry met their ears from the mountaintop, this voice belonging to Rhoda rather than the treacherous Chosen. Zakariah could have sworn he heard the words 'the Gift lives', but he dared not believe it. He rose to his feet, squinting past his tears into the setting sun to see what was happening. The screams and bellows carried by the wind were garbled and broken, the voices hardly recognizable. The small group of Anyrans that remained loyal to Rhoda began thundering down the mountain, their bodies black specks fleeing toward the city.

"What is going on?" Orchid asked, fear twisting her voice as she reached back for her sister. "Is it Adelaide?"

The small group of watching Villagers jumped in unison, scattered cries and muttered questions falling from their lips as a pillar of lava shot skyward out of the volcano, darkening the sky with ash. With great, rumbling explosions, the top of the western mountain blew off and a second pillar rose, followed almost immediately by the eastern mountain. After a moment, the lava changed course, flowing down the mountainsides toward the town below, but none spilled over toward the forest or the sea. Somehow it seemed more like an attack than a natural disaster.

"There is the fire," Orchid gasped, glancing up at Ramona. "We couldn't change it after all. The Harbinger of the end of the Totem."

At long last, the wind carried something audible to Zakariah's ears. As the lava reached Anyra below, a single word rang out from the mountaintop: "Justice." One figure was left standing as the liquid fire rushed past her legs. Adelaide's voice was unmistakable as she screamed into the sky.

"She's alive," Zakariah breathed. New tears stained his cheeks, disbelief nearly making him laugh. How was it possible? What magic had allowed her to survive? But it didn't matter. Nothing did. Adelaide Lanasting, the Gift of the Totem, had survived.

After a few moments of his twisting emotions wrapping themselves around his stomach, Zakariah made to go to her. He stepped forward, readying himself to run to her in triumph, but a hand snagged the back of his shirt.

"Zakariah, we have to wait," Edrei reprimanded him. "The heat would kill you."

"It didn't harm her, and she wouldn't let it hurt me."

"It will if she doesn't know you're there. Wait, Zakariah."

His shoulder's slumping in defeat, Zakariah turned in agreement, and their small troupe waited for the heat to dissipate.

Chapter Thirty-Two: The Gifts

When I awoke, night hung heavy around me. The stench of smoke filled the air. I sat up from where I lay nestled in the warm, gooey lava. Unconsciously, I had created a bed for myself from the still-warm sludge the magma had become.

Turning my head from my immediate surroundings, I found that the city below was almost completely decimated. The houses had been burnt to blackened husks, and where the Temple once stood eternal was completely gone. The place I had hated most, the place Sebastian had revered most, reduced to nothing.

I blinked and rubbed my eyes as I witnessed people marching up the side of the mountain. Surely no one could have survived the attack. The city was empty. Anyone loyal to the Temple was present at the sacrifice, and those who were not had been evacuated by Eliza and the Villagers. As they grew closer, I began to make out details. The people were all women, all wearing pure white gowns similar to mine before it had been singed to black ash on my skin. The striking thing was that they were all giving off a milky white glow.

I didn't move, feeling no threat with the volcano at my back, though I did not know what these apparitions were. As they approached, one woman took the lead. I peered at her to glean more information. Her features were familiar to me in some long-forgotten way. She stopped just a few feet before me, hundreds of ghostly women standing at her back. One stepped out of the crowd and stood slightly behind the first woman as if she were some form of second in command.

"Why are you here?" I questioned, not moving from my cooling nest of lava. The woman laughed, her voice ringing like a bell.

"You don't recognize me?" she asked in response. "I know it has been quite some time. And you were so very small." My eyes widened as I began to understand.

"Sylvia?" I asked. Tears like moonlight had begun to slip out of the corners of her eyes even as a wide smile spread across her face. I scrambled to my feet, but my arms phased through her when I tried to wrap her in a hug. She shook her head sadly, gazing at her own gauzy hands.

"We're not truly here, Addie," she told me sadly. "We remain only long enough to offer some explanation." She paused, reaching out as if she could cup my face in her hands. Tears fell from my eyes and sizzled when they hit the black stone at my feet. "And to give you our thanks."

"I don't understand," I sniffled, rubbing my face. I'm sure at this point it was black with soot, the remains of my hair black against my naked scalp. I felt filthy and pure, horribly old and incredibly new all at once. "Are you all of the previous Gifts?"

"Yes," the girl flanking Sylvia chimed in. She stepped forward, her slip swirling around her ankles as she moved. She had to be no more than fourteen, her face round and young. She stood about five inches shorter than both me and Sylvia, but her presence somehow exuded wisdom. I turned to give her my full attention.

"You were the first," I breathed in reverence. She nodded her confirmation, folding her hands in front of her. "Esme."

"Indeed. I was the first of hundreds of young women thrown into the mouth of this mountain," she introduced herself. Her face softened with a smile, her eyes distant. "I was much like you, my dear. I fought against those who sacrificed me."

"Those," I repeated. "So, your father didn't act alone by the Totem's will." I shook my head, remembering the lie Anyra had believed for so long.

"No. In truth, the heads of all the families in Anyra gathered. There was great famine and disease, and in order to end this plague they had to cast a mighty spell. One that must be fed and maintained over time.

"They spun the lie of the Totem to trick the Anyrans into offering up one of their own, especially one so young and innocent. A daughter fed to a goddess for the sake of her people. It was my father's idea to utilize the volcano for a virgin sacrifice, and he offered me up as the first Gift. I was the first to feed the magic of the Temple."

I drew closer, the horror of the tale shocking me. I'd grown up hearing of the first Gift, but the narrative had been warped. Romanticized by a temple reverent to the bloodthirsty false goddess. What man could willingly kill his own daughter?

"In exchange for my life, my father became the first High Priest, and in turn the leader of Anyra." I stomped in anger, a strangled growl of frustration escaping my throat, and the hardened lava at my feet heated back into liquid.

"How could they do that!?" I demanded. I peered over Esme's shoulder, or rather through it, at the plot of land where the Temple had stood. It was no more. Fear crept into my gut as the thought of the blight returning warped my mind.

"Do not be angry any longer, my dear," Esme hushed me, drawing me back to the present. "The time of Gifts, the time of the Totem is over. You have broken that tradition."

"But how?" I interjected. "How did these abilities come to me?"

"That was our doing," Sylvia began. "The last thing I saw as I fell was you. When I died, I was welcomed by my sisters." She gestured to the legion of young women whose lives were torn from them too soon. "We agreed that it had to end. I told them of you, of the great, powerful spirit I knew was inside of you. From the heart of the volcano where we were imprisoned, we gave you its power." Slowly, I nodded, accepting the gift I'd been given. The two Seers had been right, though not in a way even Orchid could predict. All along, I'd carried my own gift. The gift to end all Gifts.

"Thank you," I said, looking between Sylvia and Esme. I craned my neck to see past them to the other Gifts. I recognized a few from the past few years. I searched for a face similar to Zakariah's, but I had no clue what Elizabeth looked like. "Thank you! I will use it well."

"You already have, darling," Sylvia smiled. "I know you will do great things." Fighting off sobs, I looked into Sylvia's face.

"Is Papa in your ranks?" I asked, my voice choked. Distracted as I was by the phantoms of the previous Gifts, I had forgotten about the other lives it had claimed. Some, like my father, had thrown themselves in unceremoniously, unable to continue with the pain in their lives.

"He is not," she answered sadly.

"When he fell, his spirit was somehow rejected," Esme explained. "The same force that held our spirits within the mountain, would not allow him or anyone that was not a Gift to remain." I nodded sadly, questions still swirling in my mind. I hoped he had moved on to whatever awaited beyond this world. Something told me that, like my mother, he had not been able to move on.

"What will happen to all of you? Will you be able to rest now?" I continued.

"Yes, we are at peace." Esme assured me. I smiled, knowing that all of these women were now free. "We do not know what awaits us beyond this world, but we are very ready to find out."

The first golden rays of sunlight began to creep over the trees, reflecting brilliantly off of the gentle waves of the sea. The light seemed to cut through the ghostly figures on the mountain, causing them to appear even less corporeal than they already had. Some of them began to fade from sight entirely. Each and every girl was smiling, radiating joy and peace.

"Go then, and face what awaits you," I said. Sylvia and Esme stepped back as the sun continued its ascent. I smiled as the last of them dissipated into the air. A new sun had risen on a newly freed land. I breathed deeply, the breeze off the sea clearing the lingering smoke and filling me with a new life. The old was gone. Nearly a thousand of years of suffering were rectified in a single, catastrophic event. I began making my way down the mountain, unsure of how to go on from here.

As I approached the ruins, the stench grew stronger. I passed by the scattered remains of the Totem-fearing Anyrans, and a twinge of remorse crept into my heart. I had to remind myself that these people were murderers. They had killed countless innocent girls like me. I righted their wrong. The innocent among them would hopefully move on to wherever my predecessors went. The rest may be left to wander the land as my Sister Gifts had been left to rot in the volcano.

I entered the city proper, finding almost nothing remaining. Every house and business had been razed to the ground, leaving nothing but charred husks. Only one thing remained untouched. The Memoriam stood unharmed, each and every name still intact and perfectly legible. The slabs of black stone had somehow withstood the lava. Whether that was my unconscious doing or the action of the previous Gifts, I would never know.

"Adelaide!" I turned to the source of the cry, and Zakariah plowed into me. The pair of us nearly fell over with the force of his hug, but somehow we managed to right ourselves. He pressed a forceful kiss to my temple, clutching me fiercely in strong arms. "We saw everything! I'm so glad you're alright!"

"Me too," I agreed, tucking my face into his shoulder. When we eventually broke apart, he came away black with soot, and my dress had finally disintegrated. Shame crept into me as I looked down at my naked body, the only coverage the smears of black soot on my skin. I felt even more strange with the loss of my hair, the familiar weight gone from my head. "I need something a little more decent."

A beautiful, ringing laugh echoed from his chest as he shed his jacket and draped it around my shoulders, though I was entirely content with the temperature. I had never been one to find myself too hot or too cold. I looked at my hands, finding them entirely unmarked by burn scars as Landon's were. So many strange coincidences in my life suddenly made sense.

"Addie!" This time I didn't have time to look up before Valerie's body slammed into me. She held me for only a moment before Caleb tackled the both of us. I held on to both of them, the breath being squeezed nearly out of my lungs. "You're alive! You're alive!" Gwen wheedled her way into the huddle, sobs choking any words she would try to emit.

"Yes, I'm alive!" I laughed, pulling away from my friends. I kissed my sister's forehead, rubbing the tears from her face with my ash-covered thumbs. She giggled as the char smudged her skin, giving her the appearance of a burglar. Valerie dove her hands into her bag and pulled out a dress.

"Here, let's get you into something more suitable." I darted behind one of the tall, stone plaques and slipped into the gown, finding it too big, but that hardly mattered at the present moment. It was a lovely, simple black dress that soon would no longer fit Valerie with her growing belly. I was glad to don the overlarge dress as opposed to the wretched white slip I'd worn for the sacrifice.

I reemerged and surveyed the gathering crowd. The Villagers filled the square, their numbers making up a large portion of what Anyra's population had been before today. Soon enough, those that had left for Kantrin would be able to return home. I spotted Edrei near the front of the crowd, a child in her arms. I recognized her as Joshuah's daughter.

"Edrei!" I called, I ran to her, and she dipped her head in a makeshift bow. The child, Chandra, gave me a grin and a wave. I happily returned the girl's greeting before turning my attention back to Edrei.

"Adelaide," she greeted me, a soft smile warming her face. "You have done an incredible thing today. The innocent are now free of fear."

"Thank you, I still can hardly believe that this is real." I turned to look at the place the Temple had once stood. Its absence was jarring. For hundreds of years, the Temple was a constant, standing strong against the test of time. Now I had torn it down. "Where do we go from here?"

"I believe that is your decision," she said. I was taken aback, surprised that she was not already directing people to begin rebuilding. "Adelaide, you are the leader the people need. With your gift and your passion, you will protect and guide them well." My face must have betrayed the terror within at the prospect of becoming the leader of these people. A hearty laugh rang from her chest, and she placed a gentle, strong hand on my shoulder.

"You will not be alone my dear. I'll be at your right hand to aid you with everything you face," Edrei assured me. Slowly, I nodded, beginning to accept my newfound position in this new society. I turned, surveying the people under my care. In that moment I knew that as long as I lived, these people would be protected. "What is your direction, Adelaide?"

"Firstly, we must make camp. We need temporary accommodations as we rebuild the city," I reasoned. Edrei nodded in agreement. My focus shifted as an idea sprouted in my head, and

I began bouncing on the balls of my feet with the excitement it brought. "And I want to try something!"

I marched back toward the disheveled steps that still stood facing the square, leading up to a now empty platform. My friends called in confusion as I passed them and made my way up the stairs, taking them two or three at a time. After mere seconds, I stood at the top, the people sprawled before me. Hope filled my chest. We were safe. Chandra, the twins, everyone was safe from the threat of the Temple. I took a great breath of air into my lungs.

"My people!" I cried, echoing Edrei's words. The crowd quickly fell silent, turning to face me. Confidence filled me as if the volcano in my peripheral vision fed me with bravery.

"The old is gone! The Temple and its antiquated religion will no longer rule our lives with fear." A great cheer met my ears, the people screaming the excitement of the freedom my Sisters and I had given them. As the din continued, I raised my hands, palms angled downward, and they fell silent once more.

"My people, we are the pioneers. We shall form a new Anyra; one untouched by the theocratic hand of a temple. One ruled by justice rather than fear. And if you will have me, I will guide and protect us in this endeavor." I was nearly deafened by the shouts of approval from below. The people raised chaos just as I had, voicing their thoughts. With that, I became the Harbinger of Anyra. No longer would a High Priestess reign supreme. Now the leader would be fair and unbiased. Once the sound had subsided, I spoke once more.

"You will have a council housed within no Temple, but a City Hall where all are welcome. Any problem may be brought forth before your leaders, whether it be a theft or a land dispute or whatever you may need. You will have justice!"

As the third round of screams filled me, I looked toward the volcano and the cooled lava surrounding me. The thrill of heat and power rushed through my body as I began to raise my hands, summoning the lava to me. In my mind's eye, I could see exactly what I wanted to create. The logistics of it were miraculously clear, just as it had always been in my forge. I rarely needed plans to smelt a sword or forge a crown. I simply knew exactly what to do. This ability translated well to my newfound powers.

Where once stood the Temple, a grand City Hall took shape. The lava swirled into beautiful shapes, forming a new building. The Hall would be circular, creating no corners to hide in, with large open windows. For now, there was no glass, but those would come in time. Along the outside was a covered walkway, supported by rounded pillars. The space inside was empty but would soon be filled. I could practice my new craft later by creating statues. The roof was domed, a spire shooting from the apex. The black point could be seen throughout the city.

As the magma cooled into swirling black stone, I found the people gazing up at the structure in awe. I simply couldn't keep the grin from my face as they burst into applause. As I looked over their joyous, hopeful faces, my eyes flicked up to the treeline beyond them. There stood the buck, my buck. Though he was only a shape in the distance, I knew it was him. He dipped his head in a respectful bow, his antlers nearly touching the grass at his hooves. I gave a small nod in return. With that, he turned and disappeared back into the forest.

The cheers of the people drew my mind once again, and I beckoned them to approach. Zakariah was the first to bound up the steps, and he tilted his head back to look at what I had created. Until this point, I had only forged destruction with my power. My Gift could create beauty as well. With it, I would protect my people from any threat. Nothing and no one could stand against me, the human volcano. Nothing would touch my people of Anyra.

Chapter Thirty-Three: Anyra

"Good afternoon, my Queen," Zakariah greeted me as he sailed into the City Hall, a stack of glass panes in a multitude of colors in his arms.

"How many times will I have to ask you not to call me that?" I asked, laughing as I rose from the table. He set the glass down on the floor. "I'm not a queen, I'm called the Harbinger."

"You're a queen in my eyes," he assured me. I gave him a lopsided grin. I held a ball of semi-molten rock in one hand, practicing finer skills with the power I had been given. Large moves were easy, moving great amounts or creating basic shapes. Smaller, more detailed maneuvers were proving much more difficult. I was certain that eventually I would be able to create beautiful things as easily as I had in my forge.

"And you a king in mine," I replied. I set the now solidified rock down on the table and approached Zakariah. I hesitated as he drew nearer. Sebastian's horrified eyes flashed in my memory, the lava flowing over his body and killing him along with the others that tried to sacrifice me. In a way, we had both betrayed one another. A gentle hand met my cheek, pulling me back into the present. Zakariah's kind eyes now filled my vision, taking me in and assuring me I was safe.

"You're all right, Addie," he promised. "You did what had to be done." I nodded, breathing deeply. I let the words wash over me, trying to believe them. "You're forgiven."

"I'm forgiven," I echoed. He pulled me into his chest, holding me tightly to himself. I reveled in the safety of his arms, and his soft lips pressed against my forehead. He placed a hand aside my head, rubbing the soft fuzz of my hair beginning to grow back.

"I know it's hard. I can't begin to imagine everything in your mind right now. Just know that I'm here for you, and so many others are, too. You did a good thing."

"Thank you," I breathed, tears smarting in my eyes. I looked into his kind face, finding nearly the same sadness behind his eyes. He had lost so much, as had all the Anyrans. But we had a chance to build something better than Anyra had ever been. This was a new life. As if my body was moving on its own, I reached up to take his face in my hands, pulling it down closer to me.

His body seemed to respond to this, reciprocating without hesitation. Our lips met seemingly beyond our control, finding solace and acceptance in one another. His arms wrapped around my waist, pulling me closer into him, desperate to feel our bodies press together. I pressed my chest into his, my heart seemingly yearning to touch his. It was pure bliss.

I pulled away grinning, feeling safe and at home. This was right. Zakariah felt right. My soul felt drawn to his in a way I could not comprehend. I could not name the feeling, for it was far too powerful. I simply let it be. Zakariah's beaming smile filled me with confidence in the decision. He and I would face this and every challenge together as one.

"Do you have any meetings today?" he asked as we broke apart. I took the sphere of magma up once more. It became thick, viscous liquid once again, and I began toying with it between my hands. He laid a hand on my waist as we studied the papers laid out before us. Budgets, building plans, schedules, the Anyra-Kantrin Treaty. So much to be done, and it felt like too much to handle alone. Luckily, I wouldn't be handling it alone.

"Yes, the Kantrineirs will be here later today to discuss the terms of the treaty," I answered. I shifted the lava to one hand, twisting it around my fingers as I picked up the draft of the treaty. "I'm a little worried about it. I'm a crafter of metal, not of words."

"And lava," Zakariah chuckled, gesturing to the structure around us. I shrugged, a smile tugging at the corner of my mouth. "I can give it a once over. But speaking of craft."

He returned to his panes of colorful glass and began distributing them. He placed them under their respective windows, and I began to see his vision. He had recreated some of the windows that had been in the Temple, but many new additions had been added. I began at the window that stood left of the door, essentially the beginning of the story.

The window depicted the scene of the first Gift, Esme, mercilessly sacrificed by a cruel congregation. Her father, the first High Priest, stood at the lip of the volcano, and Esme was caught in the glass mid-fall. Zakariah had mimicked the statue of Esme we had seen in Kantrin, somehow beautifully recreating the folds of the white, linen gown.

I moved on to the following scenes. Before my eyes, immortalized in glass was the burning of the ships, the creation of the Totem's statue, the first revolt, followed by the second and the third. These had all be quashed by the Temple, their members publicly executed on the same stage where the Gifts were chosen.

One other Gift's sacrifice was painted in the glass, that of my aunt Sylvia. This was notably different than the scene of Esme's sacrifice. Rather than Sylvia depicted mid-fall, it was my father Xavier plummeting over the edge, unable to cope with his sorrow and guilt. Sylvia was below, floating in the magma as if it were water, the edges of her gown beginning to burn away. Below her form lay the swirling pool of souls, all of the former Gifts waiting to accept her.

Finally, the last window depicted a very familiar scene. This one was from the perspective of the Villagers, of Zakariah himself from where they had watched my own sacrifice and the eruption of the triplet volcanoes. Lava spewed skyward, filling the sky with ash and casting sickly red light on the ground below. Yet it was not pride that filled me gazing upon the scene.

I felt Zakariah's warm, gentle hands on my arms as he came up behind me. He kissed my bare shoulder, his lips soft against my skin. My hand drifted upward, cradling his head and the soft brown curls. I felt him press into me, wrapping his arms around my waist. I melted into his touch, pulled back from the guilt and fear I felt from the event.

"I love you," he whispered, his breath warm in my ear. I smiled as I turned to face him. He pressed a kiss to my forehead, our bodies swaying back and forth as one. I wrapped my arms around him, twisting the curls on the nape of his neck around my fingers.

"I love you," I replied, meaning every syllable. He kissed me again, lifting me off the ground in a massive hug. I laughed into his lips as he clenched me tightly to himself. I looked into his joyful face as he set me down. Peace and safety washed over me, the feeling of being known, accepted, and loved despite my past.

"So this treaty," Zakariah prompted, moving for the desk. A laugh rang out of my chest as I followed him. I handed him the paper, and he began scanning it. He nodded as he read, mouthing the words to himself. "I think it's going to be great, Addie."

On the desk beside the treaty sat the sculpture I had created from what was meant to be Rhoda's staff. Somehow, the creation had survived the razing of the city just as the Memorium had been left unharmed. Perhaps my destruction could not harm my own handiwork. After a thorough cleaning, the ruby shone as bright as ever, casting red light all around it. This would be our peace offering, a gift of friendship and gratitude.

"It will," I nodded as I hopped up onto the desk, sitting facing him. I kissed him once more, holding his head tenderly in my hands. "It will."

About the Author

Juniper M. Limerick lives in Indiana with her husband and their orange tabby cat, Butterfinger. Although *Anyra* is her debut novel, Juniper has enjoyed writing for fun since she was a child. She hopes that Anyra will be the first release in a long, successful writing career.

In her free time, Juniper enjoys many different hobbies including playing guitar, dancing, and playing video games. She crochets lots of gifts, clothing, and warm blankets for her friends and family. Juniper and her husband enjoy exploring new places and finding the best coffee shops.

You can find Juniper online at junipermlimerick.com or on social media as Juniper M. Limerick on Facebook, Twitter, and Instagram.